*intoxicating*

# intoxicating

AN

ELITE
PROTECTION
SERVICES

NOVEL

# ONLEY JAMES

INTOXICATING

*Elite Protection Services Book 1*

Copyright © 2019 Onley James
WWW.ONLEYJAMES.COM

All rights reserved. No part of this publication may be reproduced, stored in a retrieval system, or transmitted, in any form or by any means (electronic, mechanical, photocopying, recording, or otherwise), without the prior written permission of the publisher.

This book is a work of fiction and does not represent any individual living or dead. Names, characters, places, and incidents either are products of the author's imagination or are used fictitiously.

ISBN: 978-1-0822-0585-9

TRIGGER WARNING

*This book depicts situations of suicide attempts and self-harm and talk of past sexual abuse and trauma.*

# prologue

## WYATT

SEVENTY-FIVE. EIGHTY. EIGHTY-FIVE. NINETY.

As the numbers on the speedometer climbed higher, something loosened inside Wyatt Edgeworth's chest. He just wanted it over. The steamy temperature outside warred with the frigid AC pumping through the car's vents, causing the windows to fog, but he couldn't cool off. He'd lost his shirt ten minutes after he'd climbed behind the wheel, but he was still on fire.

Sweat and tears pricked his eyes until the numbers swam into a glowing red blob. He blinked rapidly to clear his vision. When that didn't work, he took both hands off the wheel, digging the heels of his palms

*intoxicating*

against his eyes until sparks danced behind his lids.

Without his guidance, the car veered into the next lane. It didn't matter, the road was dead. He hadn't seen another car in miles. Only degenerates and truckers were on the highway at four in the morning. At least, that's what his mother had told him in her most withering tone just before she'd reminded him that his behavior was inappropriate, advising him to pull over at once and wait for someone to come get him. That's when Wyatt had tossed his phone out the window. He shifted his weight, his skin sticking to the back of the butter-soft leather of his Porsche Cayenne.

Why was it so fucking hot?

The tires whirred as they connected with the white reflective warning strips on the shoulder of the road. He yanked the wheel to the left, only clipping the front quarter panel against the aluminum railing before once more finding the asphalt. He tried to concentrate on staying between the white lines, but there were so many of them.

Wyatt's head pounded, his tongue Velcroed against the roof of his mouth. His world blinked in and out of focus. He wiped at his brow and pounded on the button for the air conditioning, trying to find a lower temperature, but it was already on the lowest setting. Water. He needed water. He picked up the plastic bottle on the passenger seat, grunting his frustration when it was empty. He crunched the plastic with a scream before rolling down the window and sending it flying too. The car fishtailed, but he caught it before he lost control.

*"Jesus, I can't believe you're the one who lived."*

He swiped at the tears on his face, slamming his foot down on the gas and gripping the steering wheel with both hands. The little pink pill he'd taken earlier was at war with the half bottle of bourbon he'd ingested, leaving him tired and wired, his father's words bouncing around in his skull like a pinball.

*"What a waste you are. All the money we spent to make you normal…and for what? For you to be down on your knees in a bathroom like some two-dollar whore…at a public event? At one of my events. In front of my friends!"*

It amazed Wyatt that his father had the audacity to call *him* a whore when the event in question had a twenty-five-thousand-dollar per plate buy-in. His father had a peculiar idea of normal. Marrying a woman he hated for her trust fund. Selling his soul to appease his base. Kids in cages. Walls to keep out nobody. Yet, Wyatt was the whore. Wyatt was the abomination. What a joke. His jagged laugh was startling in the car's silence.

*"What are you even looking for? Attention? Money?*

*intoxicating*

*What's it going to take to get you to turn away from this deviant lifestyle once and for all? They have programs... Adult treatment centers. Better than the ones we sent you to before. More aggressive. Let us help you before it's too late. Your soul is in danger."*

A sob escaped. His vision was a stream of white lines that ebbed and flowed like he was in *The Matrix*. He needed to slow down, but he knew he wouldn't. He knew, way down deep in his gut—where he stuffed down all the things he used to think were possible—he wouldn't stop. His father would never leave him alone. Never let him be who he was. Never let him have anything that might fill this giant, gaping hole inside him. What was the point? Of any of it.

He flipped his headlights off, engulfing himself in darkness until the streetlights were shooting stars and the reflectors electricity and people just energy. He was just energy and atoms, and if he just let go of the wheel, it could all be over. No more pain. No more hurt. No more frustration. No more disappointment. No more Wyatt.

Wouldn't he be doing the world a fav—

Metal shrieked against metal like some prehistoric monster, and fire trailed along his cheeks and forehead, and then he was flying. Was this what it was like to die? The sudden stop stole the breath from his lungs, and pain exploded behind his eyes as his body rolled for what seemed like forever.

Was death supposed to hurt like this? Maybe this was hell. Wyatt tried to open his eyes, but only one seemed to cooperate. The night sky swimming overhead showed a world painted crimson. Maybe his father was right, and he would now spend his afterlife tortured for all eternity. He tried to laugh, but it came out as a pained wheeze, and the taste of copper flooded his mouth. Did he still have his teeth? He tried to touch them with his tongue, but his body wouldn't cooperate.

He didn't remember closing his eyes, but he must have because when he opened them again, a face appeared. He might have screamed if he could manage it, but instead, he swallowed hard, trying to focus. The man lingering above him, illuminated by the streetlights, was a round-faced guy with wire-rimmed glasses and a boater's tan. Only the skin around his deep brown eyes showed how pale the stranger's complexion was. Did people fish in heaven?

"Holy shit. Are you alive? Jesus. You're alive!" The man was shaking him, and Wyatt fought the urge to vomit. "Honey, holy shit. Holy shit! He's alive. He's looking right at me. Call 911." Then the man was back in his face. "Hey, try not to move, okay? You could have, like, a broken neck or something."

*intoxicating*

The man had so many teeth. So white. Wyatt focused on the Chiclet-like teeth as he willed his body to give him back control. "Mm fine," he tried to say, but his tongue was too big for his mouth. He tried again. "I'm fine. If…if you could just get me to my car."

The guy huffed out a startled laugh. "I don't know how to break this to you, dude, but you could fit what's left of your SUV in your pocket. It's a miracle you're alive."

Wyatt's stomach sank. He couldn't even do this right. He gripped the guy's hand. "Tell my dad… Tell my dad I tried to end it. I tried to do the right thing. Tell him."

# one

## LINCOLN

"THE SENATOR WILL SEE YOU NOW."

Lincoln Hudson stood, fighting the urge to tug at the neck of his white button-down shirt. He should have checked to see if his suit still fit before he agreed to the hasty meeting, but it was too late now. He'd been in fatigues so long the collared shirt was like a noose around his neck. Or maybe it was the job itself causing the choking sensation. Linc couldn't be sure.

He followed the petite blonde woman down a stately hall lined with ugly blue and gold carpet and painting after painting of stuffy old white men. When they reached a set of double doors, she swung them open

*intoxicating*

with a flourish and gestured for him to enter before flashing him an unenthusiastic smile and shuffling away. A man—presumably the senator—held up a finger in a 'one moment' gesture before swinging his chair away from Linc, as if that would somehow erect a cone of silence around his conversation.

Linc didn't give a shit about the man's phone call, so he prowled the room instead. He counted no less than three dead animals adorning the walls. Two from the endangered species list. Bookcases filled with leather-bound books took up the entire left wall. Linc wandered closer, trying not to roll his eyes when he noted almost every title involved the law, both secular and biblical. This guy must be a laugh at parties. The furniture was all shiny mahogany, and the man's decorator had encased anything not made of wood in brown leather. The bar in the farthest corner of the room displayed an array of crystal decanters filled with only dark liquors. Linc would bet the man had Cuban cigars stashed somewhere in his enormous desk.

"That's a beltway problem, Jerry. That's not what I'm about. Listen, I gotta go. Yep. I have a meeting. You give Clare and the kids my love, and we'll talk about this more when we meet at the club on Saturday." The man paused. "No. Wyatt won't be joining us. He's meeting with some people regarding a clerkship. Yes, we're very proud. He's a great kid. Alright. We'll talk soon."

Linc returned his attention to the senator when it sounded as if he was wrapping up his conversation. The man hung up the phone, turning to face Linc, giving him his first real glimpse of his new client. He was broad-shouldered with golden-blond hair going gray at the temples and combed just so to hide his receding hairline. He'd lost his suit jacket and just wore a pale blue button-down shirt and a navy-blue tie, loosened at the neck. When he stood, Linc noted the man's gut sagged over his belt despite the defined muscles of his arms and chest.

"Sorry about that. That man could talk the ears off corn, if you know what I mean. Montgomery Edgeworth. My friends call me Monty." When he spoke, his tone was affable, his soft Southern drawl speaking of Georgia roots, not Florida. He extended his hand, and Linc shook it, noting the way the man squeezed his hand for far too long and with more strength than necessary.

What was this guy trying to prove, anyway? Did he think Linc was looking to get into some kind of dick-measuring contest with him? Linc had met dozens of men like him in the service, insecure assholes trying to exert their dominance with these over-the-top displays of masculinity. He found the whole thing rather tiresome.

*intoxicating*

Monty gestured for Linc to sit. "Thanks for taking the time to come in and talk. You're the third bodyguard I've hired in the last six months, and quite frankly, this is taking up too much of my valuable time."

Linc gave a terse nod but said nothing. Jackson had warned him not to let Monty Edgeworth's affable nature sway him. His friend had used the words 'snake charmer.' Linc didn't care if the senator was Satan incarnate as long as his check cleared at the end of this job. "No problem at all. I was already in town visiting Jackson when the job came up for reassignment. He seems to think I'd be a good fit."

The smile slipped, and Monty nodded. "That's right. You two served together, correct?"

"Yes, sir. Two tours in Afghanistan."

"Jackson's good people, even if he spends most of his days babysitting celebrities."

Jackson Avery did a lot more than guard celebrities, but Linc wasn't about to waste his breath to say as much. Monty didn't seem like a guy who wanted people to correct him. Instead, Linc turned his focus to the job. "You need me to protect your son? Has there been some kind of threat against him?"

The senator laughed. "Oh, no. Nothing like that. Honestly, the only threat to my son is himself. He's… well, he's spoiled is what he is. My wife and I, we gave him anything he wanted because we lost our first boy when he was real young. Now, he doesn't have the sense God gave a turnip. I need somebody to keep an eye on him over the next six months."

A million questions popped into Linc's head. He started with the unusually specific time frame.

"What happens in six months?"

"Election Day. I can't afford a scandal right now. I've held this seat for six years, and I'm not about to lose to a thirty-something, guitar-playing vegan who thinks Bernie Sanders is the goddamn messiah." He snorted. "Topher Arroyo wants to legalize pot and let the gays run amuck, and if he was any more pro-choice, he'd let women drown their babies right up until their first birthday. Who the hell names their kid Topher, anyway? Hippies, that's who," he finished, his voice hitting an impressive high note.

Linc clenched his jaw, but his face remained impassive as he stared at the spot dead center of the man's forehead. Jack was right. This guy was a fucking douchebag. "So, you want me to…what? Babysit your son? I'm not great with kids."

Once again, that laugh. "My son's twenty-two years old. He might act like a toddler, but I promise there are no diaper changes. I need you to keep his name out of the papers."

*intoxicating*

Linc frowned. "No offense, but you realize you're paying six figures to babysit a grown man, right?"

"Ten minutes with my son and you'll feel like I've robbed you blind." Monty reached into his desk and grabbed something from the top drawer. He tossed a stack of pictures toward Linc. He caught them as they scattered across the glossy surface.

Linc picked them up. At first, he wasn't sure what he looked at, but then, he realized it was a car accident. The remains of a white Maserati sat crumpled on what looked to be a highway. It was nighttime, despite the artificial light flooding the pictures. As he flipped through the stack, he noted most of the photos were pictures of the car taken from different angles.

"This was his first accident two years ago. He walked away from that wreck unscathed."

"His first accident?"

Monty's face collapsed into a frown, making him look much older than his age. "Hmm. He's been in three others since then."

"Was he under the influence?"

"Not the first time. Just stupid and reckless. We convinced the judge he'd had a seizure, and they let him go."

*Of course, they did,* Linc thought, allowing himself a mental eye roll.

Linc continued to thumb through the photos. Halfway through the stack, the images changed. First, the remnants of a black BMW 2-series wrapped around a light pole and then a Lincoln Navigator sitting half in and out of what looked to be a community swimming pool. The final images showed what had once been a small white SUV. The car's front end now sat in the front seat, and the vehicle itself was folded in on all sides, like a giant had crushed it in his fist.

"This was his most recent accident. He had a fractured orbital bone, a broken femur, six shattered teeth, and a lacerated spleen. My wife had to be medicated for weeks from the stress."

*Stress, not fear,* Linc couldn't help but note. He was sure it wasn't an accidental choice of words.

The last photo showed a boy on a stretcher with an oxygen mask hiding the lower half of his face. Blood and sweat plastered matted blond hair against the boy's forehead, his left eye swollen shut. The right eye was open and looking at the camera. There was a bleakness in the look that felt like a kick to the stomach. Linc shook his head, pushing all the pictures back across the desk but one.

"The other accidents were minor enough I just paid for the property damage."

Jesus. The douche apple obviously didn't fall far

*intoxicating*

from the douche tree.

"But this last accident from eight months ago, my son totaled his Porsche going a hundred miles an hour down I-95. He lost control of the car, spun out, and once again, collided with the concrete barrier. They say the only reason he lived is that he was so goddamn intoxicated he was ejected from the car. It's a miracle he's alive," he muttered, sounding like it was inconvenient, not miraculous.

"He seems to have suffered some serious injuries," Linc noted, unable to tear his gaze from the picture of the boy.

"Not serious enough," Monty muttered. That did get Linc's attention. At his raised brow, the older man's shoulders slumped. "I didn't mean that. I'm just frustrated. He's a good kid. He's just…confused. He lacks discipline. Rules. Order. That's why Jackson thinks you'll be a good fit. He won't charm you like he did the others."

"I'm sorry if this is out of line, but your son is twenty-two years old. I can't just move into his house and watch him against his will."

"The hell you can't. My son is currently on house arrest, which he received after failing his court-mandated breathalyzer tests. He might be an adult according to the law, but he relies on me to live. Until this accident, he was finishing his final year at the University of Florida before moving on to law school. He had to take a year off to serve out his sentence, but he knows he belongs to me. He certainly doesn't have the skills or ambition needed to support himself. He'll do what I tell him. He'll do what you tell him."

Linc's eyes dropped back to the picture, his dick intrigued by the notion of the green-eyed boy doing anything Linc told him. He shook the thought away. "Sir, if he's on house arrest, what do you need me for? If he's got an ankle monitor, aren't the cops already keeping tabs on him?"

"He's left the property twice despite the damn monitor. He's got two weeks left on his house arrest, and then Miami-Dade's finest are releasing him back into society. I need you to keep him out of trouble so they don't extend his sentence, and then I need you to keep his name out of the headlines for the next five months. It's a damned miracle I've kept the house arrest a secret."

Monty sure loved to throw the word 'miracle' around. Linc suspected the senator didn't fully understand the word's definition.

"The one good thing about that Topher kid," Monty continued, unaware of Linc's inner monologue, "he's determined to run a 'clean' campaign, so he hasn't tried to dig up any dirt on me. He only wants to debate the 'issues.'"

Linc didn't trust anybody who used air quotes as much as this man did. "So, I'm not a babysitter, I'm a prison guard?"

"If you consider living in a seven-thousand-square-foot penthouse apartment overlooking Biscayne Bay a prison, then sure, you are the world's luckiest and most well-paid prison guard."

These people were everything Linc hated about the world. "Alright, then. I'm in."

The senator's face lit up, and he once again stood, extending his arm. "Excellent." Once his hand was around Linc's, he squeezed tight. "Let me be frank. I cannot stress the importance of discretion enough. Understood?"

"I signed a non-disclosure agreement when I took the job with Elite."

"Excellent. I trust you won't mind signing another one my attorney drew up on your way out."

Linc frowned but nodded. "I suppose not. That'll be fine."

"Then there's nothing else to say but welcome aboard. Once you collect your belongings, my driver will be happy to take you over to the house." Linc had a hand on the doorknob when the senator spoke once more. "Don't forget you work for me, Mr. Hudson. No matter what my son tells you."

Linc closed the door behind him, a headache throbbing behind his left eye.

He hoped this job was worth it.

## two

### WYATT

WYATT RUBBED AT THE STRAP CUFFED TO HIS RIGHT ankle. Underneath it, the skin looked raw and irritated, but he consoled himself by imagining the look on his father's face if he could see him sunning himself by the pool, a bottle of the old man's best Bordeaux beside him. He wasn't even drinking it, just had it open in case dear old Dad popped by unannounced. Not that his father ever had or ever would. He put his efforts into the things he cared about, and Wyatt hadn't been a thing Montgomery Edgeworth cared about since he was six, if ever. Pressure swelled behind Wyatt's ribs, but he pushed it back, biting down on the inside of his cheek until the taste of metal filled his mouth.

Whatever.

He flopped back onto the plush green lounge chair, throwing one last glare at his government-issued ankle bracelet before he closed his eyes, letting the warmth of the sun and the pain of his throbbing cheek push away the sick feeling he didn't want to acknowledge. He hadn't seen his father in months, not since the judge had given Wyatt a stern lecture about responsibility and then sentenced him to six months of house arrest. He had no reason to think his dad would darken his doorway, even though Wyatt had chased off another watchdog.

Without opening his eyes, Wyatt picked up the bottle of *Chateau Latour Pauillac* and sniffed it before taking a tentative sip and wincing. It tasted like plums and dirt and reminded him of wood shavings. He took another generous swig. Maybe if he got drunk enough, he could pretend the white noise of Graciela's vacuum cleaner was the beach and the upbeat Latin music pouring from his Bose speakers was a live band at a tiny island bar.

Today wasn't Graciela's cleaning day. She was only scheduled on Wednesdays, but since his incarceration at Casa de Tightass, she'd been there every day pretending to clean. In exchange, Wyatt pretended not to notice it wasn't her day. He liked the company, even

*intoxicating*

though he suspected his mother sent Graciela there in the hopes she would spill Wyatt's secrets. He couldn't fault Graciela for pretending to. His mother paid her spies generously. But Graciela was one of two people in the world who were loyal to Wyatt above anybody.

Despite the noise, Wyatt had no trouble hearing the obnoxious chime of the doorbell as it blared Beethoven's Fifth. He stayed where he was, but he forced his eyes back open. "Graciela! Doorbell!"

The housekeeper flicked her gaze in his direction, then deliberately turned her back to him, swinging her ample hips to the music.

"That will reflect in your Christmas bonus, lady," he promised as he walked past her.

"Oh, and I was so looking forward to that fifteen dollars," Graciela simpered, her accented words dripping with sarcasm.

He grinned and patted her graying bedraggled bun as he passed. He didn't bother to put on pants, instead throwing open the door in only his black boxer briefs.

Big mistake.

"Wyatt Edgeworth?"

Wyatt was certain his mouth fell open. He gaped at the six-foot-plus slab of suited muscle standing in his doorway, but he couldn't help it. It wasn't often every fantasy you ever had came to life and knocked on your front door.

The man before him had a wide stubbled jaw, gorgeous honey eyes, and thick chestnut hair shot through with silver that Wyatt decided was the perfect length for tugging. He was old. Easily forty. There were crinkles forming at the corner of his eyes and deeper lines along his forehead, but that didn't detract from long sooty lashes and a very kissable mouth. A mouth pressed into a hard line as if irritated. Shit.

Wyatt glanced over his shoulder. "Hey, Graciela. Did you hire a stripper?"

"Aye, yes. Send him in, he's late," she yelled over the noise before waving a dismissive hand. "No, you stupid boy. Your father sent you another babysitter. I hope this one is smarter than the last."

The man's lips twitched as if attempting to hold back a smile, and Wyatt tried to ignore the fluttering in his belly. Could his father really be so cruel as to send the most beautiful man Wyatt had ever seen to guard his body for the next six months? The answer was yes. What a fucking bastard. What the hell was he supposed to do with this guy?

"You could start by letting me in."

Jesus, had he said that out loud? "Uh, come on in, I guess."

The man frowned at him until Wyatt realized he

was blocking his path. He took a hasty step backward, trying to recover his equilibrium. *Pull it together, asshole. He's just another warden.* "So, you're my dad's latest super-soldier, huh? Graciela's right. The last guy was a moron. Hope you're a lot smarter, G.I. Joe."

"It's Lincoln, but you can call me Linc."

Wyatt wanted to call him a lot of things, but he needed to shut this shit down. "I'm not going to call you anything. In fact, I'm going to pretend you don't exist. You should do the same. Stay out of my way and I'll stay out of yours and we'll just do our best to get through this next six months. Cool?"

The man—Linc—snorted before closing what little distance there was between them, forcing Wyatt to take a step back or have his nose buried in the taller man's chest. Even with distance, Wyatt could smell the man, could feel the heat of his body, and that was very much not okay because he smelled like an old-school manly cologne like Old Spice, which Wyatt liked way too much for a guy wearing only skintight boxer briefs.

If Linc noticed Wyatt's predicament, he didn't say so. He leaned close, his voice a low growl. "Listen, kid. I don't know how things worked with your last babysitters and I don't really give a shit. Pay attention. When I speak, you'll acknowledge me, and when I tell you to do something, you will do it because I don't just run my mouth for no reason. I can smell the liquor on your breath, and that stops right now. If you're doing drugs, that stops now too. You'll get up at a reasonable hour every day, put on some fucking clothes, and eat something healthy because you look like you're wasting away. You'll do something productive with your time, and lights out will be midnight and not a minute after. Do I make myself clear?"

Wyatt's throat clicked as he swallowed, his mouth bone dry and his dick rock hard. *Don't look down, don't look down,* he chanted silently as he debated covering his hard-on with his hands. What was wrong with him? It was just a lack of options. It had to be. His father—and the sheriff's department—had held him captive there for months with not a man in sight, and the two attempts he'd made to venture out with his ankle monitor on had ended with him recaptured before he hit the lobby. He just needed to jerk off and he'd be fine.

He wasn't sure there was a non-humiliating way out of this situation. Too late, he forgot the man was waiting for an answer. "Yeah…yeah, sure. Whatever you say, G.I. Joe. We're good."

With that, he turned on his heel and marched down the hall, his feet sticking to the marble tile.

"Graciela will show you around," he tossed over his shoulder before entering his room and slamming the

*intoxicating*

door shut behind him. Once inside, he leaned against it as if the man might follow. "Holy shit," he muttered, sliding his hand inside his underwear and wrapping it around his cock, squeezing hard to stave off the sudden arousal. He took a few deep breaths, trying to will his body to relax, but he was too far gone.

Wyatt had never had such a visceral reaction to another human in his life. Linc's voice was gruff and growly, and it struck a chord low in Wyatt's belly. Even with the bulky fabric of Linc's cheap black suit jacket, Wyatt couldn't miss the massive size of his arms. He just knew those arms could grip him hard enough to leave a mark, could throw him around, make Wyatt bend to his will.

He turned, pressing his forearm to the door before letting his cheek rest against it. Fuck. He bit his lower lip to cut off a moan as he stroked his hand over his cock, the dry friction both painful and exactly what he needed. He pictured Linc's face, imagined his weight against Wyatt's back, his gravelly voice against his ear. Imagined him holding him down and fucking him, using him. *"If I tell you to do something, you'll do it."* His chest tightened, his breath leaving him in tight bursts as he worked himself faster. He wanted this man. Wanted his hands and his words and his demands. What would have happened if Wyatt challenged him?

Would Linc punish him? He bit back a moan at the thought. *"Do I make myself clear?"*

"Fuck. Fuck," he whispered, spilling over his hand as waves of ecstasy rolled along his body and he painted the back of the door with his cum.

He stayed where he was, panting, eyes shut tight as he caught his breath.

"What the fuck?" he whispered. After a minute, he stepped out of his underwear and made for the bathroom. Maybe a cold shower was exactly what he needed.

He settled for a lukewarm shower. As he washed his body with clinical efficiency, Wyatt fumed. Who the fuck did this guy think he was? He would not have some old man ordering him around like he was a child. He was almost twenty-three years old. He wasn't about to bend to some super-soldier who wanted to give him a bedtime.

He yanked the handle for the water hard enough to make it groan in protest. Once outside the shower, he toweled off and turned to face himself in the mirror, examining his naked body. He wasn't wasting away. Sure, he was thinner than usual, but that was because he was existing on whatever Graciela brought him to eat and he didn't know how to cook.

He leaned forward, narrowing his gaze at the bluish

*intoxicating*

circles under his eyes. When had those shown up? It wasn't like he was having trouble sleeping. Hell, he'd slept twelve hours yesterday. What else was there to do? His blond curls were now pasted flat against his scalp, making him look somewhat gaunt, but it wasn't like he was on a hunger strike. It was more like a cleanse, fruits and vegetables chased down with coffee and energy drinks. He ate when he was hungry. He just never really felt hungry anymore, not for food anyway. When his eyes fell to his thighs, he looked away, still not ready to acknowledge the scars there. Instead, he poked at his flat belly, examining himself closer. Was he too thin?

"Fuck that guy," he said to nobody.

Why was he letting a guy he'd known five minutes get into his head?

*Maybe 'cause you want him in your pants?*

"You shut up too," he told himself, stabbing the mirror with his finger.

# three

## LINCOLN

LINC DROPPED HIS BAG ON THE PLUSH KING-SIZE BED and shook his head as he took in his surroundings. He'd never seen a room so large. The ceilings soared, and all the furniture had a sparse modern look that made Linc feel like he'd just wandered into a museum's art installation. A metal bookcase ran the length of the wall to his right and two uncomfortable looking curved black chairs sat before the bank of windows that made up two walls of his room. Everything was black or white or chrome, but the bed looked comfortable enough to Linc, and that was all he cared about.

*intoxicating*

He jerked his tie loose and let it fall on the bed, followed by his jacket, shirt, and pants. The senator hadn't stated any particular dress code and Linc refused to wear a suit to babysit a spoiled rich kid in a ten million dollar condo. He slipped on a t-shirt and a pair of faded blue jeans before walking to the window and staring down at the bustling city far below.

Linc wasn't sure what he'd expected when Wyatt opened the door, but it wasn't a sullen fallen angel with sparkling green eyes and a riot of blond curls. He was all sleek muscle and sharp edges, lithe like he'd gotten those muscles swimming laps in the pool, not hitting the weights at the gym. His features were almost… delicate. High cheekbones and a perfect jawline. He was…he was pretty. Beautiful, even. Sculptors spent lifetimes trying to create that kind of perfection.

He shook the thought from his head. Wyatt was a kid, eighteen years his junior. He couldn't even think about him as anything less than a job. He was just a job. A much-needed paycheck. If he thought of him as a troublemaker, a boy in need of a firm hand and correction as his father said, then things could get out of control. Linc knew exactly what to do with boys who needed discipline, and that could absolutely not happen there. Ever. No matter how much the idea appealed to him.

He yanked the things from his bag and shoved them into drawers to keep his mind off the boy just outside the door. Fifteen minutes later, a soft knock sounded. He paused before yanking it open. Graciela stood on the other side with a large sandwich and a glass of milk. "I thought you might be hungry," she said, a placid smile on her face.

"Oh, uh, thank you." He took her offerings as she stared past him into his bedroom. "Uh, do you want to come inside?" he asked. It wasn't like it was improper; the bedroom was the size of somebody's apartment. There was a sitting area, for God's sake.

"Yes, please, for a moment. That would be wonderful."

He stepped back, gesturing with his glass for her to come inside. She made her way to one of the strangely shaped black chairs and sat. She wasn't as young as he'd thought at first glance. Her face was a roadmap of wrinkles and she wore not a stitch of makeup. He could see that her once black hair had long since ceded to the silver, even with it caught up in a knot on her head.

He sat opposite her in the other black chair and took a huge bite of the sandwich, trying not to groan in pleasure at the combination of ham and spicy mustard. "This is great. Thank you," he said around the bite.

She beamed at him for a moment before her face

*intoxicating*

grew serious. "Did Mr. Monty send you to be the next babysitter for the boy?"

Linc frowned at her words. "He hired me to watch over him for the next few months, yes."

She sat up straighter, her gaze eagle sharp. "What did he tell you about Mr. Wyatt?"

"That he's been in several accidents. And that he'd been under the influence for the last one, which is how he ended up on house arrest. He said he was… impulsive, reckless. Spoiled."

"The last two guards he sent were barely older than him and were easily manipulated—Wyatt's specialty—but I don't think you will be so easily led."

"I'll do my job," he said.

"I hope so. He's fragile. He's wandering, always wandering"—she tapped her finger against her temple—"in here."

Linc wasn't sure what that meant. "Fragile?"

"Mr. Monty refuses to see Wyatt for who he is. He's never given him what he needs."

Linc contemplated her words as he ate another bite before saying, "What do you think he needs?"

"Time. Attention."

Linc snorted. "He's a bit old to be acting out for attention, don't you think?"

Her expression grew stormy. "That boy's been

raised by one nanny after another since the day they brought him home from the hospital. He has no life skills. But more than that, his parents have treated him like an afterthought. An inconvenience since day one. Nobody more so than his father."

Linc had no idea why she was unloading all this on him, but he nodded anyway.

She wasn't finished. "I come here every day and I pretend to vacuum that floor so that I know he's okay. To make sure he hasn't done the next stupid thing. I thought having those guards around would help, but they weren't interested in seeing the truth."

"The truth?"

"You just have to look beneath his words."

"I don't understand."

She gave him a sad smile and stood. "I know you don't, but you're not the only one who signed a stupid paper. I cannot tell you what I know, but I'm hoping you'll see it anyway. Enjoy your sandwich."

With that, she left him to decrypt her message.

THE SOUND OF GLASS BREAKING IN THE DISTANCE had Linc on his feet and moving. He glanced at the clock. One-forty a.m. He'd been asleep less than an

*intoxicating*

hour. He quietly slipped open his door and padded barefoot toward the noise somewhere in the vicinity of the living room. He studied the darkened room, but nothing seemed amiss. Then he noticed the doors to the balcony were open just enough to accommodate a body, but the only light was the light sparkling beneath the water of the swimming pool.

Linc pushed the doors open enough to fit through and started his process all over again, scanning the back porch for any signs of life. His gaze snagged on a wet rust-colored stain, growing larger, spreading like blood across the stark white travertine tiles. He crept closer, noting the chunks of glass scattered through the puddle and beyond, almost to the water. Not blood. Wine. The sound of breaking must have been a wine bottle.

"Hey, G.I. Joe! Just in time. Can you grab me another bottle? I broke mine and I'm a little stuck here," he said with a giggle.

Linc's heart stopped. Just beyond the broken bottle, Wyatt lay across the concrete railing of the balcony looking at Linc with glassy eyes.

"What are you doing up there?" Linc asked, keeping his voice calm.

"I'm sleeping. Well, I was trying to sleep, but my brain just was going around and around, so I came out here for some air. Doesn't the moon look pretty tonight? Both of them." He flailed his hands toward the sky with another sharp laugh.

Before Linc could say anything, Wyatt sat up before losing his balance and almost toppling backward off the balcony. "Oopsie daisy. Nope," he said, glancing out toward the ocean. "That was close."

Blood pounded in Linc's ears. Monty Edgeworth was right; his kid was reckless. Linc took the long way around the pool to avoid the glass, and when he was close enough to rest a hand on Wyatt's knee, the boy glanced over and smiled at him. "Oh, hi, Joe," he said as if they hadn't just had a conversation sixty seconds ago.

"I'm going to guess my rule about no drinking and no drugs didn't penetrate," he grunted as he glanced over the edge of the railing to another pool eighteen stories below.

Wyatt snorted. "You said penetrate."

Linc rolled his eyes, carefully pulling Wyatt into a sitting position. Wyatt gazed down at him and gave a goofy smile. "You're old. Like way older than me and even way older than the other super-soldiers my dad hired to babysit me."

"Thanks," Linc said through gritted teeth as he tugged Wyatt from his perch before turning and depositing him on his feet safely away from the glass.

*intoxicating*

Wyatt pitched forward, the boy's smooth hands skimming across the hair on Linc's chest and over his nipples. Linc should have shoved a shirt on before investigating the sound. He wouldn't make that mistake again.

He waited for the boy to drop his hands, but, instead, he slid his palms down, tracing the grooves of his abdominal muscles, dropping his hands just before his fingertips could skate beneath the waistband of Linc's pajama pants.

Jesus.

Wyatt gazed up at him with wonder. "How can you be so old but still so hot? I bet girls line up for you, huh? Even the ones my age probably want you to be their sugar Daddy. Can you be a sugar Daddy with no money?"

Linc struggled to form a coherent thought. All the blood had rushed from his brain to his cock the moment Wyatt touched him. "I have no idea. Not really my area."

Was the boy trying to distract Linc? Make him angry? Confused? Was Wyatt confused? Linc walked him back around the pool, his hands on both arms, locking them at his sides just in case the kid got any ideas about groping him again. Linc wasn't sure he was that strong.

Wyatt stopped short, forcing Linc to do the same. "That's too bad. You'd be a good Daddy."

Linc's dick throbbed, but he just pushed Wyatt back into the house.

Once inside, the boy wriggled himself out of Linc's grasp and stumbled into the kitchen. "I'm starving."

He pulled a can of whipped cream from the fridge, upending it and spraying the contents into his mouth before moaning obscenely. Linc rolled his eyes, snatching the can and putting it back. "That's not food. Sit down, and I'll make you something."

A strange shadow crossed the kid's face before he gave him a lopsided smile. "G.I. Joe can cook," he said with a fake gasp. "Plot twist."

Linc didn't bother to answer. He opened the fridge, scrutinizing the contents. There was fettuccini on the shelf and raw spinach in the crisper drawer. With a little more digging he found cream, butter, and parmesan; everything he needed. He spent another ten minutes trying to find the spices and the pots and pans for the meal. He heated the butter in the pan and dumped the spinach in.

When he turned back around, Wyatt was amusing himself by taking all the almonds out of a bowl and arranging them to form pictures. "Come here."

Wyatt blinked at him. "What?"

*intoxicating*

"You can help. I'm not your cook."

Wyatt stood, making his way toward Linc with trepidation, like it was some elaborate scheme. Linc handed him a wooden spatula. "Just push them around in the pan so they don't burn, okay?"

Wyatt frowned but nodded, staring into the pan with the same concentration one gave bomb disposal. Linc smiled. He couldn't help himself.

He opened the cream and grated the parmesan before returning to the pan. As soon as he approached, Wyatt shoved the spatula in his face. "Here."

"Uh-uh. You're the chef. I'm the teacher. It's easy. Add this." Linc held out the cream. Wyatt stared at it stupidly before taking it and upending it into the pan with all the finesse of a toddler. It hissed as it hit the burner, and Wyatt flinched, wide eyes cutting to Linc. "It's fine. Now, you're going to just fold in the parmesan slowly while you stir. Got it?"

Wyatt didn't answer, just shook the parmesan into the sauce. *Good enough,* Linc thought. He placed the pasta in the now boiling water and pulled two plates from the cabinet.

When he'd plated the pasta, he filled two glasses with water and set them next to the plates.

Wyatt climbed up onto the stool next to Linc and picked up his fork. "No. Water first. The whole glass, then you can eat." Wyatt stared at the fettuccini longingly before picking up the water glass and draining it. "Good boy."

The words left Linc's mouth before he could stop them.

He could feel Wyatt's gaze burning into the side of his face, but he refused to look. Instead, he slipped from the stool and refilled Wyatt's glass. "Eat, or it'll get cold."

"Okay," Wyatt mumbled.

They ate in silence. Once they finished dinner, Linc rinsed the dishes and stacked them in the sink. "Bedtime," Linc said, pushing the boy toward the hallway. "Let's go."

Wyatt moved, still not speaking. When they got to his room, he turned on Linc. "Are you going to tell my dad I was drinking?"

Linc examined him, trying not to get lost in luminous green eyes. "Is that what you want? Do you want me to tell your dad you've been drinking so he can have another reason to be mad at you?"

Wyatt's face fell, and his cheeks flamed. "Good night, Linc. Thanks for the pasta."

## four

WYATT

TWO GUNSHOTS HAD WYATT ROCKETING UPRIGHT IN his bed. He couldn't see. The taste of metal filled his mouth, electricity jolting along his spine. He was blind.

"Rise and shine!"

The words exploded in his head like shrapnel from a dirty bomb. His hands flew to his face, relief washing over him as he realized he wore a black silk eye mask and the sexy-as-fuck soldier shouting at him hadn't, in fact, shot and blinded him. The loud bangs must have been Linc's fist hitting his door before entering.

His relief was short-lived as he peeled off the mask and the sun seared a hole through his already aching brain. He couldn't help the whimper that escaped. "Why?" was all he could manage. His tongue felt like he'd dragged it across a thousand dirty carpets.

What had happened last night? He didn't want to know. He slipped the mask back in place before rolling over and nestling himself deeper into the comforter trapped beneath him. There was a moment when the world righted itself before his stomach sloshed and the mattress began to rise and fall, like it rode the waves of rough seas.

"Why is the bed moving?" he groaned.

A low chuckle sounded from the vicinity of the doorway. "It's not. You're hungover."

"Why…are…you…screaming?" he asked in a desperate whisper.

"I'm not screaming. Why are you naked?"

"I'm not na—" he started.

Except, he was. Totally naked and laid out over the covers, like he was presenting himself to Linc. Oh, God. His already aching cock throbbed. He was thankful he was lying on his stomach. But that left him in a weird predicament. Did he just stay there, ass up, until Linc let him be? Did he cover himself and act like some scandalized maiden?

Another thought sent a shudder through him. Was Linc looking at him? The idea made him want to grind himself down onto the mattress. Guys like Linc... military guys...they all had girlfriends and wives. Even the ones who were gay were so deep in the closet they were frolicking with woodland creatures in Narnia.

What the hell was wrong with him? Everything. Fucking everything.

*"You'd make a good Daddy."*

Heat flooded Wyatt's face. Jesus, he'd actually said those words to Linc last night. He'd gazed up into those warm whiskey eyes and told G.I. Joe he'd be a good Daddy. What the fuck? There was nothing left for Wyatt to do but lie there, hungover and horny, and just wait to starve to death and die. He could never look Linc in the eye again. Like, who said shit like that? Not straight guys. And definitely not to another straight dude. He couldn't 'no homo' his way out of this.

He hoped his humiliation would somehow lessen his hard-on but nope. Apparently, Wyatt had all kinds of kinks. Had Linc left? Was he looking at him? God, the thought of Linc watching him had him wanting to arch up, push his hips into the air, present for him. Would he like what he saw? Would he want more? What would more look like with somebody like Linc? He wanted to know more than he wanted his next breath. More than he wanted his hangover to disappear.

Linc let out a strangled cough and then cleared his throat. "I told you yesterday. You will not sleep all day. Get up and get in the shower. I'll make you something to eat."

Wyatt swallowed. "I just need another hour. My head is pounding."

"There's a bottle of water next to your bed and some ibuprofen. Take the pills. Drink the whole bottle. Then get in the shower." When Wyatt didn't move, Linc barked, "Now."

"I'm a little naked here."

Linc snorted. "If you've got something I've never seen, I'll throw a dollar at it," he promised, his voice far more gravelly than Wyatt remembered.

It was clear Linc wasn't leaving…ever. "Yeah, fine."

Once more, he peeled off the eye mask, but this time, when he rolled over into a sitting position, he brought the covers with him, even if it looked a little ridiculous. He fought to keep the contents of his stomach where they were as the world assaulted him on every front. Linc looked fresh and clean in a pair of jeans and an olive-colored t-shirt. Wyatt had been right, Linc's arms were huge. He was huge. Was he huge everywhere? Wyatt forced the thought down before he started tenting the sheets.

Linc watched Wyatt with a strangely guarded look.

*intoxicating*

Wyatt made a show of tossing the pills back and sucking down all twelve ounces of water before turning the empty bottle over so Linc would see he was compliant. Linc snorted and shook his head but said nothing.

*"Good boy."*

Linc had said that to him last night. He'd practically purred it. Was that real? It couldn't be. Not even twenty-four hours with this guy and Wyatt was ready for the nut house. How was he going to survive six months with this man? His fucking dickhead father had finally found the perfect punishment.

Once Linc left, Wyatt practically crawled into the bathroom. He turned on the hot water and sat on the floor of the shower until some of the cobwebs in his brain finally faded away. He didn't bother to shave. He didn't trust himself around a razor. He brushed his teeth and threw on a pair of black joggers and the first t-shirt his hand touched, a white V-neck with the Chanel logo in bold black script. He didn't try to tame his damp curls. He was too busy trying to navigate walking and breathing at the same time.

How much did he even drink last night?

When he stumbled into the kitchen, he found Linc leaned against the kitchen counter with a cup of coffee in his hand as he read a folded up newspaper. Who read newspapers anymore? All that stuff could be found online. On Facebook, even. Old people loved Facebook.

On the counter was a plate with two pieces of toast with butter and a cup of black coffee. It stopped Wyatt cold, his chest constricting painfully. He swallowed hard, blinking sudden tears from his eyes. To somebody who knew nothing about them, the practical stranger standing in his kitchen could be his husband who had made Wyatt breakfast. Linc was barefoot, for fuck's sake. Wyatt didn't know why that mattered—why any of it mattered. Frustration had him wanting to turn and run but his feet seemed glued in place.

Linc glanced up. "Good, finally. Sit. Eat. All of it."

Wyatt rubbed at his eyes with probably more aggression than needed.

"You okay?"

The concern in Linc's voice was like a hand against his windpipe. He sucked in a shaky breath. "Yeah, the smell of coffee just turned my stomach. Made my eyes water. That's all."

Linc grunted but didn't respond. Wyatt was grateful. He was far too raw for anybody to be questioning him about anything. He sat at the bar and nibbled at his toast, ignoring the coffee. He preferred a little coffee with his cream and sugar, but he couldn't seem to will himself to open his mouth and ask for it. God, he was

*intoxicating*

a fucking mess.

Luckily, Linc seemed content to stand there and read his paper. Had he left and gotten the paper, or did they deliver it? Wyatt had never noticed one before. He didn't know why it mattered. He just needed something innocuous to occupy his brain rather than the man six feet away.

He was going to ask—just to fill the silence—when a strange chirping sound came from Linc's pocket. He pulled out his phone and frowned at the caller ID.

Linc flicked his eyes toward Wyatt. "I have to take this. Eat." He walked around the corner, but Wyatt could still hear every word. "Hey, sweetheart. Everything okay?"

Once more, that strange pressure in Wyatt's chest returned. Of course, he had a girlfriend, maybe even a wife. Lots of military guys didn't wear rings. He took another tentative bite of his toast, forcing himself to chew and swallow.

"I know. Tell them I'm working on it." What exactly had 'sweetheart' said? Working on what? "Okay, well, I'll call them in a little while. Try to buy us a little more time." Another pause and a huge sigh. "Look, I know. What time is his doctor's appointment?" *Whose doctor's appointment?* Wyatt silently screamed. "Make sure you give yourself an hour to get him ready. He was feisty the other day. He wants to do everything himself, but he just can't."

Jesus, a wife and a kid? Wyatt pushed his plate away, pills and water and half a piece of toast churning in his stomach.

"Yeah, I know. Call me when you leave the office. I love you, too."

Wyatt picked up his coffee and gazed into it glumly. Linc frowned when he came back around the corner, staring pointedly at Wyatt's still full plate.

"I said all of it."

Wyatt set his coffee down and leaned back against the cool iron back of the bar stool, crossing his arms. "I can't. I'll puke."

Linc stalked forward, pushing the plate toward him. "You can and you will. This is non-negotiable."

A tiny shiver raced along Wyatt's spine, his nipples going hard at Linc's stern tone. But he stuck out his chin. "I said I can't."

Linc leaned into his space until his breath puffed against his cheek. He smelled like coffee and sandalwood. "Listen, kid. I've got all day. If it takes the next six months to get you to eat two goddamn pieces of toast, well then, that's what it takes. Try me."

Wyatt licked his lips, thinking there was nothing in the world he'd like more than to try Linc. He tried not to

*intoxicating*

let his gaze fall to sleeves stretched over muscled biceps that led to perfect forearms dusted with dark hair.

Wyatt was so fucked. He pushed the thought away, sneering at the older man. "Fine. But if I puke all over the counter, you can explain it to Graciela."

Linc raised one thick brow. "If you puke on the counter, you're going to clean it up, brat. You're twenty-two years old. Time to act like it."

Something flared in Wyatt's stomach. "I'm sorry, but who the fuck are you? You're just a fucking bodyguard. You're not my fucking life coach. That chick quit, like, six months ago. I'll eat your stupid fucking toast, but you can stop acting like you give a fuck about me. We met yesterday." The minute the words left his mouth, Wyatt wanted to suck them back in. He wanted to invent a time machine and go back thirty seconds and not sound like the pathetic loser he truly was deep down.

He stared at his plate for a solid minute before he dared to look up again. Linc examined him, forehead furrowed but eyes soft...almost like he felt sorry for him. That made Wyatt want to throw something, drink something, swan dive off the balcony. Anything to get away from Linc's pitying glance.

He picked up the untouched second piece of toast, folded it up and stuffed the whole thing in his mouth, fighting the urge to gag as he chewed it defiantly.

Linc grinned, and Wyatt's heart stopped beating, all the blood in his entire body heading south. His gaze followed Linc as he walked around the counter. For a moment, Wyatt thought he was coming toward him, but then he walked past him through the living room to the hallway. He let out a shuddery breath, disappointment and relief flooding his overstimulated system in equal measure.

Sudden warmth bloomed against his back and the world tilted on its axis as Linc's face suddenly appeared next to his, his lips close enough to press his words against Wyatt's skin. "Good boy."

Wyatt bit his bottom lip, struggling against the temptation to lean into the words, but Linc was already walking away again. "Fuck you," Wyatt whispered to himself.

"Don't think that you're going to lounge by the fucking pool all day, either. You're going to make yourself useful," Linc called from somewhere down the hallway.

How the fuck was Wyatt going to do that?

## five

### LINCOLN

LINC LOCKED HIMSELF IN HIS ROOM AND HEADED straight for the bathroom. He splashed cold water on his face and cursed himself for being a goddamn idiot. Not even forty-eight hours on the job and he was already playing chicken with a kid half his age. He was a special brand of fucking stupid. Wyatt was spoiled and reckless and a hundred different kinds of damaged, but fuck if Linc's cock didn't stand at attention every time the brat stared him down, just begging Linc to make him obey.

Wyatt was perfect in every way. Beautiful, sullen, stubborn...just broken enough to not care that the war had left Linc fucked up in ways he couldn't even begin to put into words. The look on the kid's face when Linc had walked away without praising him for doing as he was told… Fuck. How could he not go back? Not give him the words he'd been so desperate for? Linc was only human.

But he needed this fucking job, needed it more than anything. People were counting on him. He couldn't get distracted. He couldn't be what Wyatt needed. He stared at himself in the mirror. Why was he even contemplating this? They didn't even know each other. He needed to get a goddamn grip on himself and his perversions.

But Wyatt wanted him. The boy was a big sucking void and Linc wanted nothing more than to fill him up, again and again, to give him what he so desperately needed. But Linc would be a monster for giving in. Wyatt was one big open wound, desperate for somebody to be all the things his father wasn't, and Linc couldn't do that, not in the way the kid needed, not the way anybody needed. There was something wrong with him; a wire had gotten crossed and he could never go back.

He needed to jerk off and fucking forget about it. Put all these thoughts in a box and put it on a shelf and just do his fucking job. He should never have gone into

*intoxicating*

Wyatt's room last night. It went far beyond the call of duty. But after seeing him on that railing, one strong wind or drunken fumble away from death, the bleakness practically radiating from him…Linc knew he wouldn't sleep without checking to make sure he was okay.

He hadn't expected to find him blindfolded and naked and laid out for him, like an offering. All that pale creamy skin set against that stark black comforter had left Linc hard and leaking just picturing all the things he could do to him. He'd even contemplated sliding his hands into his sweatpants and getting himself off as he watched the boy sleep before he came to his senses.

It would be far too easy to take the boy, to make him his. *"You'd make a good Daddy."* That's what Wyatt had said. Daddy. The word had bounced around Linc's head all night as he'd thrust into his tightened fist, eyes clenched shut, imagining Wyatt riding his cock, head thrown back, full red lips parted as he panted, begging his Daddy to give him what he needed. Fuck, Linc wanted that. He wanted to make him beg. Wanted to hear his desperate cries fall from those sinfully perfect lips. Wanted to know what Wyatt looked like bent over and covered in Linc's handprints.

Goddammit.

Linc slammed his fist against the counter. He was

a fucking soldier, and this kid was a job. He was also the son of a powerful conservative senator who had no qualms about treating his own kid as a criminal. Suddenly, the senator's remarks about his opponent rang in his head. *"The gays would run amuck."* Had this douchebag hired Linc just to make sure his kid stayed firmly in the closet?

He shook his head. He couldn't get caught up in some political family drama. He couldn't be what Wyatt needed, no matter how much the thought appealed to him.

"Get it together, asshole."

Linc needed to blow off some steam. He changed into black athletic shorts and headed down the hall toward the in-house gym Graciela had pointed out on his quick tour yesterday.

He had just crossed the threshold when he heard it. A high-pitched whine followed by a strangled distressed noise and then Wyatt chanting, "No, no, no, no, no, no!"

Linc turned, heading back toward the kitchen, frowning at the frantic thumping and slamming noises. He was almost back to the living room when Wyatt cried his name.

"Linc!"

He'd spent far too many hours last night picturing

*intoxicating*

all the ways he could make Wyatt scream his name, but none had prepared him for the sight of the boy standing in the kitchen, slowly being overtaken by a sea of white foam. Linc blinked stupidly, trying to make sense of what unfolded before him.

Wyatt's wide eyes shot to him, his lips wet and his chest heaving. Jesus, he was gorgeous even when panicked. "What are you doing?" Linc asked, voice calm.

"Making myself useful," he shouted. Linc didn't miss the accusation in his tone.

While Linc was putting the pieces together with no problem, he wasn't quite ready to rescue Wyatt.

"How, exactly?"

"I was doing the dishes," he said indignantly.

Linc couldn't help but smile as the bubbles expanded, spilling past the island. Wyatt was adorably flustered, glaring and gesturing toward the white mess as if it had wronged him. Linc took a deep breath and said goodbye to his favorite sneakers before carefully wading into the fray. He grimaced as bubbles clung to his bare legs and water soaked his shoes and socks.

He thought Wyatt would move out of his way as he approached, but he ignored Linc and stabbed uselessly at the many buttons on the device. In the kid's defense, Linc had seen missile launch pads with fewer buttons. Was this a dishwasher or a transformer?

"Move," he barked.

Wyatt threw a glare over his shoulder before attempting to comply. He stepped back, his bare foot landing on Linc's sneaker, causing him to stumble. Linc's hands shot out, closing around Wyatt's waist, gripping him tight, pulling him back against his chest with more strength than necessary. Wyatt's sharp intake of breath sent a jolt of electricity along Linc's skin, his fingers digging into the grooves of the boy's narrow hips through the thin layer of cotton fabric.

For a moment, they both froze. Wyatt felt good in his arms. He fit perfectly, his riot of curls resting just under Linc's chin. His hands flexed as Wyatt's breath punched from him in tiny gasps. Linc wanted to use those angelic curls to tug Wyatt's head to the side, bite bruises along his neck, mark him for all the world to see. The urge to drag his teeth along all that pale skin had his cock standing at attention, and there was no way the boy couldn't feel his arousal pressing against him.

Wyatt didn't move, didn't struggle to get away. He was rigid in Linc's arms, waiting—waiting on Linc's orders. The boy would do anything Linc wanted, he knew it in a way he'd never be able to explain to another soul. Wyatt was his; his to kiss, his to fuck, his to protect and discipline. Jesus, none of this made sense, but Linc knew he wasn't wrong. If he dragged

*intoxicating*

the boy's sweatpants down right then and there, Wyatt would let him. Linc could slip inside Wyatt's hot, tight channel and fuck him bent over the kitchen island, hands around his throat while Wyatt gasped for air, taking only what Linc allowed.

He needed to stop this, to let him go. Instead, he wrapped his arm farther around the boy's waist, tucking him against his chest as he leaned forward and pressed the off button. The mountain of foam stopped pouring from the sides of the machine, but it did nothing to diminish the mess already there.

The dishwasher fell silent, the green light dying. Linc could feel Wyatt's taut belly rising and falling beneath the broad spread of his fingers as they just stood there, paralyzed by whatever this was. Wyatt was so warm against him, and he smelled like spice and flowers. "What did you do?" Linc murmured, trying desperately to break the spell.

"What?" Wyatt mumbled, distracted.

Linc chuckled, his chin resting on top of Wyatt's head. "What did you use for soap?"

He made a helpless gesture, foam flying from his fingers and landing on his cheek. "I'm not stupid. I used dish soap." He snagged the bottle of viscous purple liquid and pointed to the words 'dish soap' before looking over his shoulder at Linc. "See?"

Linc's breath punched out of him at the desperation in Wyatt's eyes. He wanted Linc's approval, his validation, even for something as simple as this. Linc was playing with fire, but fuck, it was a heady feeling.

"Dish soap is for washing dishes in the sink. The detergent goes in the dishwasher," Linc said gently.

The light died in Wyatt's gaze, his perfect mouth turning down at the corners as he pushed away from Linc. He should have let him go but he held firm.

"It was an honest mistake. It was a good effort."

"Yeah, sure. Whatever," Wyatt said, dropping his gaze back to the bottle.

God, this kid was so raw, so fragile. Linc laced his fingers through Wyatt's curls, tugging his head back, forcing him to meet his gaze. "Hey, don't do that."

Linc's cock stood at attention as Wyatt trembled against him, his lips falling open. Linc dipped his head.

A sound rang out, like some unseen hand banging a gong, somewhere near the vicinity of the door, and then, suddenly, a girl with a riot of chestnut curls flounced into the living room with an enormous bag over one arm and her phone in the other.

"Wyatt! I need you. My day has been a full-on five-alarm dumpster fi…re?" She trailed off, stopping short as she took in the two of them.

Linc dropped his arms, taking two steps back.

*intoxicating*

The girl raised both brows, smirking. "Oh. Well, hi there."

Linc cleared his throat. "I think it's okay now. Why don't you visit with your friend and I'll…I'll take care of this mess. The dishwasher will be out of commission for a while."

Wyatt swallowed hard, giving Linc one last longing look before turning to the girl. "What did I tell you about barging in here?"

She scrunched up her face. "Fuck if I know. Was I sober?"

He scoffed, grabbing her by the arm and tugging her down the hall. "Are you ever?"

"True."

Linc turned back to the mess at his feet. That was close. That girl might have just saved his life.

## six

### WYATT

WYATT DRAGGED CHARLEMAGNE HASTINGS DOWN THE hall with far more speed and aggression than a girl wobbling on five-inch heels was probably used to, but he needed to put some distance between him and G.I. Joe back in the kitchen. Some small part of Wyatt felt guilty for leaving the man to clean up his mess, but another part of him was still thinking about said soldier's erection pressing against his back.

Wyatt would have bet his entire trust fund Linc had been two seconds away from kissing him before Charlie had barged in there like the hot sloppy mess she was, and Wyatt was one hundred percent sure

*intoxicating*

he would have let him and seventy-five percent sure it would have been the worst idea ever. God, what would Wyatt even do with Linc? The man was married, with a kid. Even if he was gay, he wasn't available, and Wyatt was a lot of things, but he wasn't a homewrecker.

At least, he never had been.

Once they entered his room, he locked the door. For one insane moment, he even contemplated sliding a chair under the handle. He took a deep breath and let it out, trying to calm his frayed nerves. But then a thought formed, making itself at home in his brain. He and Linc were stuck together for the next six months. Six fucking months of whatever the fuck just happened in the kitchen, or almost happened, or whatever. How was Wyatt supposed to deal with that? He wasn't strong enough to say no.

Wyatt didn't know whether he should laugh or cry. This particular problem could never have crossed his father's mind when he'd hired Linc. His old man couldn't imagine a world where somebody like Linc would ever look at someone like Wyatt as anything but weak and pathetic. Wyatt couldn't really picture it either, but he hadn't imagined Linc's fingers digging into his flesh or his breath against his neck or his rock-hard cock pressed snugly against the small of Wyatt's back.

Charlie turned on him out of nowhere, knocking him out of his thoughts before he had to deal with his own inconvenient boner.

She poked one pointy plum-colored nail into his chest. "Okay, babyface. Talk to me. What is going on with you and Mr. Sex-on-a-Stick out there? He looked like he was about to mount you on the kitchen counter."

"Shut up," he said, but there was no bite to his words.

"He's kinda old though, right?"

He didn't answer her, just rolled his eyes. Yesterday, he would've called Linc old, but today, he thought he was just old enough. Wyatt glanced down at his damp joggers and t-shirt and briefly considered changing but dismissed the idea. Maybe the cold, clinging fabric would keep him uncomfortable enough to stop reliving the last fifteen minutes in his kitchen.

"Come on, you gotta give me something. Were you two about to christen your mother's precious marble countertops?"

Wyatt sighed. He had no idea what would've happened had Charlie not barged in, and he honestly wasn't sure he wanted to know. There was something about the way Linc looked at him, like he could see through him somehow. It left Wyatt jittery and

*intoxicating*

unsettled. If Linc looking at him made him breathless and shaky, what the fuck would happen if he kissed him…or something more? Wyatt wasn't exactly a virgin but Linc made him feel like one.

"Seriously, boo-boo. What's up with you and the stranger in your kitchen? I thought your dad still had you stuffed in his closet. If I missed your coming-out party, I'm gonna be pissed."

Wyatt's stomach plummeted, and bitterness filled his tone. "You've missed nothing. I'm still a closet case, promise."

Charlie dropped her suitcase-sized handbag on his bed and walked toward the tall chair sitting in front of his vanity. She flounced onto the black leather seat, smoothing her white t-shirt dress down over long tanned legs. "That's too bad. Old Man River out there definitely wants to fuck you six ways from Sunday."

His face flushed, frustration twisting his insides. "Jesus, Charlie. Do you ever stop to think about what you say before you say it?"

"Of course not. What would be the fun in that?" She made grabby hands toward him. "Okay, enough about you. Let's talk about me."

He rolled his eyes. "You really need to stop mixing your Adderall with your Chardonnay."

She scoffed, one hand clutching her metaphorical

pearls. "How dare you? Do you think I could tolerate my mother without pharmaceuticals? Or your mother, for that matter?"

He shrugged. "That's fair. Why are you here?"

Her voice took on a high-pitched whine. "I need you to do me."

Wyatt blinked at her. "What?"

"Do me! My makeup. My hair. I got a callback on my audition, and I can't get in with Kristiane until next week, and I need to look like the ingenue that I am."

Wyatt threw a look toward the closed door as if Linc might linger on the other side, listening through the keyhole. Not that there was a keyhole. Or any reason for Linc to spy. At all. He was probably up to his well-sculpted ass in lavender-scented dish bubbles.

Wyatt sighed. "Fine. Sit. So, what are we talking about here? My-parents-stockpile-Bibles-and-guns fresh-faced or I-have-Daddy-issues slutty?"

She tapped her nail against her veneers. "Somewhere in between those two would be perfect."

"Brooke Shields in *Blue Lagoon* it is."

His stomach swooped as he gave one more nervous glance toward the locked door. He wasn't sure why he didn't want Linc to know about the makeup. But he only shared this part of himself with the people he

*intoxicating*

trusted, which at twenty-two years old was comprised of two people, Charlie and Graciela.

He busied himself pulling various palettes and brushes from drawers as Charlie ignored him, rapidly firing off texts to her mother and her agent. By the time he flipped on the white lights surrounding the vanity mirror, upbeat music spilled from the speaker of Charlie's phone. He'd learned long ago that the key to shutting the girl up was to give her a song to sing, and he just didn't want to talk about Linc anymore.

"Okay, phone down."

Charlie complied, letting her eyes fall shut, even without him asking. As stupid as it sounded, the two of them had been doing this for so long, the ritual almost felt sacred. Charlie understood what makeup meant to Wyatt more than anybody. Sure, there was an artistry to it, but there was magic in it as well. Makeup concealed, it transformed, it could make people see things that weren't there and hide things that were. It was as close to sorcery as Wyatt was ever likely to get, and he gave it the reverence it deserved.

They fell into a companionable silence. When Wyatt went to work on Charlie's hair, she switched the music so she could practice for her rehearsal. He parted sections of her hair as she flawlessly belted out numbers from the *Hamilton* soundtrack. Wyatt tried not to be jealous of her talent or her freedom, but it was hard. For as much as Charlie's mom was a 'stage mom,' she was also fiercely protective of Charlie... and even Wyatt, to an extent. A former beauty queen who'd married a hedge fund manager, she often lamented about how she'd wished for a gay son.

Wyatt tried not to dwell on the life he could have had with Charlie's accepting parents instead of his hateful father and his uninterested mother. There was no use crying over bad DNA.

When he finished with Charlie, he misted a setting spray over her face and shellacked her hair in place with a bit more flourish than necessary. "Okay, I hereby declare you just slutty enough for your callback."

Charlie bounced off the chair, snagging her phone as she gave herself a cursory once-over. "Oh, it's perfect. Somewhere between scream queen and drag queen. Once again, your genius astounds me." She snagged her enormous bag from the bed, settling it in the crook of her arm before she stopped in front of him, narrowing her eyes. "You'd tell me if you weren't okay, right?"

Adrenaline shocked through his system at her sudden change in tactics, his heartbeat tripping. "What?"

*intoxicating*

The corners of her mouth tugged downward, her heart suddenly bleeding from her big blue lemur eyes. "You don't look good."

Something twisted behind his ribcage. "Well, fuck you very much."

She wrapped her hand around his forearm, her talon-like nails digging into the skin there. "I'm serious. You have that same hollow-eyed haunted look you had just before we went to Barbados that summer... The summer you came back from—"

"I remember," he snapped. He softened his tone at her wounded look. "I'm fine. I just had a little too much to drink last night."

Her expression went from piteous to murderous in a moment, her voice dropping to a hissing whisper. "Drink? You're on house arrest for a DUI."

He rolled his eyes, waving his hand dismissively. "Do you see a car in here?"

"Don't do that. This is serious." He let his gaze drift to a spot over her shoulder, trying to mentally shield himself from her words. "You can't keep doing this to yourself. You have to get out of here, away from your father, from this place. It's not good for you."

Wyatt forced a brittle smile onto his face. "Hah. Let she who is without prescription pharmaceuticals in her Prada cast the first stone. You can't even get out of bed without amphetamines."

She sucked in a breath, her voice raising an octave. "I have a legitimate diagnosis, dickhead. You're mean when you're hungover."

He pulled a face, crossing his arms over his still-damp t-shirt. "And you're no fun when you're preachy, so I guess we're even."

They stood glaring at each other for a solid minute before Charlie's shoulders slumped and he watched her shrug off the last five minutes as if they'd never happened. A huge toothy grin spread across her face. "Anyhoo, gotta run. Let's totes do it again soon." She dropped a kiss on his cheek before opening the door. "Try not to trip and fall on Grandpa's dick out there. He might break a hip."

"Wow. You're so funny," he sneered, shoving her out his bedroom door.

"Hey, you look like the bait on *To Catch a Predator*. I'm just trying to keep you safe."

He flipped her off. "Good luck on your callback," he said, voice filled with spiteful glee.

Her eyes went wide, and she stabbed her finger into his chest. "You take that back right now."

"No."

"I'm not kidding, Wyatt Montgomery Edgeworth. You say 'break a leg' right now or we're not friends

*intoxicating*

anymore." He stared her down. "Say it!" she screeched.

After he felt she'd sufficiently twisted in the wind, he relented. "Fine. Break a leg, I guess."

She shook her head like a disappointed mom. "You're a monster."

"It's true. You know the way out," he said, shutting his bedroom door in her face.

He should go back out and help Linc, but instead, he fell backward on the bed, suddenly cognizant of his still-damp clothes and the giant knot in his belly. He couldn't do it. He couldn't go back out there and pretend they hadn't almost kissed. So, he just lay there, hiding in his room like a coward. Like he always did.

It was going to be a really long day.

## seven

### LINCOLN

LINC WAS DREAMING. HE KNEW HE WAS. IT DIDN'T STOP his heart from racing or the metallic taste from filling his mouth. It always started with blood. Copper pennies and gasoline burned his nose and throat. The desert sun seared his flesh. He tried to blink the sweat from his eyes, but he still couldn't see. His men were out there somewhere. Had they survived the blast? Wavering shapes rushed toward him. He squinted, trying to make sense of them. Did they wear fatigues? He couldn't tell. They were ghosts, or maybe he was the ghost. If it weren't for the throbbing numbness radiating down his right arm, he might have thought he was dead.

*intoxicating*

He tried to reach for his rifle just a few feet away, but his arm wasn't cooperating. They were getting closer with each passing second. His pulse skyrocketed, adrenaline sending shock waves along his body until he wasn't thinking, only reacting. When the amorphous shape appeared above him, he lashed out with his left hand, gripping their throat with everything he had and rolling them beneath him. He needed the advantage. They had weapons. They had the full use of their bodies. They had all their senses. He only had fear and training. He straddled them, squeezing with every bit of strength he could muster with just his one hand. If he was lucky, he could fracture their hyoid bone. They'd suffocate.

They fought back, their blows weak as they struggled beneath him, frantically shouting.

"Linc!"

Somewhere, the sound of his name penetrated through the fog of his memory.

"Linc. Stop! Fuck, please. Fuck. Stop!"

Linc opened his eyes, blinking to adjust to the sudden darkness after having struggled in the blazing noonday sun of his nightmare. He was back in his room at the Edgeworth penthouse, straddling a breathless, red-faced Wyatt. *Jesus. Holy fucking Christ.* Linc could have killed him. His hand still clutched Wyatt's throat. His left hand. *Thank fuck.* He let out a shaky breath. If it had been his right hand… He didn't even want to think about that. He massaged the tender skin at Wyatt's throat. The boy winced as he swallowed beneath Linc's fingers. Even in the dark, he could see it would bruise. "I'm so sorry," he whispered.

Wyatt's lips moved, but his voice sounded miles away. A lead weight crushed down on Linc's chest, and his vision tunneled, his heart slamming against his ribcage until he thought he was having a heart attack. Fuck. Not now. Not. Now. Beads of perspiration pricked at his forehead and slid along his spine, but he was ice cold. He wanted to move, to run away, but his mind held him frozen.

Wyatt's soft hands were touching his face as he spoke. Linc forced himself to concentrate on the boy's lips. "Linc. I think you're having a panic attack. Can you hear me?"

He didn't speak, just gave a jerky nod.

"Okay, dude, I have these all the time. Focus on five things you can see." Linc's gaze jerked around the room, trying to focus on anything. "Say them. Out loud."

"The lamp. The headboard." He sucked in a ragged breath, his gaze falling to Wyatt. *Your sinful mouth, your riot of curls spilling over my pillow,* he thought to

*intoxicating*

himself. He swallowed. "The...the chair. The pillows. You."

Wyatt's thumb caressed Linc's cheek, his voice a low murmur. "Tell me four things you can touch."

Four things he could touch. Okay. The sheets, the comforter, the silky material of Wyatt's pants, the soft skin of his long delicate throat, still clenched in Linc's left hand.

*Shit.* He tried to move his hand, but Wyatt captured it, holding it in place. "Don't." Linc's cock twitched at Wyatt's raw plea. "Four things."

He needed to focus. To think. To relax. To pull himself back. Focus. "The sheets. The blanket... You. I can feel you."

Wyatt's pupils dilated, his pink tongue licking over his full lower lip, goosebumps erupting across his skin. "That's three," he whispered.

"It's enough."

Wyatt gave a half nod of acceptance. "Two things you can hear."

The air conditioner humming, the fan squeaking lazily overhead, but all Linc could think to say was, "Your breathing."

"One thing you can...taste."

He leaned down, pressing his lips against Wyatt's, dipping his tongue inside for just a moment before pulling back. This time, his heart felt off-kilter for an entirely different reason. They sat there, locked in place, Linc's hand around Wyatt's throat and Wyatt's hand crushing Linc's wrist, refusing to let him go. They were both panting, both half naked. Wyatt's impressive hard-on was tenting his gray pajama bottoms underneath Linc.

This was all happening too fast. It shouldn't be happening at all. Taking this job was a mistake, but it was too late to turn back now. He needed the money. Linc should let him go, should walk away and lock himself in the bathroom and jerk off in the shower, like a person who valued his fucking job and his integrity. But he didn't. He fucking didn't.

He dipped his head lower but didn't kiss the boy, just breathed him in. With Linc looming over him, one hand still on his throat, Wyatt seemed to melt into the mattress, like every problem he'd ever had was suddenly long gone. Maybe, in that minute, it was. Maybe all Wyatt needed was a hand around his throat and somebody to use him up and take what they wanted. And Linc wanted. He wanted everything.

When he slanted his lips over Wyatt's this time, the boy moaned low, canting his hips, rubbing his needy cock against Linc's own half-hard dick. Linc took his time. It wasn't sex, Linc rationalized, just fooling

*intoxicating*

around, giving Wyatt what he needed, what they both needed. Wyatt's little noises drove Linc crazy. The boy was so pliant, so willing. He'd let Linc do anything to him. The thought had Linc hard and leaking so fast it made him dizzy.

He ripped his mouth free, biting kisses along Wyatt's jaw and throat, slowing only to press his lips a bit more gently to each of the reddened fingerprints that would be bruises tomorrow. He should be sorry—he might have been sorrier if Wyatt had seemed even a little distressed—but the idea of marking Wyatt, seeing tangible proof of what they were doing long after the sun came up tomorrow, had Linc growling, capturing Wyatt's mouth in another rough kiss.

He pulled back, gazing down at the pale expanse of Wyatt's bare torso, letting his hands smooth over his chest. Wyatt clutched at Linc, whining, trying to pull him back down. "Don't worry, greedy boy. I'm not done with you," Linc promised.

He hooked his fingers in Wyatt's waistband, tugging his pants down and off, tossing them somewhere on the other side of the room. Wyatt's cock slapped against his firm belly, and Linc wanted nothing more than to bury his face where his scent was strongest, to run his mouth along the hard length and suck him down until he came screaming beneath him. Instead, he took him in hand, wiping his thumb along the tip, using the fluid to work him slowly. Wyatt arched his back, moaning long and low like Linc had wrenched the sound from him. He was beautiful like this, head thrown back, lips parted, chest heaving. Just for Linc.

He released him, smiling when the boy whined his frustration. Linc was only getting rid of his own underwear, then he lined himself up over Wyatt again, his body pressing into him. Wyatt practically sobbed, rocking himself desperately against Linc to get more friction.

Linc could easily have just rutted against him like a teenager until he came, but some part of him wanted to test Wyatt, wanted to see how far he could push him. He leaned forward, practically bending the boy in half. God, he'd love to fuck him this way, his knees over Linc's elbows as he drove himself into the tight heat of Wyatt's pliant body again and again…but this could only be tonight, and Wyatt wasn't ready for anything more than this.

Linc braced himself over Wyatt with one hand, the other slipping back around his throat as their bodies aligned perfectly, their cocks slotting alongside each other.

"Yes," Wyatt sobbed.

"Yes, what?" Linc growled against his ear, squeezing

his throat just enough for Wyatt to struggle. "Say it. I need to hear you say it."

"Yes, Daddy," Wyatt whispered.

Linc bit at his lips, rocking their bodies faster. "Again, say it again."

"Please, Daddy."

"Beg me."

"Please. Please. I need you. I need th—" His words died on a harsh shout as Linc ground their hips together. "Please, Daddy. Please. Please. Please," he chanted, almost like he didn't even know the words were falling from his lips.

"Good boy," Linc praised, his hand slipping from Wyatt's throat to yank at the drawer beside his head. He snatched the small bottle of lube from its place tucked way in the back and sat back on his heels, pressing a hand to Wyatt's chest as he tried to follow. "Don't move," Linc commanded.

Wyatt looked like he wanted to argue but did as Linc instructed, so he rewarded the boy by taking both of their cocks in his slick fist. Wyatt worked himself against Linc's cock and the tight heat of his palm. Normally, Linc would have forced him to remain still, but he was being so good, so obedient. Linc let him chase his pleasure, once more wrapping his hand around the boy's throat and squeezing as electricity licked its way across every nerve ending. His balls tightened, and the base of his spine felt hot and tingly. He would not last much longer. He caught Wyatt's heated gaze. "Come for me. Come for Daddy."

Wyatt sucked in a breath, a look of surprise spreading across his angelic face as his body seized beneath Linc and he came hard, shooting onto his stomach and spilling over Linc's fist. Linc didn't stop. He worked him through the aftershocks before catching Wyatt's cum in his hand, working it over his own length. Wyatt stared up at Linc, glassy-eyed and sated, like he'd heard the voice of God, like Linc was a god and getting Wyatt off had been some kind of goddamn epiphany. It was the look that did it, had Linc coming with a harsh shout, painting Wyatt's belly with his own release before smearing it over the boy's skin, like he could rub his scent into his flesh, make him a permanent part of him. When he finished, he brought his hand to Wyatt's lips. He didn't have to say a word; Wyatt opened immediately, his tongue darting out to lick Linc's fingers clean.

He was so fucking obedient. Linc leaned down and kissed his forehead. "That's my sweet boy," he praised before rolling to lie beside him.

# eight

## WYATT

WYATT SAID NOTHING, JUST LAY THERE SUCKING in heavy breaths, waiting for the use of his limbs to return. His post-orgasmic haze was wearing off quickly, and the evidence of their encounter was drying on his skin, making him itch. Wyatt had never been in bed with a guy before. He'd fooled around in cars and bathrooms and even the industrial freezer at Bar Lounge but never in a bed. It was too...intimate. Too personal. He enjoyed being able to get off and get out. Before anybody figured out who he really was.

But there was no sneaking away this time. Linc was right there, pressed against him, splayed out naked with one hand behind his head and the other across his stomach, like lying in bed with Wyatt was no big deal. Maybe it wasn't a big deal to Linc. He was married. He had a kid. Wyatt's stomach churned. After Charlie left, he should have stayed in bed, like he'd planned, but after midnight, his stomach had demanded sustenance and he'd crept into the kitchen. There was a note on the microwave door. Linc had made dinner and left it for him. Who did that? They didn't even know each other and Linc had shown him more consideration than anybody in his family ever had.

That was why he went to Linc's room, to thank him for dinner. At least, that was Wyatt's story. He hadn't expected to find Linc struggling and whimpering, crying out. He only wanted to wake him. But when he'd touched his chest, Linc had rolled him underneath him and clutched his throat, and Wyatt's lizard brain had kicked in. And this lizard liked to be manhandled by hot scruffy men in their underwear, apparently.

Wyatt wanted to roll over and bury his face in the pillow and wait Linc out, but it was his bed. When the mattress shifted, Wyatt couldn't help but glance in Linc's direction, admiring the view of his sculpted ass as he strode naked across the room and opened the door to the mini fridge in the corner.

When he came back, he sat facing Wyatt. "Come on.

*intoxicating*

Up. Sit up." Linc's tone left no room for arguing. If Wyatt's cock could have rallied, it would have. "Drink this."

He stared at it for a long moment, but then he took it and sucked down half. He went to hand it back, but Linc shook his head. "All of it." Wyatt did as he was told and Linc took the empty bottle back. "Lie back down."

This time, Wyatt did roll away from Linc. He didn't want to be cared for. He didn't want Linc acting like this meant anything. These encounters never meant anything. They couldn't. What was the point? When Linc curved his body around Wyatt's and tucked him tight against him, Wyatt froze. "You don't have to do this, you know."

Lips traced the back of his neck. "I like to snuggle after an orgasm. Get over it."

Wyatt scoffed, feeling huffy. "Don't I get a say in this?"

A shiver ran across Wyatt at Linc's rough growl. "Nope. My room, my rules."

Silence blanketed the room, the only sound the rhythmic movement of the fan overhead and Wyatt's heart beating in his ears. Linc's fingers spread across Wyatt's belly, his thumb rubbing lazy circles that stirred something deep down low.

"Thanks for dinner," he finally mumbled, for lack of anything to say.

"I wasn't sure you would find it. I thought maybe you'd died in there," Linc said, voice sleep soaked like he'd dozed off or had been on the verge of doing so.

"I was avoiding you."

Air puffed against Wyatt's shoulder as Linc laughed at him. "You don't say. Why was that exactly? Afraid I'd put you to work instead of letting you tan by the pool all day?"

"No. 'Cause I was pretty sure you wanted to fuck me in my kitchen earlier." The words left Wyatt's mouth before he could stop them.

Teeth grazed Wyatt's shoulder, and his cock twitched, the hand that had been on his belly now scraping over one hard nipple. "You're imagining things. I find you repulsive," Linc rumbled.

Wyatt smiled despite himself, his hand reaching back to rub Linc's hip. "Yeah, same. When you kissed me, I almost puked."

Once again, that gruff laugh before they descended back into silence. Wyatt waited for Linc to do something more. He could feel Linc's half-hard cock resting against his ass. Linc was driving him nuts, just kissing and licking at his neck, touching him like he owned him, like he had some claim to Wyatt's body, like it was his to access any time he wanted. The thought had the blood rushing south, but Wyatt couldn't let this happen again. It just felt too good.

He turned in Linc's arms until they were practically nose to nose. "I don't know what this is that we're doing right now. I don't know what you expect from me. I don't do cuddles and kisses and just breathing in each other's space. Like…this isn't me."

Linc pressed his lips to Wyatt's forehead. "Relax. This was just a temporary moment of insanity. We just needed to get it out of our systems. You've been locked up in this house for six months and were probably bored. I haven't had the time or the energy to find a hookup since I was discharged. We've got another six months stuck together. It's good we got this out of our systems now. Right?"

Wyatt's stomach curdled like spoiled milk, his chest tightening, but he gave Linc a nod and a tight smile. "Yeah. Totally."

"In twelve days, you'll be on the outside and I'll just be the old guy lurking in the corner, keeping you out of trouble."

Wyatt rubbed his nose against Linc's before stealing a kiss. "You are pretty old," he agreed somberly. "You're, like, what? Fifty?"

Linc snorted. "Forty, you little shit."

This time, it was Wyatt who laughed. "Same difference. Old is old."

"Go to sleep. Tomorrow we go back to the real world."

Wyatt wanted to tell him there was no way he could sleep with another person hot and sweaty against him, but a yawn interrupted his plans. He tucked his head under Linc's chin. He shifted, jostling Wyatt not unpleasantly, and then the blankets were around his shoulders and Linc's arm wrapped around his waist. He drifted to sleep in the cocoon Linc had made for them, his heart beating beneath Wyatt's ear.

IT WAS A SCORCHER. JUST THE SUN REFLECTING OFF the pool's surface was enough to have Wyatt regretting his plan to sit on the patio and pretend he wasn't stalking Linc as he paced back and forth through the kitchen with the phone pressed to his ear. Three days had passed since Linc had rocked Wyatt's world, and he was equal parts frustrated and furious. He wasn't sure why he was angry, exactly. He didn't want Linc. There was no use wanting something he could never have. Nothing could come of the two of them fooling around.

*intoxicating*

*Except for maybe a few thousand orgasms.*

No. Wyatt didn't want that. He couldn't. But the fact that Linc had so easily slammed the door on their sexcapade with seemingly no regrets left Wyatt's ego as bruised and raw as his throat.

The fingerprint-shaped bruises were now purple and green, which were not Wyatt's colors, but he refused to cover them. Sometimes, he stared at himself in the bathroom mirror and wrapped his own hand around his neck and tried to remember exactly how it felt when Linc choked him as he'd jerked him off.

Linc obviously didn't think about it at all. He barely looked at Wyatt. Even now, Wyatt lay by the pool in his smallest swim trunks and Linc hadn't so much as flicked his eyes in his direction. The dick. *Well, maybe not a total dick,* a voice nagged. He made Wyatt dinner every night, even if he just left it for him in the microwave.

From somewhere deep inside the house, the front door opened and slammed shut, and then Charlie was striding toward him through the living room in a flowy belted white dress with big blue flowers and a huge wide-brimmed hat. She looked like she'd just stepped off a cruise ship. "Hey, new security dude whose name I don't remember," she sang with a wave.

Linc covered the mic on his phone. "Hey, future real housewife whose name I don't remember," he called, giving her back the same wave.

Charlie gave a delighted cackle as she made her way to the far side of the pool where Wyatt had taken up residence. She wrinkled her nose when she realized he sat in the shade. "Why are you lurking in the shadows like a creeper? Are you stalking Father Time in there?" she asked, tone suspicious as she dropped to sit in the chaise beside him.

Wyatt's eye roll was lost behind his sunglasses. "Of course not. I just don't want to look like one of your leather handbags when I'm thirty. My skin care routine takes a solid hour, and I'm not going to ruin it by scorching myself with this brutal noonday sun."

"You're ridic—" She shut her mouth abruptly, lurching forward and snatching his chin, jerking his head upward. "What the hell is that? Are those... Wyatt Edgeworth, is that a handprint around your throat?"

The blood rushing to Wyatt's face felt worse than any sunburn could. He stared at his own horrified expression in the mirrored lenses of Charlie's aviators before he cut his gaze to Linc, praying he couldn't hear Charlie's high-pitched shrieking.

"Shh, keep your voice down."

Charlie gasped, lurching to her feet. "Keep my voice down? Did he do this to you? Did he hurt you?"

Before Wyatt could say a word, she was off like a shot,

*intoxicating*

charging toward Linc as fast as her Espadrilles would allow. "What the fuck is your problem, dickface?"

Linc's brows ran for his forehead in confusion, though he looked disconcertingly unflustered. "Uh, I'm a little busy here," he said, giving his phone a jiggle in case she had somehow missed it.

Charlie plucked the phone from Linc's fingers and tossed it into the pool. "Now, you're not," she shouted. She shoved Linc with both hands, but he stood firm, staring down at her like she was a rather annoying insect ruining his picnic. That did nothing to dissuade her. "Do you think that because you're bigger than he is and stronger and…older that you can just bully him? That you can abuse him and hurt him? Do you have any idea what he's been through? Why don't you pick on somebody your own size? You're disgusting!"

Linc blinked down at Charlie stupidly as Wyatt tried to pull her back. "Charlie, it's not like that at all. Please, shut up before you make it even worse."

As soon as the words were out of his mouth, he regretted them. Both Linc and Charlie stared at him, mouths agape, which Wyatt might have found hilarious in any other situation, but which was not at all funny now. Charlie balled her fists at her sides and turned on Linc, whose eyes went wide at the horrific screech she emitted just before she punched him in the face.

"Ow," Linc muttered, putting a hand over his now injured eye.

Jesus. What the hell was happening right now?

"Charlie, stop! What is wrong with you? Let's go talk in my room, okay?"

Before she could answer, the front door once again opened and closed, and all three of them turned toward the sound. Wyatt's stomach dropped, and he did his best not to vomit. Of course, his father chose today to show up.

Wyatt prayed the entire building would suddenly collapse and take them all out in one spectacular mess. But alas, the building held firm. Money couldn't buy happiness but it could buy top-of-the-line construction materials.

Charlie's blue eyes went feral at the sight of his father, and Linc and Wyatt could only watch in horror as she marched toward the older man and poked her claw-like nail into his navy blazer. "This is all your fault. Are you just so desperate to control him that you'll let this savage kill him? Look at him! Look at his throat. You just won't be happy until he's dead, will you? Do better! Be better!"

She didn't wait for an answer, just made one last terrifying girl noise before flouncing out the door, slamming it in her wake.

*intoxicating*

"That girl is as bug-shit crazy as that heathen mother of hers. I don't know what Craig was thinking marrying that woman."

When neither he nor Linc responded, his father's gaze darted between the two of them. After a moment, he strode forward, snatching Wyatt's jaw hard enough he feared he'd incur more finger-shaped bruises. An uneasy feeling settled in the pit of his stomach as his old man turned to scrutinize Linc once more. There was nothing Wyatt could say to get Linc out of this. If he told his father how it really happened, Linc was out of a job, and if he didn't, Linc was still out of a job.

"Wyatt, go to your room. I think I need to have a talk with your new security detail."

"Dad—" Wyatt started.

His father turned on him, spitting his words between clenched teeth. "What did I say?"

Wyatt flinched back reflexively, and his father sneered at him with unbridled disgust. Wyatt's gaze dragged over his father's shoulder to Linc.

"Go," Linc mouthed.

Wyatt's heart sank, but he did as he was told, fleeing to his room, slamming the door closed behind him and sliding down it, clutching his head in his hands. He ruined everything he touched.

Now, he'd ruined Linc too.

# nine

## LINCOLN

BY THE TIME WYATT'S DOOR CLOSED, LINC WAS prepared to accept any consequence Montgomery Edgeworth doled out. He'd hurt Wyatt. Not on purpose, but the results were the same. Linc had put those bruises on the boy's neck, no matter how much he'd wanted them there, and now, he'd created an even larger problem between Wyatt and his father.

Linc never should have left the Marines. After just a few months, it was clear he had absolutely no clue how to function in the outside world. Jackson had handed him a job making six figures, and he'd managed to blow it up in a week. A job babysitting

*intoxicating*

a kid on house arrest. That had to be some kind of record. He should've just gone back overseas as a hired gun. They made good money and didn't have to pretend they still belonged in polite society. He should just start packing, but he would let the senator say his piece, for Jackson's sake.

"Lincoln, I understand more than anybody how frustrating that boy can be. He's mouthy, he's lazy, he cares more about his hair than he does about getting a degree or contributing positively to society. He never makes the right choice. He's my greatest disappointment."

Blood rushed in Linc's ears, his pulse skyrocketing. Seriously? The man was blaming Wyatt for the bruises on his own neck. That was some next-level rationalizing, even for a politician. Linc shoved his hands in his pockets to keep from giving the senator a matching set of bruises.

"There have been a million times in my life where I've wanted to throttle the boy, but I don't. You know why? Because I can't afford child abuse allegations. Nowadays, nobody understands the benefit of discipline. Of corporal punishment. It's all participation trophies and entitlement. Do you understand what I'm saying?"

"No," Linc answered honestly.

"I'm sure by now you've realized that my son has certain...proclivities."

"Proclivities?" Linc all but growled, unable to stop his lip from curling.

The senator's eyes glittered, his expression mimicking Linc's. "Yes! See? That look right there. That disgust. I get it. I understand it. It enrages me, too. That boy of mine will do anything to spite me, to make me look bad, even behaving like some...sodomite. It's completely unnatural." The man was pacing now, waving his arms like some fire and brimstone preacher. Linc knew the type. He'd spent the first ten years of his life in a tiny town in Mississippi and had been on the receiving end of more than one of these self-aggrandizing sermons. "It's...it's spiteful is what it is. Repulsive, morally reprehensible, and God knows I've tried to reason with him, tried to get him the best therapists, got him enrolled in the best programs as soon as I saw what he was. Light of God Ministries has one of the best conversion programs out there. I put him in when he was just fourteen years old. Three years in a row they had him and still...still, he behaves that way."

"What's your point?" he asked between clenched teeth before begrudgingly adding, "Sir," remembering he still represented Jackson.

"My point is, I understand your rage. I imagine

*intoxicating*

a Marine like you finds a…deviant…like my son to be an abomination. He clearly makes you angry and I understand. I do. But any discipline you dole out must be out of sight. Even now, on house arrest, that beatnik wild child he cavorts around with could run to the papers and claim he's being abused by his father's employee. You see how bad that would look for me, right? I just want one more term in office. I'll deal with everything else after November."

Linc's head spun as he tried to grasp exactly what Monty Edgeworth was saying. Was he implying he was fine with him almost killing his son? Jesus. This man was a fucking monster. A monster paying him six figures. Six figures Linc desperately needed. He mentally shook himself. "Just so we're clear, what is it you expect of me?"

The man gave him a broad grin and clapped him on the shoulder. "Discretion, soldier, as discussed. Discretion is key. No visible bruises, no life-threatening injuries. You were Special Forces. I'm sure they taught you all the best techniques. Ways to… make an impression without causing any permanent damage or disfigurement. Without leaving behind any evidence."

Linc's blood wasn't rushing, it was boiling. The only person Linc wanted to damage and disfigure was this smug piece of shit in front of him smiling while he detailed all the ways Linc could abuse his son. "You can't be serious?" Linc heard himself say.

The senator held up both hands, like a blackjack dealer signing off. "This isn't a setup. Honestly, it couldn't work out better for me. If the L.O.G. couldn't save him, maybe a little military discipline can." His voice dropped low. "Listen, if you're worried about Wyatt telling anybody or going to the police, I promise he won't. If those three summers taught him nothing else, it's how to keep his mouth shut and protect the family. Thank God for small favors."

Linc was grateful his shaking hands were in his pockets. He was ten seconds away from tossing a state senator off his own balcony, and the only thing keeping him from acting on his instincts were thoughts of his own father two hours away and the boy down the hall. If Linc left now, who knew who the man would hire next? Black market mercenaries? Linc was no saint, but Wyatt was much safer with him than with anybody else. What if the next guard found Wyatt as reprehensible as his father? What if the previous guards had already abused him?

"I'm sorry for the bruises. I assure you, they won't happen again," Linc managed, forcing the words past his lips. Chewing ground glass would have been less painful. He promised himself when all of this was over and he had penned his resignation for Jackson, he was going to punch this guy squarely in his smug fucking mouth. Twice. At least.

"Don't worry about it, son. These things happen. I think you might be just what my son needs."

He turned to walk toward the door but turned back at the last minute. "Your father must be very proud. Thank you for your service." And with a jaunty salute, he was gone.

Linc counted to thirty before he picked up the nearest object—a highball glass Wyatt had used for his orange juice—and hurled it against the wall with a shout. A bit of tension left him as it fractured, glass scattering across the floor. But it wasn't enough. It wasn't nearly enough. He wanted to rip the other man apart, wanted to torture him slowly. Linc knew the things that went on in those conversion programs. Every gay kid had heard the horror stories. Some he knew had stories of their own. He couldn't imagine what three straight summers would be like.

He needed to call Jackson. He needed to call Ellie. He reached for his cell phone before remembering it was now at the bottom of the swimming pool. Charlie. His eye throbbed a bit as if suddenly remembering the girl's fist. She was a melodramatic psychopath, but at least she actually cared about Wyatt. That still left him without a cell phone. Shit.

He cleaned up the glass and tossed it in the garbage before brushing his teeth and snagging his wallet off the dresser. On his way out, he stopped to knock gently on Wyatt's door. "He's gone." There was no response. "I need to go to the office and talk to my boss, and then I need to replace my cell phone. Are you going to be okay here by yourself?" Still nothing.

He cracked Wyatt's door open. The boy was on his stomach under the covers, a pillow on his head, only his right shoulder and left calf visible. He likely wasn't sleeping but Linc left him as he was.

Hopefully, he'd heard none of the conversations between Linc and the senator, though he imagined it was nothing the boy hadn't heard a thousand times, possibly while on the wrong side of Monty's fists.

He sighed and shook his head. "I'll be back," he said again before closing the door. Back in the kitchen, he spied Wyatt's cell phone. It was unlocked. He keyed up Wyatt's texts and found Charlie's name, quickly tapping out a text.

**Can you come back? I need you.**

He held his breath as three dots danced, shoulders easing only when he saw her response.

**On my way.**

*intoxicating*

At least Wyatt wouldn't be alone while Linc was gone. Not physically, anyway.

"THE GUY'S A COCKSUCKER, MAN." JACKSON HUFFED out a laugh from behind his desk, his deep, booming voice filling up the large office space. "All the best homophobes are."

Linc dropped into the chair on the other side of the enormous desk. "I don't think this guy's in the closet. I think he's just a sanctimonious prick. He stood there, with that fucking smirk on his face, asking me to beat the gay out of his son but not to leave bruises."

Jackson leaned forward, folding his hands on his desk, the snowy-white dress shirt rolled to the elbows drawing a sharp contrast to the ebony skin of his muscular forearms. Linc had forgotten how large the other man was, how intimidating he could be with his tattoos and shaved head. Even without a rifle in his hands, Jackson looked lethal, like he could tear a man apart. Civilian life looked good on him. He was seven years younger than Linc, but he had seen just as much time in the desert. Yet, here the man was, running one of the most successful private security companies in the country.

"While we're on the subject. You wanna tell me how

that boy actually got those bruises around his neck?"

Linc rubbed his hands over his face. "Not really, no."

Jackson opened his desk drawer, pulling out a bottle of whiskey. He opened it and took a sip before passing it to Linc. "I'm afraid I'm going to insist."

Linc took a swig, letting the fire lick down his esophagus to his stomach. "It was nothing. I had a…a nightmare. The kid was in the wrong place at the wrong time."

There was a long silence, and then Jackson asked, "Was that wrong place your bedroom?"

Linc flicked his gaze to his friend before taking another swig and handing the bottle back. "It wasn't like that. He came in to thank me for leaving him dinner. When he saw I was having a bad dream, he tried to wake me up and…couldn't."

It wasn't exactly a lie. Jackson didn't have to know everything.

"You were having another flashback." It wasn't a question.

Linc scoffed. "I don't have PTSD. It was just a nightmare."

Jackson leaned back in his chair, lacing his fingers behind his head. "A nightmare that could have cost a kid his life and me my company. You need to see

*intoxicating*

somebody, man. I shouldn't have to tell you this. Martinez ate his gun less than a year after he got out. I have a great shrink. I'll give you her card."

Linc was already shaking his head. "I can't afford your fancy-pants therapist, Avery. All my money's gotta go to Ellie right now."

"You can't afford not to go, brother. Consider it a perk of the job."

"You already do too much for me."

The chair groaned as Jackson shot forward, his face growing stormy. "Fine. Then consider it an order from your employer. I can't have you choking out the bodies I have hired you to guard...even if it's what *they* want."

Linc's whole body went hot, then cold. "Excuse me?"

Jackson sighed. "Be careful with him. I gave you this job for a reason. Two other guards couldn't handle this kid. They both said the same things. Reckless. Self-harming. Suicidal."

Linc's pulse throbbed behind his eye. He didn't like feeling he was being manipulated on all sides. "Meaning?"

"Meaning it doesn't take a rocket scientist to figure out why Wyatt is the way he is. You know what it's like to not be accepted for who you are. Some kids cut, some drink and do drugs. Some join the military and turn themselves into bullet sponges. You're uniquely qualified to watch this kid because you were this kid."

"So, you hired me so I could—what?—mentor him?"

Jackson shrugged. "I thought maybe you could give the kid something he needs. Something you both need."

Linc stared at his friend for a long time, trying to puzzle out exactly how much Jackson understood about Linc's needs. If Jackson really understood, he'd know he was the worst possible thing for Wyatt. But they were all in way too deep now. "What exactly is it you think I need?"

"Purpose. You're in free-fall, brother. I'm just trying to offer you a safe place to land."

## ten

### WYATT

WYATT WAS A GHOST HAUNTING HIS OWN HOUSE. TEN days had passed since his father and Linc had talked things out in the kitchen, and things had been weird ever since. His father had left but was never really gone. He was like a demon; even though you couldn't see him, the toxic weight of his hate permeated the place, leaving Wyatt restless.

He didn't know what his father said to Linc, but any time Graciela even so much as referenced the good senator, Linc clenched his jaw, grunted, and went to work out for an hour. At this rate, he was going to look like the Hulk before their six months were over.

Not that Wyatt was complaining…or looking…at all. Well, not much anyway. Just enough to know that Linc was definitely *not* looking at him, and it was driving Wyatt crazy. It was like living with a roommate who got along with everybody but him. A roommate who starred in his jerk-off fantasies at least twice a day.

With his bruises long gone, it felt like what happened in Linc's room had all been some elaborate wet dream. Except, it wasn't. Wyatt could recall every detail with savant-like accuracy every time his hand trailed below his waist. He remembered exactly how Linc's lips felt on his, how his teeth bit down onto Wyatt's earlobe as he growled at Wyatt to beg. Sometimes, if he closed his eyes hard enough, he could pretend it was Linc's hands on him instead of his own, but it was never the same. Wyatt wasn't trying to quote lame movies but Linc was definitely his particular brand of heroin, and Wyatt was afraid he'd be chasing that high forever. The feeling was clearly not mutual.

Okay, Linc still made Wyatt meals and left them in the microwave and he still left him water bottles with little notes reminding him to drink them. But wasn't that worse? A person shouldn't get to ignore another person after giving them the best orgasm of their life and still get to worry if they're adequately hydrated. Like, what the fuck? Who did that? People who played head games, that's who. Linc was trying to break him down psychologically.

Even now, Linc was walking around the kitchen putting away dishes in loose-fitting sweatpants that did nothing to hide the outline of his dick. Each time he reached up to put something on a high shelf, his t-shirt rode up, exposing a strip of tanned, toned belly and a happy trail Wyatt wanted to trace with his tongue. This torture had to be deliberate. It had to be. And two could play at that game.

Wyatt put on his gray joggers that Charlie had forced him to buy because they rode low on his hips and "hugged his ass to perfection" and slipped on his favorite pale green hoodie but left it unzipped. This was war. He wasn't ripped like Linc, but he was lean and toned in all the right places and tons of guys were happy to tell him so. Maybe Linc just needed to know what he was missing.

When he got to the kitchen, he went straight to the cabinet where Linc stood and wedged himself between him and the counter. "Excuse me," he said, giving no sign he meant it. He snagged a glass and tried to ignore the twinge of arousal that hit him when Linc's knuckles grazed his belly.

Linc just grunted, his preferred form of communication lately. Once Wyatt had filled his orange juice glass, he took a seat at the island, pretending to gaze out at the patio. His plan to ignore Linc until he noticed he was the one being ignored quickly went south when Linc slid something across to him on the counter.

"Eat this," Linc commanded.

Wyatt looked down to see a granola bar, grimacing. "I'm not hungry."

Linc's response was a low rumble that went straight to Wyatt's cock. "Did it sound like I was asking?"

Wyatt pursed his lips and tilted his head, glancing up at Linc through thick lashes as he deliberately pushed the bar back over to Linc. "You're not the boss of me."

Linc leaned across the island until they were almost nose to nose, and Wyatt most definitely regretted his decision to go commando. "Kid, I'm the textbook definition of the boss of you. Now, eat."

Linc slid the bar back across the island, one brow arching upward as a smirk spread across his face.

Wyatt huffed through his nose and made a show of tearing the wrapper and taking a big bite, pulling a face as he chewed. "Why does this taste like cardboard?" he asked, mouth full.

Linc chuckled. "Because it's healthy. It's packed with vitamins and healthy nutrients. You need the calories."

*intoxicating*

"'Healthy nutrients'?" he mimicked around another bite. "You're so old."

"I didn't realize nutrition was something only old people cared about. Now, eat."

Wyatt forced himself to swallow down the bite with a shudder. "I don't want to eat this. It's disgusting."

"Well, you didn't eat your dinner last night, so this is the consequence."

Wyatt's already hard cock throbbed at the word 'consequence,' his gaze darting to Linc's. "You can't be serious. Lincoln, come on. I'm twenty-two years old. I don't have to eat if I don't want to."

Linc's honey-brown eyes pinned him in place. "I don't think you want to test that theory. I'm in a mood."

Wyatt's mouth went dry, his tongue darting out to lick his lower lip. What did Linc's moods look like? Would Wyatt end up with more bruises? He couldn't remember another human being ever having this kind of effect on him.

Wyatt had no idea what would happen next, but he sure as shit wasn't going to finish that cardboard granola bar. "Well, I'll see your mood"—he stood and walked to the trash can by the island—"and raise you mine." He opened the lid and dropped in the granola bar before turning on his heel and sashaying down the hallway with as much attitude as he could muster.

He'd almost made it back to his bedroom when Linc caught him, pinning him against the door, one hand tangling in his hair, tugging his head back. "You're just begging for it, aren't you?" he growled into Wyatt's ear. "Did you think if you misbehaved, I'd jerk you off again? Hmm?"

Wyatt swallowed past the lump in his throat, grateful that his super obvious erection was being crushed against the wall. "I don't know what you mean," he said, tongue all but tripping over his lie.

"Bad boys don't get to come. Bad boys get punished. Do you understand?"

He didn't understand, not really. He gave a jerky shake of his head, suddenly not sure what to do with his hands hanging uselessly at his sides.

"Then I'll demonstrate."

Wyatt sucked in a startled breath as Linc yanked Wyatt's pants to mid-thigh, his dick slapping against his stomach and revealing his arousal. The sudden cool air had goosebumps erupting along his overheated skin. His heartbeat became erratic. "Wait."

"Too late for that."

Before Wyatt could ask what he meant, Linc's hand cracked across his bare ass. Hard. Wyatt yelped, face flushing at the sound. This wasn't how he'd seen this playing out. They were in the hallway where anybody could see…could see Linc punishing him, spanking him. His head swam, thinking of the many people who could waltz into his house any time they pleased.

"You can't—"

Two more sharp slaps turned Wyatt's words into a low moan. If this wasn't what he wanted, his fucking body wasn't getting the memo. His body bowed, pushing his hips toward Linc like a whore. Fuck, it would just figure Wyatt would like to be spanked. God, he really wasn't paying his therapist enough.

"I. Can't. What?" Linc asked, punctuating each word with another blow until Wyatt's ass burned and tears pricked at his eyes.

"Please," Wyatt heard himself whisper, breathless.

*Slap.* "Please what, baby?" Linc purred in his ear.

"I—"

*Slap. Slap. Slap.*

Tears rolled down Wyatt's cheeks, skin blazing everywhere Linc's blows landed, and all he could think about was whether he'd still see Linc's handprints on his ass tomorrow, whether he'd still feel them. It made the pain worth it. It made him crave it.

"You finished misbehaving?" Linc asked.

"I don't know," he heard himself say, his voice sounding far away.

He swore Linc chuckled before he delivered another three slaps. "How about now?"

Wyatt wiped his face against his forearm, bracing it against the door. His limbs felt heavy and numb. "Yes," he mumbled.

The barest hint of a slap had Wyatt hissing. "How do you address me?"

"Sir?"

"Wrong answer," Linc growled. "You know what I am. Say it."

"Daddy," Wyatt whispered, every nerve ending standing at attention. "Yes, Daddy."

Linc's lips grazed Wyatt's throat, his teeth tugging his earlobe. "Good boy. Kiss me."

Wyatt turned his head, crushing his lips against Linc's, kissing him like he held the cure for whatever poison had infected Wyatt. Linc spun him around, shoving him against the door, before finding Wyatt's mouth once more. He melted against him, letting Linc explore.

When Linc finally wrapped a hand around Wyatt's cock, he sobbed. Linc's thumb swiped over the tip and Wyatt moaned into his mouth. Even with the copious amount of pre-cum leaking, Linc's hand was a punishing dry friction that had Wyatt whining. He could only bury his face against Linc's throat, holding on as his knees buckled. "You want to come, sweet boy?"

*intoxicating*

"Yes, Daddy."

"Then you should learn to do what you're told the first time."

Linc's hand disappeared, and Wyatt keened, both relieved and disappointed. "Please, Daddy," he begged, his lips still against Linc's throat.

"Look at me."

Wyatt pulled back, dragging his gaze upward until he was staring up into Linc's stern face. He cupped Wyatt's cheeks, wiping his tears away with his thumbs. "Say it again."

"Please, Daddy," Wyatt begged, meaning every word.

"On your knees." Wyatt dropped so fast he was sure he'd regret it tomorrow. "Eyes on me."

Wyatt's gaze locked on Linc. He pulled his cock out with one hand, the other hand braced on the doorframe above Wyatt's head. Linc's cock was perfection: thick, cut, and leaking pre-cum. Wyatt wanted to taste it, to feel the heavy weight of it on his tongue. But he didn't dare. "Don't you dare touch yourself until I say," Linc snarled, working his hand faster.

Wyatt whimpered. He wanted to come so bad, but he wanted to touch Linc more. He wanted to wrap his hand around the velvet length and run his tongue along the thick vein that ran underneath. He wanted to be the one making Linc breathless.

"You can touch yourself, but don't you dare come until I tell you."

Wyatt was almost afraid to do as Linc commanded; he was far too close. This was all too much. He bit down on his bottom lip, moaning as his hand wrapped around his aching erection. The base of his spine was tingly and hot, and he didn't stroke himself so much as squeeze, attempting to stop the orgasm threatening to engulf him.

"Open your mouth."

Wyatt did as he was told, tipping his head back and sticking out his tongue. Linc made a choked-off noise, and then his cum was painting Wyatt's face, the bitter tang coating his lips. He swallowed it down, his eyes pleading with unspoken words.

"Now, you can come."

It only took two strokes, and Wyatt was spilling over his fist, his toes curling as waves of ecstasy crashed over him, and his brain fell temporarily offline.

## eleven

### LINCOLN

WYATT WAS CRASHING. LINC WATCHED THE ENDORPHIN rush ebb, leaving the boy dazed and listless. "Come on."

He tugged Wyatt to his feet, pushing open his bedroom door and leading him inside. Wyatt didn't fight him when he settled him in bed or when Linc brought a warm washcloth and gently cleaned the evidence of their hallway escapade from Wyatt's skin. He left Wyatt long enough to grab some water and other provisions before returning to the room and locking the door behind him. Linc's self-preservation instincts were finally kicking in somewhat now that he'd defiled Wyatt in the middle of the hallway in broad daylight.

*If your self-preservation instincts were really kicking in, you'd turn and walk away right now,* a voice nagged.

Whatever. He'd berate himself over it later. For now, he needed to take care of Wyatt, who had curled himself into a tight ball in the center of the mattress and was doing his best to convince Linc he was asleep. He sat, bracing himself against the headboard before easily maneuvering Wyatt, arranging him so his back was to Linc's chest, his head resting against his shoulder. "Drink this."

Wyatt gave a sleepy laugh. "Tell the truth. You have stock in this bottled water company, don't you?"

Linc grinned despite himself. "Yep. Can't babysit ungrateful brats forever, can I? I'm already *so old*."

Wyatt craned his head to meet Linc's gaze, and he had to remind himself this was temporary. That it was over. No matter how perfect Wyatt was. No matter how much Linc wanted to put him back together. It had to stop. They could only get away with it for so long without getting caught, and that was a Pandora's box he could never close if opened. The consequences would be too far-reaching.

When Wyatt finished his water, Linc handed him the orange slices he'd pilfered from the crystal bowl on the counter. Once again, Wyatt flicked his gaze to Linc, smirking. "Afraid I'll get scurvy?"

*intoxicating*

"I'll bet you fifty bucks you don't even know what scurvy is."

Wyatt scoffed. "A vitamin C deficiency. Most people think it only affected sailors, but it's been around since the thirteenth century. Napoleon's army got it from consuming horse meat." When Linc blinked at him, he batted his lashes. "True story."

"I'm not paying you fifty bucks," Linc warned.

"Hah, my father paid almost fifty grand a year for me to go to that pretentious-as-fuck private school. The least I could do was pay attention."

Wyatt was full of surprises, or maybe Linc had just made assumptions based on the limited information his father had supplied. Now that Linc understood what Wyatt had endured growing up, it wasn't hard to see why he acted out like he did. It wasn't any excuse for drinking and driving—he was lucky he'd hurt nobody but himself—but it shed a light on Wyatt's state of mind. Graciela had warned him that Wyatt wasn't stable. Jackson had used the word suicidal. The signs that Linc should turn and run weren't just there, they were flashing in red neon, but Linc couldn't do it. At least not professionally. Somebody had to watch over Wyatt.

Linc dropped an absent kiss onto Wyatt's curls. "Eat, you stubborn boy."

They fell silent as Wyatt gave in and ate the sections of orange. Once finished, he started to fidget, clearly uncomfortable in the quiet. "I'm fine now. You can go."

Dismissed. Linc didn't think so. "I'll go when I'm ready…when I think *you're* ready."

He peeled open the two sides of Wyatt's unzipped hoodie like he was unwrapping a present, running his fingers across his flat belly, noting the smattering of moles dotting his fair skin like constellations.

Linc relished Wyatt's sharp intake of breath, but then his hands captured Linc's wrists. "I said I'm fine," Wyatt muttered, not escaping Linc's arms but tensing within them.

"Stop," Linc warned.

"I don't want to do this with you." Wyatt's voice was small but angry.

Wyatt wasn't used to discipline, didn't know the effects what they'd done could have, but Linc did. He couldn't just leave Wyatt alone. He didn't want to.

"Look, just because you think you're fine, it doesn't mean you are." Wyatt's nails dug half-moons into Linc's wrists at those words. Maybe that wasn't the right thing to say. Linc had no idea what the right words were. He didn't do feelings or relationships or long-term, especially not with inexperienced kids like Wyatt—beautiful, broken Wyatt. Linc easily slipped

*intoxicating*

his wrists from Wyatt's grasp, tilting his chin upward. "I'm not ready to let you go just yet."

"What about what I want? Does that matter?" The rawness in Wyatt's words was a sucker punch to the gut.

"Do you even know what you want?"

Wyatt deflated, the fight draining from his body, his head falling back against Linc's shoulder. "I know nobody ever really cares what I want."

Jesus. "Turn around."

Wyatt ignored him, staring down at Linc's hands.

"Turn around and look at me. Now."

Wyatt begrudgingly turned until he was straddling Linc's lap, dragging his eyes upward. This close, he could see the smattering of freckles across his nose and that his sea-glass eyes were ringed with gold.

"I care," he finally said. It wasn't a lie. Linc really cared about Wyatt, wanted him to have a life out from under his father. The life he deserved. "What do you want?"

Wyatt looked startled at Linc's question, his full lips pulling down at the corners. "It doesn't matter."

"It matters to me." Linc didn't know why it mattered or why Wyatt should care that it mattered to Linc. It shouldn't. But he needed Wyatt to know that under different circumstances, he'd want this. Them. Whatever they fucking were. "I care about what you want. So, what do you want, sweet boy?"

Wyatt opened his mouth, like he was about to confess a secret, and Linc saw the exact moment the boy chickened out. Instead, he cupped Linc's face, running his tongue over Linc's lower lip. "What if I said all I want is you?"

Linc wondered what shameful, secret desire Wyatt hid, but he let it go. They barely knew each other, even though it didn't feel that way to Linc. Instead, he addressed Wyatt's words. "I want you, too. Just because we can't keep doing this doesn't mean I don't *want* to keep doing this," Linc insisted, pressing his lips to Wyatt's forehead, his cheeks, his chin, before finally pressing a kiss to his pouty, unrelenting mouth. "There are so many things I want to do to you that it would take me the next five and a half months just to list them, but we both know if your father found out, it would be a nightmare—for both of us—and I can't afford to lose this assignment."

Wyatt's face was a storm cloud, his mood darkening. "Because of your family?"

Linc frowned. How did Wyatt know that? "Yes, because of my family."

"How does your wife feel about you fucking men?" Wyatt asked, tone icy.

Linc's brain froze. "My…what?"

*intoxicating*

Wyatt looked at him then. His eyes were glinting with anger, his jaw thrust forward. "Don't lie. I heard you on the phone with your wife talking about your kid."

Linc tried to think back to the numerous calls he'd had but couldn't pinpoint one that would have given Wyatt the idea that Linc was married…to a woman… and had a kid?

He should let him believe it. It would be easier if Wyatt thought Linc was a liar and a cheater. Maybe he'd hate Linc enough to dismiss him from his mind entirely and never look back. But Linc just couldn't have him thinking that way. He hated dishonesty. "I'm not married, and I definitely don't have a kid."

Wyatt searched Linc's face like the truth was written on his forehead. "You told her you were doing everything you could, and you said your kid would try to dress himself. I'm guessing he's pretty young. You don't have to lie… This isn't a thing, remember?"

Understanding dawned, and Linc dropped his face into the crook of Wyatt's shoulder, placing a kiss there before he lifted his head to meet Wyatt's accusatory gaze. "I was talking to my sister, Ellie, about my father."

Wyatt frowned, his expression leery. "Your dad was trying to dress himself? That's not even a good lie."

Linc shook his head. He didn't want to talk about this—not with Wyatt, not with anybody—but he needed Wyatt to understand why this couldn't keep happening, no matter how much Linc wanted it. Wyatt needed to know what was at stake.

"My father has a disease called Korsakoff Syndrome, which has caused severe and permanent dementia. He lives with Ellie in Orlando, but he's getting so bad she's having a hard time on her own, and we need to put him in a home where people can care for him."

Wyatt's mouth formed a perfect O, his hands splaying over Linc's t-shirt. "There's nothing anybody can do for him? No treatment?"

Linc's chest suddenly felt tight, a lump forming in his throat. He locked it down. He didn't have time to get emotional. It solved nothing. He was a Marine. Marines sucked it the fuck up and did what needed to be done. "No. By the time my sister found him, he was too far gone," he forced himself to say.

"Found him?" Wyatt asked.

"Yeah. It's a long story. My father has a lot of problems. Alcohol was the biggest, and now, it will ultimately be what kills him."

The silence stretched between them, like a rope pulled taut, until finally, Wyatt said, "You don't really want to talk about this, do you?"

Pressure exploded behind Linc's ribs, the sorrow he'd kept at bay threatening to overwhelm him. He

*intoxicating*

gave a stilted shake of his head, fighting to find his control once more. Wyatt's hands slid lower, fingering the hem of Linc's t-shirt, silently asking permission.

"Go ahead."

Wyatt peeled Linc's shirt off and tossed it aside, splaying his hands over Linc's now bare skin, his look filled with wonder. He leaned forward, dragging his lips along Linc's collarbone. His dick took notice, and Wyatt was hard again, too. Linc closed his eyes, cupping Wyatt's ass and yanking him flush against him until they both groaned.

Wyatt rocked against him as he dipped his head to tongue at the hard peak of Linc's nipple, biting down until Linc hissed. Wyatt's thumbs teased over Linc's hip bones as he turned his attention to Linc's other nipple. Linc squeezed the globes of Wyatt's ass, grinding their cocks together through the thin layers of fabric.

Wyatt lifted his head, eyes molten as he brushed his lips across Linc's cheek to his ear. "I want more, Daddy."

Fuck. The boy was perfect, so perfect. His perfect boy. "You're relentless," he growled, teeth grazing Wyatt's shoulder. "What do you want?"

Wyatt made a half-bitten-off sound, cheeks flushing. "I want to make you come. Please."

"I don't know. Do you think you deserve that?"

Once again, Wyatt hit him with the full force of those puppy eyes. "Please, Daddy. I'll make it so good for you."

Linc's dick throbbed. Jesus, this fucking kid. "I don't know. You didn't finish your granola bar. You've been kind of a brat."

Wyatt dropped his head then looked up at him through his lashes, his tone almost a whine. "Please? I won't even come, I promise. Let me make you feel good."

Well, that was an offer Linc hadn't seen coming. He had already spanked him for disobeying him about his breakfast. "Take my cock out."

Wyatt hurried to do as he was told, sliding out of Linc's lap and kneeling between his splayed knees before hooking his fingers in Linc's pants. He lifted his hips just enough for Wyatt to push them out of the way and free his already leaking erection.

Wyatt didn't put his mouth on Linc's cock, instead pressing his face against his groin and inhaling, like the scent of Linc alone was enough to get him off. Fuck. Wyatt trailed his tongue along the seam where Linc's thigh and pelvis met, fingers digging into the grooves of Linc's hip bones. It occurred to Linc then—Wyatt was waiting for permission.

Linc glanced at the clock sitting on the bedside

*intoxicating*

table. It was one in the afternoon. They shouldn't be doing this in the middle of the day. They shouldn't be fucking doing this at all. Somehow, that made it easier for him to say, "Do it. Suck me. Make me come."

Wyatt didn't hesitate. He fisted the base of Linc's cock and sucked him into the back of his throat like a goddamn porn star. "Jesus, kid," he muttered, his abs flexing, body curling inward against his will.

There was no finesse, but what he lacked in technique he made up for with enthusiasm and a nonexistent gag reflex. Wyatt pulled off, eyes wet and lips cherry red as he trailed his mouth along the underside of Linc's straining cock, giving him 'fuck me' eyes as he dipped his tongue into the slit before sucking him down once more.

Linc couldn't help but arch his hips, couldn't help the way he fisted his hands in Wyatt's curls, fucking up into the hot suction of the boy's perfect mouth, driving his cock into his throat and holding him there until tears trailed down his face. "Good boy."

Linc released him, and Wyatt pulled in a few ragged breaths before taking Linc into his mouth once more. He forced Wyatt to take it slow, holding him steady and fucking into his mouth with short, shallow thrusts. Wyatt's greedy little sucking noises had Linc's balls pulling tight against his body.

He could see Wyatt's hard-on tenting those ridiculously tight pants, but Wyatt didn't try to touch himself. Linc was his sole focus. As soon as Linc released him, Wyatt sucked him back down, his head bobbing as he worked Linc over with a single-minded intensity that had Linc squeezing his eyes shut. "I want you to swallow it all. Every fucking drop."

Wyatt took Linc down his throat, the muscles there convulsing in ways that had Linc's vision whiting out. He pinned him in place, driving his cock into Wyatt's mouth again and again before he came hard, spilling himself so deep Wyatt had no choice but to swallow or choke. He took it all, his wide green eyes locking on Linc's as he pulled off with a pop, licking every drop off his lips before giving him a huge smile.

"Come here." Wyatt climbed back up in Linc's lap, and he captured the boy's mouth in a filthy kiss, wanting to taste himself on his tongue. "You did good, sweet boy." He shoved his hand into Wyatt's pants, taking his cock and working it over at a punishing pace. "Come," he growled against the boy's lips.

Wyatt tensed, a surprised cry escaping as he did as Linc commanded, a full-body shudder rolling over him.

They sat there in each other's arms, trying to catch their breath, Wyatt's forehead on Linc's shoulder. After a moment, Wyatt slipped out of Linc's grasp, flopping

*intoxicating*

onto his back beside him. The intimate bubble they'd existed in for the last few minutes seemed to pop, leaving only awkward silence and something else... Something that felt a lot like loss or regret.

Time to get back to the real world.

"Is Graciela coming today?" he finally asked.

Wyatt shrugged. "She's not scheduled to come, but that never stopped her before. She's here a lot less now that you're here, and when she is here, it's to talk to you, not me."

Link huffed a laugh. "Are you jealous of my time with her?"

"Maybe, yeah," Wyatt grumbled.

"Well, don't be. Tomorrow, you are a free man, and you'll return to your old life and your old friends and I'll just be another of your father's employees."

Wyatt audibly swallowed, voice tight. "Sure."

"This can't happen again," Linc said, more to himself than Wyatt.

Wyatt sat up, throwing a hurt look over his shoulder. "I heard you the first ten times. I'm going to take a shower. Maybe you shouldn't be here when I get back."

"Yeah, kid. Whatever you want."

"What I want. Right."

# twelve

## WYATT

WYATT LAY UPSIDE DOWN ON HIS BED, HIS FEET resting against the wall, watching the glowing red light of his ankle monitor blink on and off the way he'd done a thousand times over the last one hundred and eighty days. In just six short hours, he'd be free from this gilded prison. The thought should have pleased him, but it caused a pit in his stomach, growing wider with each passing minute. Wyatt hoped it swallowed him whole.

Somewhere in the kitchen, Linc was running the blender, making one of his disgusting green smoothies, while Graciela pretended to vacuum for the fourth time that week, and music blared from the recessed house speakers. Wyatt was on overload. There was a pressure building inside him, threatening to rip him in half. He had spent so much time trapped in this apartment, he wasn't sure he could cope with the outside world. If coping had been one of his strengths, he wouldn't have ended up on house arrest in the first place.

He didn't know how to be a functioning person. He just wasn't good at it. He'd spent twenty-two years living a life where somebody—his father—made every decision for him, where there was always somebody to do everything *for him*. He had never once had to worry about paying a bill or changing a tire or even doing his own laundry. Once the cops removed his ankle monitor, none of that would change. Graciela would keep doing the chores, and his father's business manager would keep paying his bills, and his father would keep telling him what he would do with his life. Just like before. The thought had Wyatt spiraling. Every single day, the same. Nothing changing. Wyatt never allowed to be a whole person, never allowed to be himself, whoever that was.

His nails dug half-moons into his palms, pain converting his panic into endorphins, giving him just a few seconds of peace. He needed to stop feeling sorry for himself. People would kill to have his life. Nobody cared about the poor little rich boy and his rich boy problems. Not even the rich boy's parents.

He swung himself into a sitting position, his gaze drawn to his vanity. He hadn't dabbled with his makeup in days, not since Charlie's callback. He glanced at the door. It wasn't like Linc would barge in. He'd been doing his best to pretend Wyatt didn't exist since he'd taken Wyatt at his word and left while he was in the shower yesterday. The deputy wouldn't be there for hours to take the monitor off. There was no reason he couldn't play for a while.

Fuck it.

He sat in the chair, opening drawers and extracting palettes of richly hued powders and creams and setting them out. Warmth and anticipation rushed over him, soothing his frazzled nerves. Time disappeared when he had the brushes in his hand. Makeup took precision and skill and artistry. There was depth and dimension, blending shades to camouflage any perceived imperfections and highlight desirable assets. When he was doing makeup—his or somebody else's—his mind just quieted and the rest of the world fell away.

He could do a full face in an hour or less, but he wasn't in a hurry. He started with a primer, ensuring his foundation would glide on like silk. He built from there, layering and contouring until he was somebody else, somebody confident and capable. Somebody who

*intoxicating*

handled their shit, who wasn't afraid to be himself. His smoky purple eyeshadow made his pale green irises look almost supernatural, and he cat-eyed his liner until it was sharp enough to slit a man's throat.

Makeup was a mask to hide behind, but it also made him feel like a superhero in disguise. He'd managed a lot of anonymous hookups in darkened clubs, and nobody had ever figured out who he was behind all the paint. Or maybe, they just hadn't cared. He finished his look with a matte mauve lipstick Charlie had gotten him for his birthday, then realized there was nothing more he could do other than wipe it off and start over. That thought depressed him even more.

He wished he could take pictures, could show off his skills on Instagram like other artists, could create tutorials on YouTube and help people understand that anybody could wear makeup, anybody could be beautiful, more confident, feel better about themselves. That's what he wanted... That's all he'd ever wanted from the time he'd sat at his mother's vanity and tried on her red lip gloss. But no matter what Linc said, it didn't matter what Wyatt wanted. He raised his phone to take a selfie to send to Charlie, the flash going off just as the door opened behind him.

"I've got a surprise for yo—What the fuck?"

Wyatt froze, his arm raised, and his eyes locked on

his father's reflection in the mirror. After a minute, his body came back online, and he jumped to his feet, his brain cycling through a hundred different ways to defuse the situation. Somehow, he landed on snarky indifference. "Don't have a fucking coronary, Dad. It's just—" His father's fist connected with his diaphragm, and his words died on a ragged gasp, his breath forced from his lungs, like he'd plummeted from a ten-story building. His chest was on fire, his lungs paralyzed, but it didn't stop him from trying to suck much-needed air back into his body. His phone slipped from his fingers, and he clawed at his chest as if he could will his lungs to come back online.

He should have seen the blow coming. It was his father's favorite strike zone. No visible bruises but all the trauma. His panic came rocketing back. In some dark corner of his mind, he understood his body wouldn't allow him to stand there and suffocate, that his lungs would eventually cooperate and allow him to breathe, but it wasn't helping just then. It would serve his father right if he died like this, right in front of him. *Good luck explaining the fist-sized bruise on your dead son's chest, Monty.*

His father wasn't even in the room when Wyatt finally managed his first agonizing breath. He could hear him rummaging around in his bathroom, but he

*intoxicating*

staggered to the bed, resting on the edge as he practiced pulling air into his abused lungs and pushing it back out. Each breath burned, like his chest was filled with gasoline, but his father was unconcerned. He flung a wet rag at Wyatt, the edge catching the corner of his eye and setting off another fiery reaction.

"Wipe that shit off your face. What the fuck is wrong with you? Are you really this stupid?"

Wyatt assumed the question was rhetorical. They both knew nothing Wyatt said would convince his father of his mental acuity, so he just sat there, waiting for his father to explain himself. When his father said nothing, Wyatt rasped, "Why are you here?"

"Well, I stupidly thought you might be in a hurry to get that thing off your ankle, so I called in a favor, and there are two of Miami-Dade's finest out there waiting to take that thing off of you and get rid of the equipment. I didn't expect to find you in here playing makeup and painting yourself up like some two-bit harlot."

Wyatt forced himself not to snicker at the word harlot. Who even used that word anymore? "Gosh, Dad, what a nice thing for you to do. So out of character. Was that the only reason you stopped by?" Wyatt asked, his voice full of mock appreciation.

His father's blue eyes shifted to the floor, and Wyatt

scoffed. Of course, it wasn't.

"Now that you mention it, I need to talk to you about some things coming up with the campaign."

Before Wyatt could ask for further explanation, the door to his bedroom creaked open to accommodate Linc's large frame. Wyatt's gaze dragged to him almost against his will. Linc frowned at Wyatt, and he felt another little piece of himself die. Now, his chest hurt for two reasons: his father's abuse and Linc's disapproval. He didn't know which was worse. But Wyatt supposed it didn't matter. He and Linc weren't a thing.

When the senator noticed Linc standing there, he shielded Wyatt with his body like Linc hadn't already seen him in enough makeup to make a drag queen jealous. "Wash your goddamn face and meet us in the living room when you're presentable."

Wyatt waited until they'd both left before he threw the towel across the room and reached for the makeup wipes in the first drawer of his vanity. As he erased his hours of work in a matter of minutes, he focused on making himself numb. If he didn't care, his father had no power over him and neither did Linc. At least, that's what he told himself. He was tired of feeling like a raw nerve all the time.

When he was barefaced again, he threw on a pair of white jeans and a navy and white long-sleeved striped sweater. His hand was on the doorknob when his phone chirped from the floor.

He picked it up, frowning at a text message alert from an out-of-state number. There was just a single line, but his heart tripped in his chest just the same.

**I thought you looked hot.**

He left the room with the barest hint of a smile on his face. Two plain-clothes officers stood in the kitchen with his father. Linc was also there, off to the side, arms crossed over his chest, like a sentry. He seemed to be doing his best to make himself invisible, but Wyatt could feel his eyes on him like a caress. It made it easier to smile and make small talk with the officers as they removed the contraption from his leg.

Once his father had taken the time to sufficiently kiss the deputies' asses and ask for their vote in November, he walked them out. As soon as the door shut, his father's affable nature and good ol' boy smile slid off his face like melting wax, leaving only a sneer of disgust. "You could've cost me this election just now, boy."

Wyatt resisted the urge to rub at the spot where his father had sucker-punched him. He refused to apologize. "You said you wanted to talk about the campaign?"

For a moment, it seemed his father wasn't ready to let it go, but then he sighed and reached into his suit pocket. "This is an itinerary of all my speeches and state dinners. My campaign manager says it looks suspicious that you haven't been to any of the fundraisers, and several people have commented on your absence."

Wyatt found that hard to believe. Nobody ever seemed to notice he wasn't in attendance. "Okay."

His father's cheek twitched in an aborted sneer. "Every event with a star next to it is a family event. You will make yourself available." He turned on Linc, pointing a finger in his direction. "You will ensure he shows up and that he dresses and acts appropriately the entire time. Do I make myself clear?"

"Crystal," Linc grunted.

Wyatt wanted to puke. It was a fundraising dinner that had started the events leading to his accident that night. The incident with the cater-waiter in the bathroom. He hated those dinners. It was just shaking hands and kissing old ladies while they begged him to let them set him up with their granddaughters. He didn't want to do that shit anymore. He just couldn't. "I don't think you want me around there, Dad. What if I do something super gay?"

His father gripped him by the back of the neck, dragging him forward until their foreheads touched and Wyatt could smell the coffee on his father's breath.

*intoxicating*

"Wyatt Edgeworth, you will show up when you're told and you will do as you're told or so help me, the next program you enter will make Light of God look like goddamn Disney. Do you fucking understand me?"

Something deep inside Wyatt withered, but he bared his teeth in a demented smile. "Yeah, sure, Dad. Whatever you say."

When his father released him, Wyatt looked at Linc over the man's shoulder. Every vein in Linc's arms strained under his skin, and he clenched his jaw tight enough for Wyatt to worry he might hurt himself.

"Things would be so much easier for you if you'd just learn to do as you're told and stop all this attention-seeking nonsense," his father muttered.

"Sure, Dad." Wyatt didn't have the strength to fight with him today. "I need to go get ready. Charlie and I are meeting for a late lunch," he lied.

His father puffed out his chest, like some preening bird, giving a dismissive sniff. "I need to get back to my office, anyway."

Once he left, Wyatt closed the door and leaned against it in case his father tried to come back. When he was certain the man was long gone, he gave one last look in Linc's direction, then went back into his room and closed the door.

He was wrong. This fucking apartment wasn't his prison, his family was. As long as his father was alive, Wyatt would never be free. The thought had him crawling back into his bed and pulling the covers over his head. He just needed sleep.

He'd worry about everything else tomorrow.

# thirteen

## LINCOLN

"I'M TELLING YOU, JACKSON, IT'S A BAD IDEA. HAVING Wyatt at his father's speaking engagements and fundraising dinners? It's a recipe for disaster. The kid's gonna snap."

Jackson rested his arms on his desk, his fingers steepled together in front of his chin. "The kid's gonna snap? It's you who looks too tightly wound, brother."

He wasn't wrong. Linc was a wire on the verge of snapping, his shoulders tight, his jaw aching from his clenched teeth. He needed an outlet. Something other than punching a heavy bag or bench-pressing extra weights. If Wyatt had truly belonged to Linc—in every sense of the word—Linc would have poured all this energy and rage into fucking Wyatt, taking him apart and putting him back together, using him over and over until they were both too exhausted to think about the mess their lives had become.

But he'd ended it…because it was the right thing to do. The *smart* thing to do. Necessary. He needed to finish this job; his sister needed him to finish this job. But everything in Linc screamed that Wyatt needed him more. Of course, that could just be his dick talking. He just didn't fucking know anymore.

"He hurt him," he finally said, continuing to pace the length of Jackson's office.

That had his friend's attention. "Hurt him physically? You saw this?"

Linc gave a single jerk of his head. "No, I didn't see it, but I could tell. He's abusive. The guy gave me carte blanche to beat the gay out of his kid. It's not a real leap to think that he'd put his hands on him."

Jackson gave a heavy sigh, pinching the bridge of his nose between his thumb and forefinger. "Linc—"

"Don't tell me it's not my business, Jack. I'm not going to stand by and watch that fucker hurt him," Linc barked.

Jackson's head snapped up. "You think I'd tell you to ignore something like that? Am I that kind of guy?

*intoxicating*

I got into this business to help people, to protect them. But you need to be careful."

"Careful?" Linc repeated.

"Yeah, careful. That man is a state senator. Yes, he's a son of a bitch and yes, most people loathe him, but he has reach. We're in a very red state. He could make your life and mine very complicated...never mind what he could do to his son. If you think you're getting too close to this, I'll find you another client, one you're less likely to become attached to. Believe me, I have plenty of those."

That brought Linc up short. He wasn't giving up Wyatt. He couldn't trust that another guard would understand him, would know what he needed. That wasn't happening. "No way," he growled, slapping his hands on the desk.

Jackson's brow arched. "Take a seat."

Linc wanted to tell him to fuck off—he'd been this kid's battalion leader—but instead, he just dropped into the chair before raking his hands across his face. "This kid has been through enough. His father's an abusive, controlling asshole. He has one real friend." *Who hates me,* Linc silently added, not sure why that mattered. "He's lonely and depressed. I don't know if he's strong enough to handle these events and keep it together."

"That's not our call."

"Can't you tell the senator that it will be a logistics nightmare trying to keep him and Wyatt safe at these functions?"

Jackson snorted a laugh. "He's not the fucking president. He's a dick, but nobody's actively gunning for him. Except, maybe you," he added, giving Linc a pointed look.

"So, what do I do?"

"What can you do? SITFU, brother."

*Suck it the fuck up.* He'd said it to his men a hundred times. Stop complaining and get the job done. He dug his thumbs into his eyes until colorful spots danced across his lids. "You're right. But, man, on my mother's grave, the minute I resign, I'm going to lay that motherfucker out. I don't care if I go to prison."

"And on that day, I'll be there with bail money and a good attorney. Until then, adapt and overcome, Marine."

Linc nodded. "I need to get back. It doesn't pay to leave the kid alone for too long."

His hand was on the doorknob when Jackson spoke one final time. "Whatever you're doing with that boy…make sure you don't get caught with your dick out, for all our sakes."

"There's nothing going on."

"Bullshit."

*intoxicating*

Linc's face flushed. "I squashed it. I told him we can't. It's over."

"Uh-huh. If you say so."

Linc didn't bother to argue, just jerked the door open and left. He really did want to get back to Wyatt. He'd been in his room for hours, ever since his father had dropped the campaign bomb on his head. History had proven leaving Wyatt alone with his thoughts for too long never ended well for anybody. Technically, he shouldn't ever leave Wyatt alone, but Linc had needed to talk to Jackson before he committed a felony against a seated member of congress.

He called his sister in the Uber on the way back to the penthouse, but she didn't answer, so he left a message and responded to some forgotten emails—mostly old Marine buddies congratulating him on his new civilian life. Before he'd retired, he'd looked forward to getting out and never seeing another fucking desert again. Now, he wasn't sure he'd ever adapt to this world or if he even wanted to.

Linc should have figured out something was amiss when he passed a girl in the lobby wearing a cocktail dress and a flamingo-shaped pool float, but his mind was on the sad boy currently moping in the penthouse. Only when said girl followed him onto the elevator did he look up and frown. She grinned with way too many teeth and waved maniacally. She wasn't alone. A girl in a dress so skimpy it looked like she'd fashioned it from men's belts stood next to a guy in eyeliner, a red top hat, and a pair of skintight black leather pants that made Linc's balls ache with sympathy.

Linc frowned. "This a private elevator. Penthouse only."

"Duh. Wyatt throws the craziest parties. We're so stoked he's back!"

Linc could feel the enamel on his teeth eroding as he clenched his jaw until it popped in protest. So much for his sad mopey boy. Wyatt had rocketed straight into self-destruct mode. Linc glanced at his watch. He'd only been gone a little over two hours. Nobody could throw together a party that fast.

When they all stepped off the elevator, Linc stopped short. This was definitely a party. The double doors to the penthouse were thrown wide, and a loud thumping bass throbbed in time with the strobe lights flashing from somewhere in the corners of the living room. Bodies crushed together in the kitchen, and on the patio, topless girls ran around the pool, screaming and laughing. Couples were full-on fucking on the couch he'd drunk his coffee on not twelve hours ago.

Linc was too old for this shit. The vein in his temple throbbed along with the beat. He wanted nothing

*intoxicating*

more in the world than to go find the source of the noise they called music and kill it. The girl in the flamingo pool float took tiny baby steps on her too-high heels, almost falling onto another girl's lap. She pulled the lid off a bowl in the middle of the coffee table and gave a delighted squeal. "Oh, party favors."

Linc strode to the table. Inside the bowl were prescription pills of every imaginable shape, size, and color. The girl took two or three without looking and dropped them into her mouth, swallowing them down with a cup she found sitting on the table beside the bowl. The wire inside him finally snapped.

He prowled the party until he found the source of the music, a guy with two turntables hidden in the darkest corner of the patio. "Party's over," he shouted when the deejay lifted one headphone.

"Fuck off, man. We're just getting started."

Linc didn't have time for this. He lifted his hoodie, flashing the Glock holstered on his hip. "Party's. Over."

The guy's eyes went wide, and he threw his hands up in surrender. Linc's ears rang in the sudden silence as a hundred bodies froze at once, looking around in confusion. Linc stalked back to flamingo girl.

"Where's Wyatt?" he asked.

"I think he went to his room with some girl."

Some girl?

"You need to take your friends and your pills and get the fuck out of here now."

She scoffed. "Who are you, even? Like, you're not his dad…are you?"

Linc rolled his eyes. "I'm a cop, and I'm here to shut this party down. Do I need to show you my badge? Because I just watched you pull a handful of pills from a bowl and take them."

Luckily, she didn't call Linc's bluff. "Fine."

She stood on top of the table and waved her hands. "The party's canceled. Grandpa here is a fucking narc."

Linc watched as people started to mumble to themselves, as if unsure whether she was telling the truth or not. Linc lifted the waistband of his hoodie once more, wanting this fiasco over and done with before somebody called the real cops and a scandal broke out.

Things moved quickly after that, people filing out until all that was left behind was the typical post-party debris of food and half-empty cups. If Linc didn't kill Wyatt, Graciela would. When the last person was gone, he called the front desk and informed them the party was over and nobody else was permitted to use the private elevator. Then he went to find Wyatt.

Wyatt's bedroom was dark and empty. He frowned. Maybe pool float girl was wrong. Maybe Wyatt was in another bedroom. He was about to leave when

*intoxicating*

he heard a pained hiss from the bathroom and a girl croon, "There ya go, baby. Feels good, huh?"

The door to the bathroom was almost closed, but a dim light wavered in the mirror's reflection. His stomach churned, steeling himself for whatever Wyatt and this girl were doing to pass the time. He pushed the door wide, frowning at what he saw. Wyatt was lying in the large empty bathtub in only his unfastened jeans. The girl—woman, really—sat on the rim of the tub behind his head, naked but for a pair of black panties. Linc's gaze dragged to the huge bruise over Wyatt's diaphragm, but he forced himself to let it go, for now.

Wyatt's eyes were glassy, his pupils so blown his pale green eyes looked black in the dim light. He held the remnants of a joint in one hand, but it was what the girl held in her hand that had Linc's guts twisting. The razor blade pinched between her long black nails still dripped with blood—Wyatt's blood, judging from the brownish smears on his neck and shoulder. *Jesus Christ.*

"You. Put your clothes on and get the fuck out. Now."

"Who the fuck are you?" the girl asked, her gaze darting between him and Wyatt. She was clearly on something as well, but Linc's only concern was Wyatt.

"The guy who's going to have you arrested for assault if you don't put your fucking clothes on and get the fuck out of here," he said, voice a low rumble as he tried to control the adrenaline racing through his system telling him to pick the girl up and throw her out the door.

Wyatt snickered, his head lolling on his shoulders. "G.I. Joe!" he exclaimed in a faraway voice. "I was just thinking about you."

The girl jostled Wyatt in her attempt to hurry to do as Linc said, dropping the razor blade into the bathtub as she clutched the red fabric Linc assumed was a dress to her overinflated breasts. "Just so you know, he asked me to cut him. I know what I'm doing. Would you rather he did it himself? That's how accidents happen."

"Go," Linc all but roared, pointing to the door.

When he finally heard the front door close, he turned to Wyatt. "What the hell have you done to yourself?"

"What do you care?" he asked then giggled before taking another long drag from the joint in his hand.

Linc did care. Too much. And it was going to ruin both their lives.

He reached for the medicine cabinet, looking for something to disinfect the wounds. He was both relieved and alarmed when he found everything he needed. He disposed of the bloody razor sitting next to Wyatt's hip. "Sit up."

# fourteen

## WYATT

WYATT WANTED TO COMPLY WITH LINC'S ORDERS—HE always wanted to do what Daddy said—but his bones had evaporated and each time he attempted to move, his limbs refused to cooperate. "What's happening to me?" he asked, bemused as he tried again to sit up.

"What did you take?" Linc asked, nudging Wyatt forward and sitting behind him where Cherry had sat just moments before…or was it Ginger?

It was something Wyatt hated to eat. The thought made him snicker.

"Wyatt, what did you take?"

Linc's terse question had Wyatt trying to blink the

cobwebs from his brain. He flopped his head back until it rested on Linc's thigh and gazed up into Linc's perfect face. "A bright pink pill and a teeny blue one." He pinched his fingers together in an approximation of the blue pill. Maybe if Linc knew how little it was he'd be in less trouble. Wyatt's heart tripped at Linc's expression. "You're mad at me. Your face is all frowny. Why are you so hot like this? Why are you so hot all the time? I just want to touch you all the time." He tried once more to pick up his arms to touch Linc… to show him he was serious. When they still refused to cooperate, he started to worry. "Now, I can't touch you at all. I think the blue pill stole my arms. It looked sus-suspic-sus… It looked like a bad blue pill."

A reluctant smile tugged at Linc's mouth, the smallest of chuckles escaping, and Wyatt's heart felt like it would float right out of his chest. He had the overwhelming urge to smush his face against Linc's so he could feel the scratch and burn of the dark stubble of his flawlessly chiseled jaw against his own.

"I like when you laugh. You have good teeth. Straight. White. Shiny. Like Chiclets."

Linc ignored Wyatt's rambling, once more moving Wyatt where he wanted him. He suddenly found himself staring at white subway tile as his shoulder caught fire. He whimpered, but it was Linc who swore under his breath. "Shit, baby. What did you do to yourself?"

Wyatt's heart plummeted into his stomach. Linc was mad at him again. He hated that. "I'm sorry," he whispered.

Linc said nothing, and Wyatt had no choice but to sit still while Linc dressed his wounds. He drifted in and out, his brain warm and fuzzy as he floated in the stars, far removed from all the shit awaiting him back on Earth. He only forced his heavy lids back open when Linc's hands dug into his armpits, hauling him to his feet, before swinging him into his arms like he was Whitney Houston and Linc was Kevin Costner in *The Bodyguard*. It would have been a very swoony moment if Wyatt's whole body wasn't already feeling wonky.

He must have said that out loud because Linc snorted. "One: you are far too young to understand that reference, and two: Whitney died in her bathtub of a drug overdose, so maybe we don't dwell on any similarities there given your current state of intoxication, huh?"

"You say so many words," Wyatt muttered, his lids fluttering closed. He moaned when his body connected with the icy cool softness of his Egyptian cotton sheets. Wyatt found his hips worked just fine when Linc yanked down his jeans and underwear. He arched up to help with the process, the feel of Linc's hands on his bare skin making him groan.

Linc covered him with the comforter, but Wyatt kicked it off like a toddler. "No. It's too hot."

When Linc said nothing, Wyatt pried his lids open. Pressure built in his chest, in that spot where his father had punched him, when he saw Linc walking toward the bedroom door.

He couldn't stop the words spilling from his lips. "You can't leave. You have to bring me water and oranges. You have to take care of me."

Linc turned and the hopeless look in his eyes made Wyatt feel small, but Linc's words soothed the ragged edges of his anxiety. "I'm not leaving you. I'm just going to change my clothes. And get you some water and maybe even some oranges." His voice grew stern. "I couldn't leave you even if I wanted to because I don't know what poison is flowing in your veins or if I'll have to take you to the ER to have your stomach pumped later."

Wyatt didn't care about anything Linc said after "I'm not leaving you," but the pressure in his chest didn't ease until Linc slid into bed, gathering him in his arms and holding the bottle of water to his lips. Wyatt sucked it all down. He didn't realize how thirsty he'd been. He ate the fruit Linc had brought—apple slices this time—without protest.

*intoxicating*

When Linc laid him down, Wyatt wiggled himself into little spoon position, nestling against Linc's solid frame, noting Linc now wore a threadbare t-shirt and soft sweatpants that felt good against Wyatt's overheated skin. They fit together like puzzle pieces. If Wyatt wasn't so high, he might have felt strange lying naked in Linc's arms while he was fully clothed. Instead, it just sort of turned him on, or it would have if the drugs hadn't stolen his ability to get hard. Linc's arm wrapped around Wyatt's waist, his thumb caressing circles on the soft skin beneath Wyatt's belly button, making him shiver.

They weren't a thing. They'd never be a thing. He told himself this over and over on a loop as they lay there in the dark. But when Linc's lips skimmed across his neck, Wyatt tilted his head to give him better access.

"You can't keep doing this to yourself," Linc warned, pressing the words into Wyatt's skin like a spell that could make it true somehow.

But Wyatt knew better.

"Sure, I can. I've been doing it my whole life," he assured him.

"Your whole life," Linc muttered. "You're twenty-two. Your life hasn't even started yet."

Tears welled in Wyatt's eyes from nowhere, his throat tight. "My life ended when I was six and my older brother, Landon, died. If he had lived, he would've been the heir my father demands and I could have escaped. My father never would have looked for me."

Linc's arms tightened around him, pressing soothing kisses against his bandaged shoulder.

"I hate my brother," Wyatt confessed in a whisper. "I'm a monster, right? Like, who hates an eight-year-old for getting cancer and dying? Me. I do. He fucking escaped. He got out." He should stop talking but he couldn't. Panic crushed in on him. If he didn't get the words out, he was sure he'd choke on them. "The night I got arrested…do you know what my dad said?"

Linc's hand flattened over the bruise his father had left. "Wyatt, don't."

"Don't what? Tell the truth? You don't get it. Not talking is why the people in my family are the way they are. My mom still whispers the word 'cancer' like it's a curse and clutches her pearls whenever somebody mentions abortion or immigration or rape. Anything that intrudes on her perfect palace of privilege." Hot tears tracked down his cheeks, but his caged arms made it impossible to wipe them away. He sniffled. "He said, 'I can't believe you're the one who lived.'"

Linc shifted, tugging at Wyatt until he found his face tucked under Linc's chin. A raw keening noise slipped from his lips and then another. He couldn't stop. He buried his face against Linc's chest to hide his ugly-cry face. But there was no hiding the way his body shook or the snot and tears leaking all over Linc's t-shirt. He whispered words into Wyatt's hair, but he had no idea what he said. He didn't care. He just wanted Linc's arms and the heat of his body and to feel like one person in the whole fucking world gave a shit if he lived or died. Didn't he deserve just one?

Sometime later, he opened his burning eyes, his throat raw and his nose stuffy. "Do you know why he said it?" he managed, not sure why he needed Linc to know this part.

"What?" Linc asked, voice sleep-soaked.

"Do you know why he said he couldn't believe I was the one who lived?"

"No," Linc whispered, the arm around Wyatt's shoulders tightening, almost like Linc didn't know he did it.

"Because he caught me blowing the cater-waiter at his fundraising dinner." Linc didn't react, didn't say a word. Wyatt gave a humorless laugh. "My dad got downright biblical, calling me everything from a harlot to a sodomite, but the joke's on him 'cause I'm a virgin in the truest definition of the word." That got a reaction. Linc's body went rigid beneath him. "Didn't see that coming, did ya?"

"No," Linc said, voice wooden.

"It's not for lack of trying. I have no interest in topping a guy, but thanks to my father, any time a guy so much as attempts to touch me there, my body locks up. It's like that camp…those people…rewired my brain, sabotaged my body… It's been five years but the minute a guy touches me, I'm right back there with that needle in my arm and those fingers and… and I just can't get out of my head enough to just be with somebody that way."

Linc's hand trailed soothing circles on his back.

"It's like, even if I could be somebody else…even if I could get away from my father and this toxic penthouse prison and have a normal life…I'll never be normal, not in any real way."

"You're not…abnormal. Penetrative sex isn't the only way to have sex, not the only way to be intimate with somebody."

Wyatt scoffed. "I know that, but I want that, and they took it from me."

"You don't know that. You just need to be with somebody who's patient, somebody who will take the time to help you relax. Somebody you trust."

"I wanted that with you. I trust you," Wyatt confessed.

*intoxicating*

Linc's hand fisted in Wyatt's hair, claiming his mouth in a hot openmouthed kiss that had Wyatt whimpering, his hands clinging to Linc's shoulders by the time he released him. "You cannot say things like that," Linc growled before smacking another hard kiss against his lips.

That stupid blue pill must've been truth serum because he couldn't seem to stop confessing everything, even when Linc had never asked and probably had never wanted to know. The thought made Wyatt's heart shrivel in his chest.

He ducked his head once more, inhaling Linc's scent, like he could somehow commit it to memory. "I wanna go to sleep," he mumbled. "Stay with me, Daddy."

"I'm not going anywhere, kid. I promise. Go to sleep."

# fifteen

## LINCOLN

"HEY, FUCK-NUGGET!"

Given that Wyatt's yappy little friend—Chance? Chelsea?—was scowling in his direction, Linc assumed he was the fuck-nugget to which she referred. He took a sip of his black coffee, heaving a mental sigh before setting down his cup. He'd hoped for an hour or two of peace and sunshine before having to deal with the emotional fallout from Wyatt's rough night, but it seemed the universe still plotted against him.

Linc watched as the boy's friend marched toward him with her tiny purse tucked under one arm, like a girl on a mission. Her strange wide-legged, pinstriped

*intoxicating*

pants billowed behind her, somewhat impeding her progress, ruining whatever tough-girl persona she attempted to convey.

He stood as she approached, hoping his full six-foot-three height might cause her to hesitate. It did not. She craned her head back, her blue eyes full of righteous fury, and her bright red lips pulled back in full snarl.

His brows went up at her murderous expression, and he took a step back, voice firm. "Full disclosure, Malibu Barbie. If you punch me in the face again, I'm gonna toss you in the pool."

She narrowed her eyes. "Punch you in the face? I'm two seconds away from shoving my taser up your ass."

Wyatt emerged from inside wearing basketball shorts and nothing else. Linc briefly forgot about the girl threatening to violate him with a taser, trying to gauge whether Wyatt was okay. His face was puffy, and his hair was a rat's nest. The bruise from his father was now the size and shape of an eggplant, and the bandage Linc had secured to his shoulder curled up at one edge. Other than that, he seemed okay—exhausted and maybe a little raw, but okay. Somehow, that was worse. How many nights like that had Wyatt had?

"Charlie—" Wyatt started, but she gestured for him to shut up, never taking her eyes off Linc.

"Look, I know Senator Shitcunt likes to hire goons

like you to do his dirty work for him. Alpha males who think it's fun to shove Wyatt around under the guise of toughening him up…but not on my watch! I'll fucking kill you, and my family has enough money for me to get away with a murder or two, so don't test me." She emphasized the last four words by drilling her too-sharp nail into his chest. "Got it, crotch-weasel?"

"Your insults are terrible. You're just shoving two unrelated words together," Linc observed. "But your threats are persuasive," he added begrudgingly. "Unnecessary but persuasive."

"I'm serious. I might be small, but I will fuck you up."

"Charlie! Stop." She whirled on Wyatt, like he was next on her verbal beatdown list, but this time, Wyatt slapped a hand over her mouth. "He didn't hurt me. He didn't. Now, stop."

Charlie! That was her name. Charlie's gaze flicked from Linc to Wyatt and back again, her hands falling to her sides, shoulders deflating. Wyatt dropped his hand.

"What happened?" she finally asked. "And I'll know if you're lying."

Wyatt rubbed the back of his neck. "My dad happened. He caught me wearing makeup when the cops came to pull my monitor. He was mad I almost embarrassed him."

*intoxicating*

Charlie's face went as red as her lipstick, and her fury made Linc like her just a little more. "If there's any karma in this world, your dad will get face raped by a chainsaw," she swore.

"God willing," Linc muttered.

Charlie's gaze strayed to the bandage on Wyatt's shoulder. "Did he hurt your shoulder, too?"

Wyatt once more looked to Linc. The boy's despair had Linc wanting to take the blame just to keep Wyatt from having to explain himself. But it wasn't Linc's story to tell. Whether Wyatt told Charlie the truth or a lie, Linc would swear to it.

"Ginger."

The girl's nostrils flared, and before Linc could stop her, she reached out and ripped the bandage from Wyatt's shoulder.

"Ow!"

"You let that cracked-out slag cut you? Again?" she shrieked.

Again? The word bounced around Linc's skull. He hadn't noticed any other scars on Wyatt, but he hadn't had the opportunity to explore his body as thoroughly as he'd wanted. How many times had this happened before? Would Wyatt do it again?

"It was a pill party. I took something… It messed with my head."

Charlie slung her purse off her shoulder and smacked Wyatt with it to punctuate her words. "Are you really this fucking stupid? What the fuck, Wyatt? You promised me you wouldn't do this shit anymore. You fucking promised."

Linc waited longer than he should have before yanking the purse from her hands and firmly pushing her down onto one of the lounge chairs. "Sit. Stop doing…everything. Stop screeching, stop hitting, just—just stop. You're giving me a migraine."

Charlie crossed her arms, glaring at Wyatt and Linc. Her brows suddenly shot toward her hairline, and she jerked her head back to Wyatt. "Did your father put those bruises on your neck? If he did, you should've called the cops. There needs to be a paper trail."

Wyatt flushed to the tips of his ears, his hand fluttering to his throat almost against his will. Almost like he was remembering. Fuck. Now, Linc remembered, too. Wyatt under him, naked and begging, as Linc jerked him to orgasm, his fingers flexing around Wyatt's throat. Wyatt licked his lower lip, his heated gaze making Linc glad he wore jeans, even if his cock would have a permanent imprint of his zipper.

Linc tried to will the thoughts from his head, turning his attention back to Wyatt's nosy friend. He knew

*intoxicating*

the exact moment Charlie dropped all the pieces into place, and she sucked in a breath, her hands clapping together with delight. "Wait…was this a *sex thing*? Are you two having a sex thing?"

"Oh, my God, will you shut up?" Wyatt pleaded, throwing a look into the house, like his father might lurk somewhere within, eavesdropping.

"It *is*," she hissed before cackling. "That's amazing, you kinky little shits."

"It's not. Stop saying that."

Charlie's brow furrowed. "What's the big deal? If anybody needs to get laid, it's you. You are way too tightly wound."

Wyatt looked like he was praying a hole would just open and swallow him down. "It's not like that."

"He didn't choke you during a sex thing? 'Cause the way you two were just now eye-fucking each other and the rather impressive hard-ons you're both sporting at the mention of said choking tells me you're both either really kinky or psychopaths. But if you're saying Linc choked you for a different reason, I will still kick his ass. So, which is it, boo?"

Wyatt's hands flailed. "This is so none of your business."

She scoffed. "Everything about you is my business. Why are you guys acting like this is such a big deal?

You're both adults."

"I've been entombed in the closet for life, and Linc works for my dad. If anybody finds out, it would ruin both our lives," Wyatt confessed before clapping a hand over his own mouth. His gaze cut to Linc, brows furrowed like he thought Linc would be angry. He wasn't, but Wyatt looked so adorable, Linc temporarily forgot they weren't alone and put a hand on Wyatt's shoulder. Wyatt's face relaxed, though his eyes still seemed sad.

Linc should've panicked over Wyatt's confession, but having Charlie in the loop made Wyatt happy and she was clearly Wyatt's fiercest defender. She'd never do anything to hurt him. Wyatt hated secrets, hated that nobody in his family ever talked to each other.

"How would your dad find out? Are you going to tell him?"

Linc now understood why Charlie was so important to Wyatt. She had never met a thought she didn't speak, and she'd rearrange the universe to make sure Wyatt was okay. Linc couldn't ask for anything more than that. Charlie was probably the only person Wyatt could count on.

Charlie wasn't done pleading their case. "You guys spend like ninety percent of your time alone. Graciela isn't going to tell. I'm certainly not going to tell. Lock

*intoxicating*

the front door. Problem solved."

This time, when Wyatt looked at him, there was this small flicker of hope, a silent question. Could they? Could they make it work? Linc shook his head. "I only have this job for the next five months, and then I have to go back to Orlando. That's non-negotiable."

Charlie wiggled her brows. "Even better. Have a fling. A super hot affair. They write movies about stuff like this. You guys have five months to fuck each other's brains out. Chances are, by the time those five months are done, you'll both be ready to say goodbye. I know I usually am."

"It's not that simple," Linc assured her…and himself. It couldn't be that easy.

Charlie waved off his statement. "Fucking is never simple, but it's almost always worth it."

"Still none of your business," Wyatt groaned.

"Fine, whatever," she conceded. "Anyway, I stopped by to let you know I'm your plus one for your father's stupid fundraising dinner tomorrow."

"You already know about that?" Wyatt asked.

Once more, she scoffed. "Duh, Graciela told Natasha, who told my mom, who told me. So, I came straight away to tell you I'll be reporting tomorrow night for beard duty."

"My dad hates you," Wyatt reminded her.

"Yeah, but he hates that you're gay more. So, straight son dating the rich daughter of liberal actress trumps gay son who secretly likes to get choked and fucked by his big, beefy bodyguard. He'll deal."

Wyatt winced. "Stop saying that."

"Mm, no. You obviously want to bone each other. I hate subtext and innuendo. Just do it. I'll be your cover. Tell your dad it will sell the whole straight playboy thing if I'm your fake girlfriend. He'll be so annoyed by you choosing me, he'll never even notice you banging Captain America."

Linc should have shut down the entire conversation. Having Charlie on board was helpful but not foolproof. It was still dangerous. They could still lose everything if anybody found out. Besides, Wyatt wasn't stable enough for the kind of relationship Linc demanded of the boys he played with. Linc wasn't sure he was stable enough, either. He always insisted on a layer of protection—no attachments, just scenes and aftercare, and then they went their separate ways. The others had understood the arrangement. But Linc was already too attached to Wyatt. He already cared. He held his tongue, though. He wanted Wyatt, and if Wyatt wanted to take the risk, Linc knew, deep in his gut, he'd never be able to tell him no.

Wyatt watched Linc's face, so he tried to keep his

*intoxicating*

expression neutral. Wyatt's disappointment in Linc's lack of response was obvious. Finally, he said to Charlie, "I can't ask you to do that."

She huffed. "Ask? Please, I volunteered. You're not a true celebrity until you've bearded for at least one closet case, anyway. I consider it another box to check on my Road-to-Hollywood checklist. Anyhoo, I'm gonna go try to find an appropriately inappropriate dress for your father's dinner tomorrow. You guys probably have a lot to talk about."

And then she left, leaving them on the patio with a mountain of tension between them.

# sixteen

## WYATT

WYATT'S VEINS THRUMMED LIKE SOMEBODY HAD electrified his blood. He didn't speak. He couldn't. What the fuck was he even supposed to say? Charlie had pulled the pin on a grenade and tossed it to Wyatt as she walked away. But Linc had to know Wyatt wanted him, wanted this…more than anything. He had to. It was Linc who kept saying it couldn't work between them, that it was too risky. Wyatt had accepted Linc at his word, but now that Charlie had put the offer on the table between them, Wyatt couldn't remember ever needing anything more. Five months of Linc as his Daddy was more than he'd ever dared hope for,

*intoxicating*

and if he said no, Wyatt wasn't sure he'd recover.

"Do you want—" Linc started.

"Yes," Wyatt interrupted.

Linc tilted his head, narrowing his eyes. "You don't even know what I was going to say."

Wyatt's hands flailed. "Don't you get it? It doesn't matter what you were going to say. The answer is yes. Whatever you want…I'll always say yes."

Linc closed the distance between them, locking his hands in Wyatt's hair and crushing their mouths together. He melted into him, tasting the coffee on Linc's tongue and reveling in the scratch and burn of Linc's stubble on his tender skin. Linc walked them backward toward the house, never breaking the kiss. When Wyatt stumbled, Linc's hands hooked under his thighs, lifting him like he weighed nothing. Wyatt's legs encircled Linc's waist, their lower bodies aligning in a way that had Wyatt moaning.

When Linc finally tore his mouth away, his gaze bore into Wyatt. "You have to be sure. You don't really understand how these arrangements work; there are contracts and limits. You're a virgin, and I've never done something like this with somebody inexperienced."

Wyatt held his gaze. "I'm only a virgin in the technical sense. My hard limits are no humiliation, no water sports, no sharing me with anybody else. My soft limits are what we talked about last night. I want to…bottom…with you, but I don't know if my body will…" He broke off, looking over Linc's shoulder, sure it would be a deal-breaker.

Linc dragged his thumb over Wyatt's lower lip. "Understood."

Linc dropped them both onto the sofa, bringing Wyatt down to straddle his lap. Linc studied him until Wyatt couldn't help but ask, "What?"

"You know more about this stuff than I thought."

Wyatt rolled his eyes with a smile. "I told you you'd make a good Daddy the first night we met. Did you think I hadn't done my fair share of Googling? Porn's free now, old man."

"Is that how you get yourself off at night? Watching Daddies dominate their boys?" Linc rumbled, one hand fisting in Wyatt's hair, the other yanking him closer until they were flush against each other.

Wyatt couldn't help but rock himself against Linc's half-hard cock. Linc slapped his ass hard enough to make him hiss.

"Stop that. We're talking now," Linc said even as his rough hands skimmed Wyatt's torso and chest, his thumbs tracing over Wyatt's flat nipples. "Daddy asked you a question."

*intoxicating*

"Yes, Daddy," Wyatt said on a moan, arching his back at Linc's touch, his eyes drifting closed as Linc placed a kiss in the center of his chest.

"Pay attention, sweet boy."

"I'm trying," Wyatt whined. How was he supposed to concentrate with Linc's thumbs tracing the grooves of his hip bones, Linc's hard cock jutting against his own, and Linc's tongue teasing over the stiff peak of one nipple? Linc wasn't playing fair.

Linc's mouth disappeared, his hands traveling to Wyatt's ass, squeezing hard enough to make Wyatt yelp. "Eyes on me." Wyatt cut his eyes to Linc, mouth a sudden desert. He was trying to behave, but there was too much talking. He forced himself to concentrate, watching Linc's lips as he spoke, afraid to miss even a word. "If we do this, I expect complete obedience. You belong to me in every sense of the word. When we're alone, I own you; you exist just to please me. If I want you, I take you. You come only when I feel you've earned it, and if you disobey me, you will be punished severely. Is that understood?"

If Linc was hoping to scare Wyatt off, he clearly hadn't been paying attention. Wyatt's cock throbbed. He wanted to touch himself so badly, but he just nodded. "Yes."

Linc leaned forward, biting Wyatt's nipple until he

cried out. "Yes, what?"

"Yes, Daddy," he moaned.

Linc tongued over Wyatt's tender flesh. "Good boy." He leaned back. "We use the traffic light system. Green means go. Yellow means pause. Red means everything stops. Understand?"

Wyatt couldn't ever imagine a world where he'd stop Linc from doing anything he wanted to him.

"Yes, Daddy."

Linc gripped his chin, forcing him to meet his gaze. "This one's important. You will not self-harm under any circumstances. That's my hard limit. No cutting, no drugs, no putting yourself in dangerous situations. Don't test me on this."

Wyatt hesitated. He couldn't promise that. He wouldn't. When the world got to be too much…it was the only way to quiet the noise. The drinking, the drugs, none of those things mattered. They were a distraction. But the cutting…he couldn't agree to that. When his thoughts grew toxic, his hatred and panic and self-loathing leaching into his blood until he felt sick and sluggish, there was only one way to let it out, to cleanse himself of the poison. He was safe. He was careful. It was only one little cut. It wasn't that Wyatt liked it or that he even wanted it. He needed it. Without it, he might die.

*intoxicating*

There was no way somebody like Linc could ever understand. He possessed a strength Wyatt could only dream of. Linc would leave in five months and be whoever he wished to be, but Wyatt would still be there, being whoever his father demanded. But Linc said it was a hard limit, and Wyatt wanted Linc more than he wanted to tell the truth. He gave a hesitant nod. *It's only five months.*

Linc released him. "Say the words."

Wyatt closed his eyes, burying his face against Linc's throat. "Yes, Daddy."

"If I think you can't handle this or that it's doing more harm than good, I'll end it. I won't be another person who hurts you. Understand?"

Wyatt had never understood the words bittersweet until right then. He pressed a kiss to Linc's shoulder and then his throat. "Yes, Daddy. Whatever you want. Yes. Can we play now?"

"So impatient," Linc muttered even as he shifted Wyatt, letting him rut his cock against Linc's perfect abs. Any friction was good friction. Wyatt had never been more ready to go in his life.

Wyatt moaned. "More, please."

"What do you want, baby?"

"Whatever you want, Daddy."

Linc chuckled. "Good answer. Bedroom. Now. I

want you naked on the bed before I get in there."

Wyatt rushed to comply, shucking his shorts halfway to his destination, grateful Linc missed him tripping and face planting into the mattress. Once on the bed, his mind raced with possibilities. He had wanted a Daddy for longer than he could remember, and he'd wanted Linc since the moment they'd met, but never in his wildest dreams had he imagined he could have both. It was overwhelming in the best possible way.

What would Linc want from him? Would he want him to bottom? He said he understood Wyatt's issue, but that didn't mean he wouldn't try to get him past it. The thought made him shiver. Linc on top of him, inside of him, taking him and using him up. Jesus. His hand went to his hard and leaking cock, eyes closing as he bit his lip to stave off the noises threatening to spill out.

"Did I say you could touch yourself?"

His eyes flew open. Linc filled his doorway, forearm propped against the frame as he drank his fill of Wyatt's naked form. He flushed, not sure if it was because Linc caught him touching himself or because Linc watched him do it. He made Wyatt feel like a virgin, despite his many and varied experiences.

"What are you thinking about?"

Wyatt wanted to wrap himself in the warmth of Linc's raspy tone. "You, Daddy."

*intoxicating*

Linc prowled closer, hands slipping into his pockets. Wyatt's gaze fell to the outline of Linc's thick cock through the well-worn denim. He bit down on his bottom lip, giving Linc his best 'fuck me' eyes, but he didn't seem in any hurry to undress as he stood at the end of the bed. Wyatt fought the urge to cover himself as Linc's hungry gaze roamed his flesh, like he had a claim to him. He did have a claim, Wyatt supposed. Linc owned him body and soul…at least, for now. "What about me?"

He'd had all kinds of hookups, always in the dark, usually standing up or crammed into the back seat of somebody's too small sports car. Nobody had ever seen him naked, never seen him laid out with the sunlight streaming through the blinds, leaving nowhere to hide. It left him shaky and vulnerable. "Thinking about you fucking me, Daddy."

Linc's brows flew upward, like Wyatt's candor surprised him, and a small wet spot formed on the front of his jeans. Wyatt's belly fluttered at shaking Linc's control just a little. His triumph was short-lived as Linc hit the bed and crawled closer, his thighs catching under Wyatt's, forcing his legs wide. He swallowed, captivated by the desire on Linc's face hovering just above his. "Like this? Is this how you want me to fuck you, baby?"

Linc rocked their bodies together in some filthy pantomime of sex, like Linc was filling him up, driving into him, owning him. Wyatt whimpered, his erection jerking at the thought only to meet the unforgiving metal teeth of Linc's zipper. He gave a shaky nod, but Linc was no longer looking at his face but at Wyatt's leaking cock. Why was that so hot?

"Oh, yeah. You *do* like that, don't you, dirty boy? I bet I could make you come without even touching you. Hmm? Just my words? My voice? Telling you all the dirty things I'm gonna do to you?"

"Daddy…" It was a plea.

Wyatt wanted to be good, but Linc was killing him. He needed to touch him somewhere, anywhere. Every muscle in Wyatt's body was on edge. Was he being a tease? Did Linc think he could get Wyatt so hot his body would let go…and give in? Wyatt wanted that more than anything. It would be so much easier if the choice wasn't his. But if Linc tried and Wyatt couldn't…

Linc's mouth grazed Wyatt's. "Relax. I can hear you thinking from here. We're not there yet."

Relief and disappointment warred within him. What if they never got there? The thought of never having Linc inside him was a pit in his belly. So, he pushed it away. "Touch me, Daddy. Please?"

*intoxicating*

Linc cut his eyes to Wyatt, his expression stern. "Who makes the rules?"

Wyatt shivered. "You do, Daddy."

Linc's thumb slipped into Wyatt's mouth. He sucked it without thought, relishing the roughness against his tongue and the salty tang of his skin. Everything was too much and not enough, and they hadn't even started yet.

"Who do you belong to?" Linc asked, dragging his thumb across Wyatt's lower lip.

Wyatt's insides shook as he managed a breathy, "You, Daddy."

"I'll touch you when I'm ready. Right now, I want to look at what's mine."

Wyatt dug his nails into his thighs, trying to use the pain to stave off his arousal. Linc's voice startled him. "Hands on the headboard. If you move them, I'll tie you to the bed and you will not like what happens after that. Understand?"

As soon as his hands hit the headboard, Linc was on him. There was no rhyme or reason, no rhythm to his assault. Linc would kiss the delicate skin behind his ear, then bite his lobe hard enough to make him whine. He'd dip his tongue into the hollow of Wyatt's throat only to scrape his teeth across Wyatt's nipples, leaving Wyatt keening. It was a full-on assault on

Wyatt's senses as Linc touched him everywhere, except where he needed it most.

"Daddy. Oh, God. Please, just…please…please…I need…"

Linc kissed him, fucking his tongue into Wyatt's mouth. "Shh, baby. Daddy knows what you need."

Then Linc was no longer above him but between his splayed legs, pushing his knees up to his chest. Wyatt wailed as Linc's tongue ran along the underside of his cock before sucking the tip between his lips. His hands flailed as pleasure ripped through him, but Linc slapped them back against the headboard. "I'm sorry, Daddy. Please, don't stop. Please. I'm sorry."

Linc did stop, though. Wyatt couldn't help his sob of frustration. Then Linc's palms were gripping his ass, spreading him.

Wyatt's eyes flew open, panic seizing his heart. "Wait!"

Linc froze. "Color?"

Wyatt frowned at the word. Color? Color? Color! He didn't really want Linc to wait. He didn't know what he wanted. "Gr-green," he stuttered out. "Green. So green. Green means go. Go!"

Once again, that maddening chuckle, and then Linc's tongue swept over that tight ring of muscle. Wyatt's hips jerked upward in surprise. How the fuck did that feel so good? How had he not known that it would? His hands fisted in his own hair and he prayed Linc didn't care about the headboard anymore because Wyatt needed to hold onto something, even if it was only himself.

Linc's tongue laved over Wyatt's hole in broad sweeping strokes and tiny darting movements. If Wyatt still had any sense of reason, the noises pouring from his lips would have humiliated the fuck out of him, but he didn't care. He didn't care about anything but Linc's fingertips digging into his hips hard enough to leave bruises and Linc's wicked mouth and sinful tongue working against him again and again. "Please, Daddy."

"Don't you come until I say."

Wyatt sobbed, his hands twisting the pillows, his hips working himself against Linc's perfect fucking tongue. "Please, I can't."

"You will." With those words, Linc sucked Wyatt's cock into the tight heat of his mouth, and Wyatt couldn't hold back any longer, coming down Linc's throat without warning. Waves of ecstasy broke over him until his vision tunneled and he lost himself in a perfect nothingness.

When he opened his eyes, Linc straddled Wyatt's chest, one hand gripping the headboard and the other fisting his cock. "Open your mouth. I wanna dirty up that angel face."

Wyatt stuck out his tongue, gaze riveted on Linc as he lost himself in chasing his own pleasure, his mouth slack and body rigid. It was the hottest thing Wyatt had ever witnessed, and if his cock could have rallied, it would have. Linc grunted, his abdominal muscles flexing as he curled forward. Wyatt closed his eyes as the first splashes of cum hit his face and tongue, Linc shuddering above him. Wyatt supposed he should feel dirty but he didn't. He felt wanted and safe, and he didn't care if that was wrong or weird.

Linc's mouth found his in a dirty kiss. "You didn't wait for permission, bad boy. Now, I have to punish you."

"Sorry, Daddy," Wyatt said, unable to help the satisfied smile spreading across his sticky face.

Linc laughed. "No, you're not…but you will be."

## seventeen

### LINCOLN

BY THE TIME LINC WENT TO CLEAN WYATT UP, THE BOY was Jell-O. He allowed Linc to pull him to his feet and guide him into the bathroom, standing by silently while Linc turned on the shower and waited for the water to heat. Once under the spray, Wyatt swayed on his feet, lids at half-mast. Linc gently washed his face with a washcloth before turning him toward the spray. As Linc set about working shampoo through Wyatt's curls, he gave a contented sigh, leaning his back against Linc's chest.

An ache formed behind Linc's ribs. Had anybody ever just shown an interest in Wyatt without an ulterior motive? Had anybody cared for him when he was sick or just hugged him for no reason? Even the simplest gesture seemed enormous to the boy. Linc had at least had his sister to look out for him, even with his lunatic mother and absentee father. Wyatt had grown up with nobody in his corner, and that knowledge ate at something inside Linc.

Once Wyatt's hair was clean, Linc soaped him up, washing him carefully, his gaze snagging on the dozens of scars marring both his thighs. A sharp pain knifed through him as he imagined Wyatt taking a blade to himself in a desperate attempt to feel better. He ran his fingers over them, noting how Wyatt stiffened. Linc didn't say anything. What was there to say? He placed a gentle kiss over each set of scars before rinsing Wyatt off with clinical efficiency and bundling him in one of the huge bath sheets Graciela replaced under the sink every other day. Linc didn't bother getting him dressed since he was only putting him to bed, even if it was barely the afternoon. He pushed back the covers and gestured for Wyatt to get in.

Wyatt did as instructed without fuss but then gazed up at Linc with those huge green eyes. "Are you staying in here with me?"

Linc slipped in beside him. Wyatt curved himself into Linc's side, like it was something they did every night, nestling his head against his shoulder and throwing one leg over Linc's. Once again, that weird pang hit him. "I'll stay until you fall asleep, but I don't want to risk hurting you again. My nightmares are unpredictable."

Wyatt ran his hand over Linc's chest, his fingers combing through the hair dusted there. "I like when you hurt me, though."

Linc smiled but shook his head. "Not like that. I can't risk it."

Wyatt pouted. "But you'll stay until I fall asleep?"

Linc kissed his forehead. "Yes, sweet boy."

Wyatt was asleep almost instantly. Linc must have drifted off soon after because when he opened his eyes again, the sun was down and the light of the full moon poured in through the windows, drenching the room in shades of gray. It was hot beneath the heavy comforter, leaving them both damp, but Linc made no effort to move, even with his arm trapped painfully beneath Wyatt's head.

Wyatt had turned himself away from Linc, but his face tipped upward, caught in the moonlight. Linc couldn't help but stare. Wyatt was beautiful anytime but while he slept, the usual tension slipped from his face. His furrowed brow smoothed without his ever-present anxiety, his long lashes casting half-moons on his pale skin. He looked much younger in sleep, one hand beneath his face and the other curled around Linc's forearm trapped beneath him, like even in sleep he worried Linc would leave.

He *should* leave. He needed to get up and cook dinner, but he curled his body against Wyatt's, his tongue tracing the shell of his ear, biting his earlobe as his free hand traced the curve of Wyatt's satiny skin beneath the blankets, his knuckles sliding from his ribs to the groove of his hip and back again.

Wyatt gave a shuddery sigh, shifting himself closer, giving Linc more access to his naked, sweaty body. Linc traced biting kisses against Wyatt's jaw, his hand sliding along Wyatt's belly to wrap his palm around his semi-erect cock, stroking him at a glacial pace. Wyatt moaned low.

Linc had been with a lot of guys, but he'd never shared a bed, never stayed overnight. There was no time for relationships with weeks of training and deployments and missions. At least, that's what he'd told himself. But this—having access to Wyatt's body whenever he pleased…taking what he wanted, giving pleasure when he wanted—could become addictive. For the next five months, Wyatt belonged only to him, and Linc planned on taking advantage of every opportunity. He tightened his grip, twisting on

*intoxicating*

the upstroke, swiping his thumb over the tip before sliding back down.

Wyatt whimpered, his hips pushing upward, working himself into Linc's sweat-slick fist, chasing his pleasure even in sleep. Linc didn't stop him. He licked and bit at Wyatt's neck and throat, caught up in the salty tang of his skin, his own cock already at attention and gliding between the globes of Wyatt's ass.

Wyatt's hand suddenly tightened where he held Linc's forearm, his breath tripping as he reached back for Linc's hip. "Linc?" he whispered, turning his face toward him.

"Is that what you call me?" Linc rumbled against his ear.

"Daddy," Wyatt moaned, pushing himself back against Linc's cock before rocking himself forward into Linc's hand. "Oh, fuck, please, Daddy."

"Color?" Linc asked.

"Green, so green," he panted.

Linc captured his mouth, fucking his tongue inside before biting gently at Wyatt's lower lip. "You can come whenever you want, but you have to do the work," Linc whispered against his mouth.

Linc stopped moving his hand, but Wyatt didn't seem to notice, his fingers gripping Linc's hip as he fucked himself into Linc's tightened fist. Linc rocked his hips forward, matching Wyatt's rhythm as he worked his length between Wyatt's ass cheeks. "Fuck, you feel so good," Linc muttered.

Wyatt made a half-bitten-off sound, his muscles flexing with every forward thrust, enclosing Linc's cock in a constricted heat that had his balls tightening against his body. He drove himself against Wyatt almost as blindly as Wyatt fucked into Linc's fist, tiny noises of pleasure falling from the boy's lips as he chased his release.

"Come on, sweet boy. Work for it. Take it."

"Daddy," Wyatt breathed, almost without thought. "I…want… Fuck, fuck."

Wyatt never finished his sentence, just moaned low, his whole body trembling as his cum spilled over Linc's hand. Linc worked the fluid over Wyatt's cock, thrusting against him three more times before he buried his face in the boy's throat with a hoarse shout, pleasure rolling along every nerve ending as his own release coated Wyatt's ass and lower back.

When Linc could finally bring himself to move, he pressed his hand to Wyatt's lips, letting the boy taste himself before wiping the rest on the sheet. He pushed the covers off, giving Wyatt room now that they were both sticky. Wyatt looked over at him and grinned. "Hi."

"Hey," Linc managed, still feeling winded and a

*intoxicating*

little shaky.

"I thought you were going back to your room?"

Linc laughed. "It's only"—he glanced at the clock beside Wyatt's bed—"eight-thirty."

Wyatt yawned hard enough to make his jaw pop. "I'm hungry."

"Of course, you are," Linc said, shaking his head. "Did Graciela leave anything to eat?"

Wyatt scratched at his belly. "Doubtful. We could order in? There are a bunch of takeout menus in the kitchen drawer. What do you like?"

Linc shrugged, rolling himself into a sitting position. "Anything but Thai food. Too spicy."

"What's the matter? Give you heartburn, old man?" Wyatt snarked, exiting the bed on Linc's side.

The slap to Wyatt's ass was gunshot loud in the silence and left a perfect imprint of Linc's palm. Wyatt hissed, but the look he gave Linc could have melted steel. He leaned forward and kissed the print he'd left behind before gently shoving Wyatt toward the bathroom. "Get cleaned up, and I'll find the menus."

Wyatt threw a look over his shoulder that had Linc half tempted to follow him, but then his stomach growled, and he remembered they had to eat. He shoved his legs into the pair of jeans he'd abandoned by the bed and headed toward the kitchen.

When Wyatt returned in a pair of soft-looking olive-green pants, they ordered Chinese food and settled onto the sofa to wait. Wyatt flipped on the television and lay down with his head on Linc's thigh. Linc's fingers folded into Wyatt's curls, blunt nails scratching along his scalp. Wyatt sighed, content for the moment.

On the screen, a masked man dressed in all black rolled down the side of a mountain in dramatic fashion. Wyatt flipped the channel, and Linc snatched the remote and flipped it back. "You did not just flip past the best movie ever made."

Wyatt scoffed. "You mean the oldest movie ever made? When was this? The eighties? It's so grainy."

Linc balked. "I ought to put you over my knee just for disrespecting *The Princess Bride* like that."

Wyatt's mouth hung open as he stared up at Linc in shock. "I can't tell whether you're joking."

"Not. And if you don't like this movie, I don't know if I'll ever trust your judgment about anything, ever." Linc shook his head.

"I've never seen this movie, so I have no idea if I like it or not," Wyatt said hesitantly, as if he couldn't believe this was the hill Linc was willing to die on.

"We're starting it over from the beginning and watching it over dinner," Linc stated, leaving no room for argument. "My sister used to play it for me all the

*intoxicating*

time growing up. We'd watch this and *Goonies* on repeat whenever my mother was in one of her moods."

As soon as the words were out of his mouth, Linc wished he could suck them back in. One glance at Wyatt's face told him he hadn't missed the comment.

"Moods?" Wyatt asked, his voice an octave higher than normal as if trying for casual.

Linc shrugged. "Yeah, my mother had a temper."

Wyatt's expression went soft. "I know how that goes. Did she drink…like your dad?"

Linc tried but failed to keep the bitterness from his tone. "Yeah, among other things. My mom was a rapid-cycling bipolar who drank when she was manic and did speed when she was depressed. My father was probably too drunk to notice something was off about her at first, and by the time he did, my sister was four and I was two. So, he left."

"Left you behind with your crazy mom?" Wyatt stated, pity shining in his bright sea-glass eyes.

"Yeah." Linc rocketed to his feet, dumping Wyatt on the couch. "Want a drink?" he asked, attempting to deflect his sudden abandonment.

Wyatt scurried into an upright position, peering at him over the back of the sofa. "Yeah, I'll have a beer."

"You'll have water, diet soda, or juice."

Wyatt rolled his eyes. "Diet soda, I guess."

Linc opened the fridge and peered inside, like some new contents would spring forth at any moment.

"We don't have to talk about it. I get what it's like to have psycho parents," Wyatt reassured him.

Linc grunted. "It's—"

The doorbell rang, cutting off whatever stupid platitude Linc was about to throw at Wyatt. He walked to the door, yanking it open, grateful for the interruption. He gawked at a tiny dark-haired woman in a full face of makeup and a sharp black business suit. Whoever she was, she wasn't there to deliver Chinese food. Linc stiffened, closing the door until only his body was visible.

"Can I help you?" he asked, tone making it clear he had no intention of doing so.

"Is Wyatt home?" she asked, smiling with too many teeth, peeking under Linc's arm, like she was hoping to glimpse the boy.

In his periphery, he could see Wyatt move to the kitchen, clearly still thinking it was their dinner. It occurred to Linc then that their no shirt, no shoes look was too casual for an employee and employer relationship. He hoped this woman did not work for the senator.

"What's taking so long? I'm starving. You need tip money or something?" Wyatt called. When he saw the

*intoxicating*

woman in the doorway, he frowned.

"Wyatt," the woman called with a wave. "Miranda Rodrigues for the *Miami Sun*. I was hoping to ask you a few questions about your father's campaign." She looked Linc up and down, one brow raised and a smirk spreading across her face. "If this is a bad time, I can come back later."

Linc's blood pounded in his ears. "He's not answering questions for the press. How did you get up here?"

She shrugged, once more attempting to look around Linc's massive frame. "So, you have no comment about your father's recent decision to vote no on a bill for equal pay for women?" she asked, voice raised.

Behind her, the elevator dinged, and a teenage boy with greasy brown hair and acne stepped off with a box full of food in his hands. When he got to where Linc and the woman stood, he frowned in confusion. "Uh, delivery?"

Wyatt appeared at Linc's side, snatching the box from the guy and sliding him a fifty before disappearing once more. "Hey, guys. Food's here," Wyatt yelled over his shoulder, like there was a room full of people hidden behind the door. The delivery kid was already at the elevators, not interested in whatever drama unfolded behind him.

"Wyatt—" the woman started, but Linc cut her off.

"Listen, he's not interested in answering your questions. This is private property. If you come back here again, I'll have you arrested for trespassing."

"Well, aren't you the protective one," she said with a snicker.

"That's my job, lady."

"Well, my job is to report the news. The senator's son has been nowhere to be found for months, and suddenly, he's back on the list for every major function. I just thought there might be a story here."

Linc glared at the woman, but she was unimpressed. "There's no story. Don't come back."

He closed the door in her face, locking it and sliding the deadbolt into place before he returned to the living room. He needed to pull his head out of his ass. He should never have answered the door without looking. Sure, there was no actual physical threat to Wyatt, but anybody could have been on the other side, including the senator himself. Could they have justified their lack of clothing? Sure, but if anybody, including that reporter, had seen the fingerprint bruises on Wyatt's hips or the bite marks on his chest and shoulders, they couldn't have explained those away.

They both sat in silence for a few minutes as Linc placed the plastic to-go containers on the table and

*intoxicating*

handed Wyatt a set of chopsticks. Wyatt studied the side of Linc's face as if trying to gauge his mood. Linc took the remote Wyatt had abandoned and set the movie back to the beginning, waiting for his heart rate to return to normal.

Wyatt popped open the lo mein container, digging in with his chopsticks. "So, what's so great about this movie, anyway?" he asked, voice hesitant, like he wasn't sure Linc wanted him to speak.

Linc glanced over at him, reaching for the rice. "Uh, sword fights, pirates, sarcasm, torture, giants, Mandy Patinkin?"

Wyatt held the noodles in the air then tipped them into his mouth and chewed thoughtfully before he smirked at Linc. "The dude from *Criminal Minds*? Oh, yeah. He's cool, I guess."

Linc scoffed. "Pay attention. This movie's gonna blow your mind."

Wyatt slapped a sloppy kiss on Linc's jaw. "If you say so, Daddy."

Linc chuckled. "Brat."

# eighteen

## WYATT

WYATT WAS HAVING THE BEST DREAM EVER. LINC'S mouth was on him, sucking him like he was attempting to pull Wyatt's brain out through his dick. Wyatt tried to thrust deeper into the hot suction, but Linc's hands held him in place, gripping him tight enough to bruise. Wyatt fisted his hands into Linc's hair, begging him to take more, to let him push deeper, but each time Wyatt spoke, Linc would pull off, content to wait Wyatt out until he quieted.

It was maddening—each time Wyatt went silent, Linc's mouth started again, working him harder, driving Wyatt toward his climax until he was a

*intoxicating*

babbling mess, which would only cause Linc to stop once more. Whenever Wyatt begged, Linc would laugh and play with him more, licking and sucking at the crease of his thigh or the spot behind his balls—anywhere but where Wyatt needed it most—until Wyatt was a sobbing, panting mess.

"Tell me when you're about to come," Linc demanded in a low rumble, biting at the inside of Wyatt's thigh hard enough to rip him from sleep and show him he wasn't dreaming at all. Wyatt blinked heavy lids at Linc, who kneeled at the foot of the bed, Wyatt's thighs over his massive shoulders.

"Oh, God," Wyatt moaned.

"Daddy will do," Linc said around a smirk. "Tell me when you're close. Understand?"

"Yes, Daddy," Wyatt promised, tossing his head back as Linc took him to the back of his throat.

Linc was the best Daddy ever. First, the rimming and then the hand job last night and another in the shower before he tucked him back in, and now, the perfect suction of Linc's mouth as he gave him the hottest blow job of his life. Wyatt arched his hips, and this time, Linc let him. He lost himself in the sensation, fucking deeper without thought, caught up in the feel of Linc's lips working him over and the way he tongued at his slit, his stubble burning against all

Wyatt's most sensitive spots.

"I'm close... I'm so close... Daddy—"

The perfect heat of Linc's mouth disappeared. Wyatt tried to force his brain to process the sudden absence. Linc hovered above him now, resting his weight on his hands, a self-satisfied smile on his stupid, flawless face. Wyatt blinked up at him in confusion.

"You don't get to come again until I give you permission. Your punishment begins now."

Wyatt felt his face collapse. "Punishment?"

"You came without permission."

Linc's words were ice water dumped over his head. Wyatt glared at Linc, trying to kill him with his thoughts. Linc seemed unfazed. "Don't pout. I warned you there'd be consequences."

Wyatt contemplated kicking Linc in the balls, consequences or not. He hadn't known it was possible to be this horny and this enraged at the same time. "I'm not pouting."

"Tell that to your bottom lip," Linc teased, leaning down to bite Wyatt's pushed-out lower lip before pulling him to his feet.

He had a right to pout, he assured himself. His balls ached and his cock was hard enough to break a window, yet some stupid part of him was still desperate to please his Daddy. If Linc wanted to

*intoxicating*

punish him, Wyatt couldn't stop him, but that didn't mean he had to be happy about it. He was the opposite of happy and it was his right to behave accordingly.

He side-stepped Linc, hitting him with the most frigid look he could muster. "Fine, then I'll just go take a cold shower...*Linc*."

Using Linc's name was petty, but it gave him a small measure of satisfaction as he sauntered past. Linc caught him by the upper arm, his other hand swatting Wyatt's backside twice. He bit his lip to keep from moaning, even as his cock leaked, betraying him. Linc spun him back around. "If you need to shower, you can shower with me so I can keep an eye on you. I won't have you getting yourself off all alone in there."

"I wouldn't," Wyatt fumed.

Linc snickered. "Oh, you would. Instead, I think you should get on your knees and blow me."

Wyatt glowered at him. "Oh, do you?"

Linc smirked. "Mm-hmm. Right now."

Wyatt cocked his head to the side, lips pursed. "No."

"Are you disobeying me again?" Linc questioned, threading a hand in Wyatt's hair, forcing his head back.

Why did he like this so much? "I'm already being punished. What does it matter?"

Linc grinned, stepping into Wyatt's space, pressing kisses into his throat and along his jaw. "Do you think

I can't make it worse? I could bend you over this bed and spank your bottom until it's raw, jerk myself off while I tell you all the things I would've done to you if you'd just behaved, put your cock in a cage, make sure you don't come again for a week, maybe more. Is that what you want? Me, using you for only my benefit? That doesn't sound like much fun for you."

Wyatt's nipples tingled, every nerve ending on alert. Was this a negotiation tactic? "So, if I blow you, you'll let me come?"

Once more, that maddening chuckle as Linc ran his hand over Wyatt's ass, squeezing tight. "Oh, no. Is that what you thought? No. You'll blow me because you want to make me happy and you agreed to my rules. I'm going to bring you to the edge of orgasm as many times as I please throughout the day until I feel you've learned your lesson. Then, if you're a very good boy at this party tonight, I will bring you home, tie you up, spread you open and eat you out until you beg me to let you come."

Wyatt went light-headed at the thought. If Linc wasn't careful, Wyatt was going to orgasm right there on the spot, untouched. That would show him. "Then I can come?"

Linc kissed him, tongue darting into his mouth before he dragged his lips to Wyatt's ear. "The only

*intoxicating*

way you're going to come again is with my fingers in your ass, so I guess that's up to you."

Wyatt had never wanted anything so much in his whole life. He rubbed himself against Linc's jean-clad thigh, moaning like a porn star at the perfect friction until Linc swatted his behind once more.

"Stop that."

"Then stop talking," Wyatt whined.

"Then get on your knees and do as you're told."

Wyatt dropped to the floor before him, staring up at Linc, expression sullen.

"Color," Linc murmured, already undoing his jeans.

"Green," Wyatt grumbled.

Linc fisted his hand in Wyatt's hair, tapping the head of his cock against Wyatt's lips. "Green what, brat?"

"Green, Daddy," Wyatt murmured, opening his mouth for Linc.

"Suck Daddy's cock like a good boy."

Wyatt didn't blow Linc so much as allow Linc to use him as a fuck toy, his hands knotted in Wyatt's curls as he fucked his way into Wyatt's mouth over and over until tears leaked from his eyes and his jaw and knees ached, and Wyatt could do nothing but grip Linc's hips for stability.

"Yeah, that's my good boy. You love this, don't you?

You love Daddy using that smart mouth of yours." Wyatt could only moan. He did love it. He loved being good for his Daddy, loved being used for Linc's pleasure, loved how much Linc wanted him and only him. "That's it. Take Daddy's cock, my sweet boy. My sweet, perfect boy."

Linc came hard down the back of his throat, and he swallowed it down. When Linc released him, he went back for more, licking every last drop from Linc's spent cock and then looking up at him to see if he'd made him happy.

The pride and adoration on Linc's face made the ache in his throat and his still painfully swollen cock worth it. He'd made his Daddy happy. That was enough. Linc pulled him to his feet and kissed him. "Let's go take that shower."

Thus began the most frustrating day of Wyatt's life. Linc jerked him slowly in the shower while whispering filth in his ear, letting Wyatt work himself against the loose circle of his fist even though it did nothing to relieve his need. Later, when Wyatt's cock had given up hope, Linc pinned him to the counter and blew him right there in the kitchen, bringing him to the edge once more before again leaving him wanting. Just before Graciela was due back, Linc made good on his promise to spank Wyatt, bending him over the

*intoxicating*

bed and tormenting him for what felt like hours before jerking himself off over Wyatt's ass and rubbing it into his skin as if marking him.

By the time Linc sent Wyatt off to dress for the party, Wyatt was far too preoccupied with his own blue balls to worry about his father's fundraising ball. Wyatt wasn't allowed to shower again, despite the dried cum flaking on his back, so he contented himself with taming his riot of curls before swiping on deodorant and brushing his teeth.

He slipped into a custom slim-fit navy-blue Brooks Brothers suit bought for him by his father, one of many he kept crammed in the back of his closet after an image consultant had deemed them appropriate and not too flamboyant. Wyatt skipped the tie, wearing a snowy white button-down open at the neck, which guaranteed his mother would be in full-on pearl-clutching mode before appetizers.

Wearing it open also meant dabbing concealer on the bites and bruises Linc had left at the juncture where his neck met his shoulder. He pressed his fingers against each one, praying Linc deemed him a good boy tonight and finally let him come. Wyatt shuddered, equal parts aggravated and aroused. He now regretted how form-fitting the suit pants were since he'd sported an erection most of the day.

Wyatt found Linc standing in the living room with Graciela fussing over him, like he was going to prom and she was his doting grandmother. Linc wore the same basic *Men in Black* suit as the first day they'd met—the suit worn by most security details at these events. Graciela had asked her sister to let it out so it now fit Linc as intended, hugging him in all the right places. He looked hot. So hot. Wyatt vowed that before the night was over, he would climb Linc like a tree.

Before Wyatt could announce his presence, Graciela saw him and rushed over, smoothing over his jacket and frowning at his open collar. "Why must you make your mother crazy? Now, she will take too many pills and then I scoop her up off the bathroom floor tomorrow. You're a bad boy," she finished, swatting his shoulder. Wyatt was grateful she hadn't aimed for his abused backside. As it was, Wyatt already dreaded having to sit for dinner. Still, his cock twitched at her words. Linc smirked behind her, his eyes raking over Wyatt, like he stood there naked and not dressed in more clothes than he'd had on in days.

A key turned in the lock, and then Charlie swept in, looking more like she was about to attend the Oscars than a stuffy fundraising gala with decrepit old billionaires and their shriveled-up wives. She'd swept her hair up into a smooth bun and highlighted her

*intoxicating*

cornflower-blue eyes with bronzes and golds, which complemented her always perfect tan. But it was her dress that was truly fascinating. If Wyatt's open collar would have his mother sloppy by morning, she'd positively hurl herself off a roof at Charlie's golden bedazzled one-shoulder gown that hugged her curves all the way to the knee before spilling into a puddle of sequins at her feet. It was stunning. It was scandalous. His father would have a stroke...which made it perfect.

"Wow," Linc said before Wyatt could find the appropriate words.

Charlie blushed and curtsied before giving a spin, making the bottom swirl around her. "Aw, thanks. We should get going though. The car's downstairs."

Wyatt suddenly felt like an anvil had dropped on his head. He hadn't had to deal with his father or his cronies for almost a year in public. He no longer had the emotional fortitude for this. He wanted to back out, to send word he was ill and hide there in the penthouse with Linc where it was safe. Where *he* felt safe.

But it was too late. Charlie was hooking her arms through theirs and walking them toward the doors. "Let's get this shitshow on the road, gentlemen."

# nineteen

## LINCOLN

IN THE CAR, WYATT SAT BETWEEN LINC AND CHARLIE, shivering like a high-strung Chihuahua. He chewed his bottom lip, jiggled his leg, and fidgeted with his hands until Linc entwined their fingers and squeezed tight. His head shot up, his bleak eyes locking on Linc. A small pang of guilt needled at him. Maybe he shouldn't have spent the day edging Wyatt into oblivion. Maybe he should have done everything he could to make him as relaxed as possible. But Wyatt needed to understand his actions had consequences, and if Linc didn't follow through, Wyatt might stop believing his threats. Besides, it was far too late to worry about it now.

*intoxicating*

When they pulled up alongside the hotel, chaos ensued. There was the usual line of cars at these events, limos dropping people right at the doors. God forbid, they have to walk anywhere. A group of about thirty protesters stood outside, holding signs over their heads, booing each time another couple passed in their finery. The partygoers seemed unfazed, and some even smiled and waved in true let-them-eat-cake fashion. Charlie was right. This was a shitshow of epic proportions.

Linc exited before Wyatt, shielding him as he helped Charlie from the car in her ridiculously tight dress. Once she was on her feet, Linc ushered them inside, an arm around each of them like a shield. They ducked their heads as bulbs from cameras flashed and local reporters thrust microphones in their faces. Questions swirled around them, but none discernible enough to warrant an answer. Not that they would have answered, anyway.

Inside, the hotel lobby was a different feel altogether. Classical music flowed from speakers above. The only people visible were the senator's party guests, laughing and chatting as they made their way toward the main ballroom, like Rome wasn't burning right outside the gilded hotel doors. Linc steered Wyatt and Charlie in the direction of the party, walking behind them, a hand on each of their shoulders. Just before they passed the threshold, a woman stepped forward. Wyatt stopped short rather than run into her. Charlie frowned at the smaller woman in confusion.

"Wyatt, Miranda Rodrigues with the *Miami Sun*. We met last night. I was wondering if you'd be willing to talk now that you both have your clothes on?" she asked, raising her voice loud enough to turn heads around them.

Wyatt's cheeks burned, but Charlie curled herself into Wyatt possessively with a sly smile as if the comment pertained to her and Wyatt and not Linc and Wyatt. The people close enough to overhear gave Charlie's revealing dress a once-over before turning up their noses and moving on.

Linc lowered his voice. "He has no comment. He will never have a comment, and if you print one word that even hints at whatever you're implying, my client will sue you for libel."

She snickered. "Libel? Only if I can't prove my allegations."

Linc opened his mouth, but it was Charlie who stepped forward. "You write for the *Miami Sun*, you say?"

The woman flicked her gaze to Charlie. "Yes, that's right," she said dismissively.

*intoxicating*

Charlie smiled. "Oh, then I'm surprised you don't recognize me."

The woman shifted uncomfortably, her cocky demeanor cracking just a bit. "Why would I know who you are?"

"Because my father is your boss."

Both Linc and the woman turned to stare at the younger girl, dumbstruck.

The reporter scoffed. "My boss is a woman, and she doesn't have children."

"Oh, maybe I wasn't clear. My father is your boss's boss's…etcetera. You get the point. Your paper is owned by Stavros Holdings, LTD. That company is one of many companies owned by my father. I can get him on the phone if you'd like to confirm?" She jiggled the little purse at her wrist.

The woman paled a little but narrowed her eyes at Wyatt, like she was trying to look inside his head. "I'm not sure what you and your father are so hell-bent on hiding, but I'm not letting this go. If the story's good enough, my boss won't care who your father is."

Charlie gave the woman a frigid smile, her tone saccharine sweet. "I'd be very careful how you tread, Miranda, sweetie. Sometimes, a person focuses so hard on what's in front of them, they fail to see the danger closing in from the sides."

"Yeah, I'll keep that in mind," the woman said, expression implying she had no intention of letting this go. "I hope you all enjoy your evening."

Jesus. Women were vicious. Linc was convinced if they let women interrogate prisoners of war, they'd cut the time to break them by half. Wyatt hadn't uttered a single word during the exchange. When Linc looked at him, the boy looked resigned to his fate. Linc nudged him forward. "Come on, let's get this over with."

Once they entered the ballroom, Charlie swatted Wyatt on the butt, earning her a pained hiss and a startled glance. "Get your game face on, boo, or these hags will eat you alive."

Wyatt seemed to realize they'd entered the snake pit. His shoulders went back, his head went up, and he plastered a cocky grin on his face. It was like a cab flipping its light on. Suddenly, all eyes were on them.

The next two hours were a blur of rubbery chicken, cold vegetables, and elderly women with huge fake breasts and overly tightened faces fawning over Wyatt, like they didn't know if they wanted to swaddle him or fuck him. Linc did his best to not clothesline these old ladies as they kissed and pinched at Wyatt, like they had some claim to what was his.

"Check your face, G.I. Joe, 'cause right now, you're looking a little less like an impartial bodyguard

*intoxicating*

and a little more like a jealous boyfriend," Charlie whispered, the amusement in her voice grating on Linc's nerves.

Linc grunted in response but tried to relax his arms at his sides and look less like he wanted to kick puppies. He spotted a woman with icy blonde hair cutting a path directly toward Wyatt and braced for another onslaught. The change in the boy was immediate. He sucked in a sharp breath, like he was already preparing himself for battle. As she approached, Linc knew with certainty that this was Wyatt's mother. They shared the same sharp jawline and wide jade eyes. Linc suspected she shared his curls as well when her hair wasn't straightened into submission and cascading like a waterfall over her narrow shoulders.

"Oh, you are alive. Would it kill you to at least call me every now and again?" she asked, air kissing each of his cheeks before letting her gaze fall pointedly to the boy's open collar. "Seriously? It's like wolves raised you. This is a black-tie function and you aren't even wearing one. Are you trying to embarrass your father?" Wyatt opened his mouth, but she raised one skeletal hand. "Don't. I think your actions over the last ten years speak for themselves. Who are you?" she asked without taking a breath, examining Linc like he was some homeless man who'd wandered into the facility.

"Lincoln Hudson, ma'am," he said.

Her face soured. "Who?"

"Dad's latest babysitter," Wyatt reminded her through gritted teeth. "Linc, meet my mom, Eugenia Edgeworth."

"Oh, that's right. The soldier," she said, immediately forgetting him. "Charlemagne, darling, what happened to the rest of your dress? Did it go missing along with my son's tie?"

"Yes, there was a terrible accident. We barely made it out with our lives," Charlie shot back without missing a beat.

"Hmm," Wyatt's mother muttered. "Ansel Abrams is here, and he plans on writing a huge check tonight. I expect you to go say hello. You might still get a clerkship from him yet."

Wyatt pulled a face, like he'd rather die, but his mother either didn't notice or didn't care. Linc suspected the latter.

"He's over there with the swamp witch."

"Fuck yeah, Violet's here?" Charlie said, craning her head to look around the room.

"Charming as always, Charlemagne. Your mother must be so proud."

"She thinks I'm the fucking tits," Charlie assured her, goosing her own breasts for emphasis. Linc bit down

*intoxicating*

on the inside of his cheek until he teared up, just to keep from laughing. He had to admit, if women were his thing, Charlie would have been an absolute keeper.

Wyatt shook his head with a laugh. "Mother, please stop calling Nana a swamp witch."

She scoffed. "I'll stop calling her that when she stops acting like one," his mother countered. "Do you know she told Eloise it would just be cheaper if the woman got a knob installed on the back of her head, so the plastic surgeons could just twist and tighten her face periodically without all the hassle?" Wyatt snickered, earning a scowl from his mother. "It's not funny. She's a huge donor. She also confused the mayor's wife with his daughter and when Jacob Murphy informed her his wife passed away, she told him his wife had probably faked her own death to get away from a boring old coot like him. Honestly, her mouth is going to cost us a fortune."

"Then why did you invite her?" Wyatt asked.

Eugenia looked at her son as if he was stupid. "The image consultant said there were rumors we had stuffed her in a nursing home so we could siphon all her money into your father's campaign."

Wyatt arched a brow. "So...not a rumor so much as another one of Dad's inconvenient truths?"

"You're incorrigible, darling. I swear you don't even

care how much stress I'm under. These campaign parties are not cheap, and putting all this together is exhausting."

"You have a party planner, two personal assistants, three housekeepers, and a personal chef. My heart bleeds for you, Mother."

She shot him a look of betrayal. "You have no idea how hard my life is. I chair seven committees, I'm a volunteer docent at the museum, I have several luncheons and parties I'm expected to attend for your father, and my interior designer left right in the middle of my closet rebuild, Wyatt. It's all too much."

"Wow. That does sound terrible, Mother."

She waved her hand at a waiter a couple of feet away. "Ugh, just say hello to your grandmother before you leave. I need another drink."

"I'm going to find Violet," Charlie announced before taking off into the crowd.

Wyatt stared after the girl as if she'd just trudged off into enemy territory without a weapon and expected Wyatt to follow. He seemed almost frozen.

Linc leaned down, dropping his voice to a whisper. "Have I told you what a good boy you've been tonight?" Wyatt's only response was a shuddery sigh and a slight shift of his lower body. "Let's go say hello to your grandmother, and then we'll get out of here

*intoxicating*

and finish what we started this morning."

Wyatt made a low noise, almost like a groan. "You better mean it," he muttered before wading into the crowd after Charlie. Linc followed behind at a reasonable distance.

That's what he told himself, anyway.

# twenty

## WYATT

IT WASN'T THAT WYATT DIDN'T LOVE HIS GRANDmother. He did, as much as a person could love somebody they hardly knew. She was the closest thing to a human one was likely to find swinging in his family tree. But Violet Dufresne was what Charlie liked to call a ball-buster. She was old and half blind and sat in a wheelchair that looked like she'd pulled it straight from the attic of a horror movie. Wyatt could count on one hand the number of times he'd had more than a passing conversation with the woman since birth. His mother and grandmother didn't speak, though Wyatt didn't know why. He assumed

*intoxicating*

whatever had happened was his mother's fault. Eugenia was a handful, even on a triple dose of Xanax.

When he caught up to Charlie, she sat crouched beside his grandmother's wicker wheelchair, her hand clutching Violet's gnarled fingers and laughing at something the woman said. Wyatt had no idea why Charlie loved the woman so much. They'd only met twice, but they looked like old friends. Maybe his grandmother was senile and thought Charlie was somebody else? Maybe Charlie was a bit senile, too.

The woman looked much like an aged version of his mother, only her silver hair was caught up in a complicated configuration of swoops and waves, all decorated with a garish ruby hairpin. Wyatt and his mother both favored Violet in skin tone and eye color, but everything about his nana was brittle, including her personality.

He leaned down and kissed her cheek, and she didn't so much pat his cheek as slap it. "Well, if it isn't my missing grandson. I thought maybe they'd shoved you in a home as well and absconded with your trust fund." Wyatt's eyes went wide, and Charlie giggled. She wasn't wrong, but people surrounded them on all sides. People who would like nothing more than to gossip about Wyatt and his family.

Judge Ansel Abrams stood beside his grandmother.

He was one of his father's golf buddies. An evangelical with an agenda. His father's favorite kind. "Yes, Wyatt. We thought perhaps you were doing a stint in rehab and your father was too embarrassed to tell us," the man joked, shaking his empty highball glass.

Wyatt's stomach churned, but he plastered a phony smile on his face, turning to his grandmother. "I've been busy with school, Nana. That's all."

Ansel's eyes glinted in the glow of a hundred chandeliers. "That's funny. Justine said she hadn't seen you around campus in almost a year."

Justine was a pointy-faced little snitch. "Your daughter is a Tri-Delta. I'm not much for Greek life."

"Coulda fooled me," Violet muttered, looking Linc up and down with a knowing glance that made Wyatt sweat.

Before he could think of a decent reply, Ansel's wife joined them. She was a middle-aged woman wearing a foundation two shades too dark and a yellow dress that made her complexion sallow, like she had a medical condition. "There you are. I swear, there was a line for the ladies' room almost out to the lobby. Some of those crazy feminists made it into the hotel, I think."

"Why do you say that?" Ansel asked, peering over his shoulder as if a feminist might lurk just behind him.

"Well, the woman in the stall beside me was wearing

*intoxicating*

the most masculine shoes. I think she might have been a lesbian."

"Oh, do shut up, Martha. Wearing sensible shoes doesn't make a woman a feminist or a lesbian any more than wearing that hideous yellow dress makes you a goddamn banana," Violet snarked, shaking her head. "I swear, with women like you, I don't know why my mother fought so hard to win the right to vote."

Had anybody else had the audacity to say such a thing, Martha Abrams would have had a full-on meltdown and banished them from the ballroom. But his grandmother still wielded a great deal of power, even half blind in a wicker wheelchair. "Really, Violet. I'm just saying, some of those women out there were holding signs about their right to kill babies. That will never be okay in the eyes of God."

Violet cackled. "If only your mother had chosen that road, dear."

"Nana!" Wyatt choked.

She gazed at him, expression droll, waving a hand. "What? It's a joke."

It wasn't a joke, and everybody standing in that circle knew it. "Some people don't understand your humor," Wyatt said, attempting to defuse the situation.

"Abortion isn't a joke," a voice said from behind him.

An icy finger of awareness slid along Wyatt's spine, a metallic taste flooding his mouth. Martha's eyes got big, and she grinned over Wyatt's shoulder. "Victor! You made it."

The man in question brushed against Wyatt to get to the Abrams, shaking hands with Ansel and brushing the barest hint of a kiss on Martha's cheek. She touched her face like Victor Osborne was Harry Styles and she would never wash her cheek again. Victor was no Harry Styles. He was older than Wyatt's father by at least ten years, and his gut flounced over the waistband of his suit, buttons straining to contain his girth. He'd slicked back his thick silver hair in a half-assed attempt to cover the bald spot he hoped nobody would notice. Maybe nobody had noticed. Nobody but Wyatt who'd spent weeks looking at that spot on the top of that man's head as he'd knelt between Wyatt's legs...

Victor's gaze found his, a slippery smile spreading across his thin lips. "When Monty said Wyatt would be here, I knew I had to drop everything, especially when he said he was bringing his new girlfriend." He turned his smile on Charlie, offering a hand to help her to her feet. She took it, grimacing when he brushed his lips across her knuckles. "You must be Charlemagne."

"Charlie. Yes. Who are you?"

"Victor Osborne. Light of God Ministries. I believe

*intoxicating*

I've met your father."

Charlie's gaze jerked to Wyatt, her mouth falling open. Wyatt didn't know what his face was doing, but he had lost control of his ability to function. Whatever expression he carried was enough to have Charlie looking at him like he was two seconds away from passing out. Maybe he was. His palms were sweaty, but he was cold all over. The lights overhead seemed to blur above him.

"Wyatt, baby. Are you alright?" Charlie's voice seemed miles away.

It took a Herculean effort for Wyatt to open his mouth and say, "Dizzy. Too much champagne on an empty stomach, I think."

"Why don't you let me help you to the restroom? Splash some water on your face," Victor volunteered.

Wyatt couldn't breathe. He shook his head, but his mouth wouldn't work. It was like being punched in the chest all over again. Wyatt turned his head, looking for Linc. Where was Linc?

"I don't think that's necessary," Charlie snapped.

"Please, I insist. Wyatt was in my care plenty of times," Victor said. Wyatt felt like he was at the bottom of a well, listening to people argue while he drowned.

His grandmother's voice cut through the fog in his head. "For Christ's sake, Victor. She said no."

The knot in his chest loosened just a little as a hand found the small of his back. Linc. Linc was right behind him.

"You there. Yes, you. The one built like a mountain," Violet barked.

Linc was beside him now. "Yes, ma'am."

"You're his security detail. Please ensure my grandson and his date get home at once." Wyatt swayed on his feet, relief flooding over him. "On second thought, perhaps stop at a drive-thru and get some food in his system."

"Of course, ma'am," Linc said curtly. "Ms. Hastings, if you would come with me?"

Charlie nodded, flanking Wyatt's other side. Together, the two of them guided him out of the room and out of the hotel. Wyatt sagged against Charlie as Linc called for the car. Wyatt didn't remember much after that. Just lying on the seat, his head resting on someone's lap as they threaded their hands through his sweaty hair.

"I just wasn't expecting him," Wyatt said to nobody in particular.

"I know, baby. It's fine. You're fine," Charlie assured him from somewhere above.

Somehow, they made it home and up to the penthouse. Wyatt collapsed on the sofa.

*intoxicating*

"I've got it from here. Don't keep the car waiting," Linc told Charlie somewhere in the vicinity of the front door. He only half listened as they said their goodbyes.

When Linc scooped Wyatt into his arms, he didn't fight him. The warmth of the body beneath him and the reassuring thump of Linc's heartbeat gave Wyatt something to focus on, an anchor to cling to in his sea of panic.

Wyatt wasn't sure how long they sat there on the couch in the dark, Linc muttering nonsense into his hair, like he was reassuring a child after a nightmare. Maybe that wasn't far off. Victor Osborne was the architect of every one of Wyatt's nightmares, and no matter how much time passed, the man could yank him back down into that blackness any time he wanted.

"You okay?" Linc asked finally.

Wyatt gave a humorless laugh. "Not even a little."

"That was the man from the conversion camps, wasn't it?"

Wyatt's head jerked to Linc. "What did you say?"

"Your father mentioned that you attended camp at Light of God. Your father alluded to it being a conversion camp."

"Reparative therapy program," Wyatt muttered. "That's what they call themselves. 'Letting God fix what's broken inside us.' That's what Victor used to say. He said God had fixed him and had tasked him with 'fixing' us."

His pulse thudded heavy but slow, Wyatt reciting these things like it was something that happened to somebody else.

"Is that what he called it?"

Wyatt nodded, something twisting deep inside him. Linc wasn't supposed to be sitting there babying Wyatt. He'd promised Wyatt a night of rimming and at least one mind-blowing orgasm. Victor Osborne was the reason Wyatt panicked anytime somebody tried to touch him. He'd ruined that experience for Wyatt, and just when Wyatt was ready to try, he'd appeared out of the blue to rob him once again, like some fairy tale villain. It wasn't fair.

It wasn't happening.

"I don't want to talk about Victor," Wyatt stated.

Linc frowned. "Okay. What do you want?"

"You. The night you promised me. You said if I was a good boy that you'd tie me up and eat me out and give me orgasms." Wyatt sounded like a bratty child, but he didn't care. He wanted the night Linc promised. "Wasn't I good, Daddy?" he asked, turning in Linc's arms to straddle his thighs.

Linc brushed Wyatt's hair from his eyes, studying his face like he wasn't sure Wyatt was ready for whatever followed. Wyatt wasn't sure either, but he wanted it, anyway. He wanted Linc. "Yes, baby. You were perfect."

"Then I want my reward."

"I told you that you wouldn't come again unless it was with my fingers inside you, but if—"

"I remember what you said. I remember everything. I want that."

"Wyatt, after what happened—"

"No!" Wyatt cut him off. "He's not taking this from me too. I want it all. I want it with you. Stop stalling. I'm not being self-destructive. Can't I have something that's just for me? Can't I just take back this one thing he took from me?"

Wyatt held his breath as Linc seemed to war with himself. Some part of Wyatt felt bad for putting him in this position, but the other part knew he'd never feel safer than he did with Linc. If he didn't do this here, now, with Linc, he might never get up the nerve to do it again.

"Please, Linc," he whispered, pressing a kiss against his chin. "Please, Daddy."

He saw the exact moment he won.

"Bedroom. Now."

# twenty-one

## LINCOLN

LINC MIGHT HAVE FOUND WYATT'S SPEED WALK TO the bedroom amusing if he weren't so concerned about his current mental state. He followed along at a more leisurely pace, reaching the bedroom about the time one of Wyatt's shoes sailed past the doorway. He'd already discarded his jacket and shirt on the floor, and his pants sat pooled around one ankle as he hopped around, trying to rid himself of his other shoe. Linc didn't interrupt, just leaned against the doorway, a smirk on his face.

Wyatt had spent the night trying so hard to be flawless, but Linc preferred him like this, clumsy, eager, desperate to please. Wyatt had dazzled his father's friends. Every person had gravitated to him like a beacon, and Wyatt had regaled them all with carefully rehearsed stories and phony anecdotes about his father. Linc's smile slipped as he recalled Wyatt's clenched fists and the smile that never quite reached his eyes. Years of abuse had conditioned Wyatt to act like the obedient son, but he'd never lost himself, never let his father bury who he was…at least, not yet. Linc needed to protect that part of Wyatt—that flawed, fragile part of his soul his father hadn't obliterated just yet.

Wyatt trusted Linc enough to think he could somehow push past this mental roadblock his body had thrown up to protect him. If Linc did this wrong, if he rushed Wyatt or hurt him, Wyatt might never trust him again. He might not trust anybody ever again. He didn't want to screw this up, but Linc had no clue what it would take for Wyatt's body to relent, to let Linc in. He wouldn't take it by force. He wouldn't manipulate Wyatt or coerce him into something his body wasn't ready for. He wouldn't be another person who hurt him. He couldn't be.

Watching Wyatt wear that mask of money and privilege his father forced upon him made Linc determined to make tonight everything Wyatt wanted, and maybe, if Linc did it right, the night would end with him buried inside his boy. His gaze raked over Wyatt's naked flesh. He'd made a mess of him over the last few days. Bite marks marred his shoulders and ribs, fingerprint bruises still visible on the globes of his ass. He was the most beautiful thing Linc had ever seen.

When he dragged his eyes upward, the boy turned, his bottom lip trapped between his teeth, pupils blown as he gazed at Linc with an almost bashful expression. It shook something loose in him. He strode across the room, gripping his face and slanting their lips together, his tongue plundering Wyatt's mouth in a kiss that left the boy fisting his hands in Linc's shirt.

He pushed Wyatt back onto the mattress, yanking his tie loose and sliding it free as the boy scurried up the bed to rest his head on the pillows. Wyatt's eyes locked on the tie in Linc's hand before flicking to his face, expression adorably hopeful. The bed dipped as Linc straddled Wyatt's chest, still fully clothed. "Hands."

Wyatt shoved them toward him, wrists pressed together, lips parted, the tip of his pink tongue visible.

Linc chuckled, capturing his wrists with his tie and securing them to the headboard. He pressed his thumb to Wyatt's lips, and the boy sucked it without hesitation. "Do I need to tie your feet, or are you going to behave?" he asked, slipping his finger free.

*intoxicating*

"I'll behave, Daddy. I promise."

"Good boy."

Linc left the bed. "Don't move," he commanded, knowing full well the boy couldn't if he wanted to. He headed to his own bedroom where he grabbed lube and condoms. Upon his return, Wyatt's eyes went wide at the items in Linc's hand. He threaded his fingers through Wyatt's curls, hoping to reassure him a little. He dropped the items on the nightstand. "On your stomach, baby boy."

Wyatt rushed to comply, fisting the black tie as if he needed a lifeline. Linc stood, admiring the picture Wyatt made, all that lithe muscle and creamy skin against the backdrop of his soft black comforter. Linc caressed Wyatt's ass, pressing his fingers to the earlier bruises, smiling at the remnants of his cum still flaking on Wyatt's skin.

He stepped back, causing Wyatt to whine. Linc slid his jacket off, hanging it on the back of Wyatt's chair, before rolling his sleeves to the elbow and slipping free of his shoes. Wyatt studied him, his face only half visible, his curls falling across his forehead like some fallen angel.

"You're not getting undressed?" Wyatt asked, disappointment soaking his voice.

Linc sauntered closer, sliding a finger along Wyatt's

inner thigh, stopping just short of his balls. "Are you questioning me?"

Wyatt groaned, rocking his hips against the mattress. "No, Daddy."

Linc dropped a sharp slap on Wyatt's bruised bottom. "Stop that, or we can just pick this up tomorrow when you have a little more control. Is that what you want?"

Wyatt ground his cock into the mattress once more like he couldn't help it, his voice a low moan. "No, Daddy."

Linc laughed low, tugging Wyatt's head up for a rough kiss. "Then behave."

Wyatt made a needy little noise, but Linc ignored him, kneeling on the bed between Wyatt's thighs and hovering over him, his hands bracketing either side of Wyatt's head. He didn't touch him, just leaned in close, his breath ruffling the hair at the nape of Wyatt's neck.

"Who do you belong to?" he murmured against his ear.

"You, Daddy," Wyatt sighed.

"That's right. What do you want, sweet boy?"

"Just you, Daddy."

"You've got me," Linc vowed, meaning it more than he would ever admit.

Wyatt sucked in a breath but said nothing.

*intoxicating*

"You're gorgeous like this," Linc rumbled, tracing the shell of his ear with his tongue. "You were born for this, to be owned, possessed, marked…used." As he spoke, he punctuated each word with a biting kiss along Wyatt's neck, the knobs of his spine, his hip. Wyatt didn't respond, just gripped his bindings, pulling ragged breaths into his lungs. Linc pressed a kiss between his shoulder blades and lowered his hips, rubbing his clothed cock against his ass. "See what you do to Daddy? See how hard you make me?"

"Daddy, please."

Linc bit back a groan as he allowed himself a minute to grind his erection against the boy. "You want to be good for me, don't you?"

"Yes, Daddy," Wyatt said through a sob.

Linc pressed a tender kiss against his temple. "Then relax for me, baby. I want to taste you."

Wyatt seemed to melt, his hands loosening their death grip as Linc sat back on his feet, taking a moment to look at the picture Wyatt presented. He let his fingertips tease over Wyatt's ankles, the backs of his knees, his inner thighs, before hauling Wyatt's hips up, spreading him open. He leaned close, letting his breath fan across Wyatt's tight little hole.

"Is this what you want? You want my mouth on you?"

Wyatt arched his back, pushing his ass higher like a cat in heat. "Please, Daddy."

"Say it again," Linc teased, leaning down to bite the globes of his ass.

"Please, Daddy. Please. You promised," Wyatt moaned. "You promised," he said again, almost like he didn't know he was talking.

Linc had promised and Wyatt had done everything Linc had asked. He leaned forward, sweeping the flat of his tongue over Wyatt's tight pucker. He keened, pushing himself back on Linc's face. He held him in place, nibbling, licking, and sucking until Wyatt was a sobbing, shivering mess beneath him.

He reached between Wyatt's legs, wrapping his fist around Wyatt's neglected cock, working him slowly until the boy babbled. "I need more. I want more. Please. You said. You promised, Linc. Please."

Linc's imprisoned cock leaked at his name on Wyatt's tongue. Wyatt had never uttered Linc's name like that before, like a prayer, like he was the only person who could give Wyatt just what he needed. Linc growled, stabbing his tongue against Wyatt's greedy hole, feeling it give just the slightest bit. He squeezed his own cock, trying to pull himself together enough to take care of his boy.

He snagged the lube from the side table. "Daddy's

*intoxicating*

gonna take care of you." He coated his fingers, massaging Wyatt's hole with his thumb, applying pressure but not enough to penetrate him. "Color?"

Wyatt's response was one long, drawn out, "Green."

Linc pressed his thumb past that first tight ring of muscle. Wyatt hissed, body tensing until Linc's finger was in a vice grip. *Jesus fuck.* Linc rubbed circles on Wyatt's hip until his body adjusted to the minor invasion. Once he relaxed, Linc pressed farther, all the while studying Wyatt for signs of distress, hyperaware of the boy's ragged breathing and the light sheen of perspiration on his skin. Linc watched, transfixed, biting his tongue until he could taste blood. He could probably come just watching his finger disappearing in and out of Wyatt's body. But it wasn't about him, Linc reminded himself, taking Wyatt's cock in hand once more, working his flagging erection back to hardness.

Wyatt fucked himself into Linc's fist, and Linc allowed it. He pulled his thumb free and replaced it with his finger, probing deeper until he found Wyatt's prostate, applying pressure to the spongy gland.

Words spilled from Wyatt's lips without thought. "Fuck! Oh, fuck. Oh, fuck. That's… Oh, God. More. Don't stop. Please…" He trailed off, his hips losing their rhythm as if he couldn't decide whether to shove himself back on Linc's finger or forward into his slick fist. When Linc pulled his finger free, he pressed two back inside.

Wyatt hissed in discomfort, but it didn't stop his desperate rhythm as he chased his orgasm. Linc wanted to pull his fingers free and drive his cock into Wyatt's tight channel until he spilled inside him, breeding him, marking him as his. But this was about rewarding Wyatt for his good behavior, for letting Linc in. "Come for Daddy, sweet boy."

The noise Wyatt made was somewhere between a shout and a scream as his body shuddered and his cum spattered the comforter below. He collapsed on the bed, burying his face in the pillow, shoulders shaking as he cried. Linc lay on top of him, peppering kisses in his hair and along the side of his face. "You did so good, baby. So good. You were perfect."

Linc reached between them and freed his own aching cock, content to just rub himself off on his boy. Wyatt had done well, but Linc didn't want to push it. He shoved his pants and underwear out of the way before wrapping his arms around Wyatt and working his cock against him, eyes rolling at the friction. It wasn't long before he came, spilling his seed onto Wyatt's lower back once more.

By the time Linc recovered enough to release Wyatt's hands, the boy was out cold, snoring softly beneath

*intoxicating*

him. Linc massaged Wyatt's wrists, making sure the blood had returned to his hands, before shifting to stand up. Wyatt reached out to snag Linc's hand, pulling him back down and linking their fingers, nestling his face deeper into the pillows.

Linc sighed, kissing the boy's sweaty shoulder and closing his eyes. His pants were still around his knees, his shirt twisted around him, cum drying on his skin and pubic hair, but he made no move to untangle himself. Getting changed could wait. Getting cleaned up could wait. For Wyatt, the entire world could wait, and Linc wasn't sure what to do with that.

## twenty-two

### WYATT

WYATT DIDN'T REMEMBER FALLING ASLEEP, BUT WHEN he opened his eyes again, the room was dark, the moon outside a faint glow behind a sea of dark clouds. Linc spooned him, one arm under Wyatt's pillow and the other wrapped around his waist, snoring softly against his neck. Warmth crawled along his body as he remembered what they'd done. What he'd let Linc do. It was a strange thing to be proud of, Wyatt knew, but he'd let Linc inside, had come so hard on Linc's fingers. He could still feel him. It was a strange, almost pleasant ache, nothing like how he used to feel after…

He shook the thought away before it could take root.

*intoxicating*

He wasn't about to ruin this. He shifted his weight, grimacing as his bladder protested. He tried to slide from under Linc's arm without disturbing him, but it tightened around him. "Where do you think you're going?" Linc growled against his skin.

Wyatt laughed. "Bathroom. I'll be right back."

Linc released him, pinching his hip. "You'd better be."

Wyatt rolled his eyes. "So bossy," he quipped, a strange weightless feeling in his chest as he dropped a kiss on Linc's stubbly chin and headed to the bathroom.

Once he'd relieved himself, he stared at his reflection in the mirror. His hair stood on end, and faint shadows formed half-moons under his eyes. And then there were the bruises… If anybody saw him, he'd never be able to convince them he'd wanted this, but each mark sent a thrill through him, served as a reminder that he belonged to Linc…at least, for now.

He headed back into his bedroom where Linc lay just as he left him, on his side, eyes closed, full lips parted. Even in sleep, Linc looked intimidating, like some sleeping Roman god had wandered into Wyatt's bed and fallen asleep. He crawled back into bed, worming his way under Linc's heavy arm, facing him this time, fitting his head under Linc's chin. Wyatt's body fit perfectly. He pressed his nose to Linc's throat. Why did he always smell so good? And why was he always so warm?

Wyatt's hand smoothed over the muscles of Linc's back, working his thigh between Linc's knees. Linc's arms crushed him closer, his hand smoothing over Wyatt's ass. "Don't start anything you aren't willing to finish, kid," he murmured in his ear.

Wyatt shivered, nipples stiffening at just the sound of Linc's voice. "I'm not trying to start anything," Wyatt claimed even as he rocked against him, rubbing his half-hard cock against the groove of Linc's hip. "You just feel so good."

Linc chuckled, making no attempt to stop Wyatt humping his leg. "Oh, yeah?"

Wyatt nodded beneath his chin, trailing his tongue along Linc's collarbone, enjoying the tang of his skin. "Yeah. It's kind of my new favorite thing."

Linc leaned back, tipping Wyatt's chin to kiss him, but there was no heat behind it. "Seriously. Are you okay after what happened earlier?"

Wyatt's heart tripped behind his ribs, his hips going still. "Yeah, I'm fine. Really. Better than fine."

Linc examined him like the truth of his words lay somewhere on his skin. Whatever he saw seemed to reassure him. He kissed his forehead before tucking

*intoxicating*

Wyatt's head back beneath his chin. They lay there in the quiet, Linc's fingers tracing patterns along his back and Wyatt's hand trailing fingers along Linc's spine.

"Can I ask you a question?" Linc asked after a while.

Wyatt's pulse sped up, but he gave a jerky nod. "I guess so."

"What's the deal with your grandmother?"

Wyatt couldn't help the surprised laugh that burst from his lips. "I'm not sure I want to know how long you've been lying here thinking about my nana."

Linc chuckled. "Not long enough to cause concern… at least, I don't think. It just seems like you don't know her well. How does that work?"

Wyatt sighed. "I guess because we don't know each other. She and my mom don't get along. I don't know why, but if I had to guess I'd say it was my dad's fault. We used to see her at fundraisers and charity balls. She's a pretty powerful player in certain circles, or she was until they had her declared demented and were somehow granted power of attorney."

Linc gave a disgusted grunt, which Wyatt found sounded similar to his not-listening grunt but nothing like his horny or hungry grunts. Wyatt didn't blame Linc. His family was awful. "I guess I pictured you guys being the type to have awkward Sunday dinners in some grand mansion."

Wyatt sighed. "I don't know if you'd call Nana's six-million-dollar condo a mansion, but it is right on the ocean. When I was little, we would go to dinners there, and my brother and I would run around on the beach while the adults did whatever they did inside. I don't remember much about it, except, it usually ended up with my mother drunk and screaming and my father ranting in the car all the way home. After my brother died, we just stopped going."

"She and Charlie seem close," Linc observed.

Wyatt snorted, tucking his head against Linc's chest. "Charlie has met her twice, including tonight. She just knows how much my parents hate her, and that makes her an ally in Charlie's book. The enemy of my enemy and all that."

Linc's voice vibrated against his cheek. "Your grandmother seems fond of you, though."

Wyatt pondered that. "Does she? I feel like she's polite out of obligation. She doesn't even know me."

"She doesn't seem like a woman who does anything out of obligation, and she seems to know enough."

Wyatt supposed that was true, but he doubted any shred of affection—should it exist—would survive if she found out her only grandson was same-sex oriented. His mother had given birth to him and even she wasn't a fan. She ignored that part of him, hoping

*intoxicating*

it would go away. He imagined his grandmother's reaction wouldn't be much different.

"After Landon died, I used to dream that somebody would come rescue me. I would make up these elaborate fantasies about how my dad wasn't my dad and some other man would eventually take me away, or that there was a mix-up at the hospital and I'd find out I went to the wrong family and I actually belonged to a nice family. That one was definitely wish fulfillment because I look just like good old Eugenia, much to her delight." Wyatt hated talking about this shit, but he couldn't seem to shut up now. "Of all the people I thought might come and rescue me from my parents, Nana was never one of them. She was never a big part of my life. I don't even remember ever getting a hug from her. She would just get down on one knee and shake my hand and tell me a good handshake was important, that it was a sign of strength and trustworthiness. Then she'd usually just glare at my dad. When my dad got into politics, my mom mentioned her less and less. Even when they ran into each other at charity functions and galas, they acted like semi-hostile acquaintances more than family."

"Have you ever tried talking to her outside of campaign dinners?"

"Tonight was the first time I've seen my grandmother

in forever, and that's only because my father's image consultant clearly has no idea how our family works."

"Maybe you should try talking to her. It might be nice to have somebody in your corner."

Wyatt trailed his lips along Linc's collarbone. "I don't think you understand how my family works either."

"It's just a thought."

"Are you close with your grandmother?" Wyatt countered, uncomfortable with the direction of their conversation.

"My grandparents are all dead."

Wyatt probably should have stopped prying there, but he didn't. "What about your mom? When you talked about her, the one time you said… Is she…" He trailed off.

He felt Linc nod above him. "Yeah. She died of a drug overdose when I was seventeen."

"Jeez. I'm sorry. That sucks." Linc rarely talked about himself or his family. Wyatt didn't have that luxury since Linc had a front-row ticket to all of Wyatt's family drama. "Growing up with a drug-addicted mentally ill mom couldn't have been easy."

Wyatt's mom was cold, but she wasn't an abusive drug addict.

"I had my sister. Ellie did what she could to shield

me. She took the brunt of my mom's reign of terror."

Wyatt curled his hand over Linc's hip, nestling closer. He didn't know what to say about that. "Tell me about Ellie."

"She's amazing. She's a costume designer in Los Angeles. Or she was, anyway. She was just getting some recognition for her work when she reconnected with my dad and learned how sick he was. She left a great job to come to Orlando and take care of him."

Wyatt pulled back to look at Linc. "Why?"

Linc frowned in the shadows. "Why what?"

"Why sacrifice her own dreams to take care of somebody who left her behind?"

Linc's hand cupped the side of Wyatt's face, brushing over his mouth with the rough pad of his thumb. "I imagine for the same reason you hide your sexuality and your makeup for the sake of a man who would never do the same for you. Because he's our father, and deep down, that means something to her."

The words weren't said with any malice but they felt like gravel under Wyatt's skin, and he wanted to pick at it to get it out. Linc was right. Wyatt was no better than Linc and his sister. He hid away for his father's comfort, his father's career, knowing full well his father wouldn't piss on him if he was on fire. *"I can't believe you're the one who lived."* His father would have exchanged Wyatt's life for Landon's. Wyatt had a scar on his hip to prove it. Deep down, his father still blamed him for Landon's transplant failing as if Wyatt had willed his cells not to work, had somehow murdered his own brother.

Wyatt suddenly felt trapped, suffocated. The reassuring heat of Linc's body was now a furnace setting Wyatt ablaze. "I'll be right back," he muttered, disentangling himself from Linc's body and shutting himself in the bathroom.

Once the lock clicked into place, he paced, fisting his hands until the blunt edges of his nails made half-moons in his palms, trying to use the pain to distract from the insects crawling under his skin and the cold sweat making him shiver, but nothing quelled his shaking insides. He couldn't stay in there forever. Linc would come to make sure he was okay. He wasn't okay, not by a long shot, but he couldn't do the thing that made it better. He'd promised.

He glanced toward the locked door before slipping his hand between the medicine cabinet and the wall. He slipped free the tiny paper taped there and hopped onto the counter to stare at it. He just needed to look, to hold it in his hand. Maybe that would be enough. He opened the packet, palming the shiny new razor blade. Something shuddered within him, and the compulsion

*intoxicating*

to press the blade to his skin became a living thing inside him, a demon whispering in his head that only the slicing of his flesh would make it all better.

But he couldn't. Linc had made him promise. He'd said he'd end it if Wyatt hurt himself. Linc had never commented on the hash-mark scars on each of Wyatt's inner thighs, but he'd licked over them, pressed his lips against them. He'd made it clear he knew what Wyatt was capable of.

He let the back of his head thud against the mirror, closing his eyes and trying to picture the blade against his skin, cutting him open, relieving the pressure, letting all the pain and anxiety flow down the drain, easing the lead weight in his stomach.

It didn't work. Nothing in Wyatt's imagination felt the way cutting did. Nothing relieved the pressure the way a sharp edge did. But he couldn't disobey Linc. If he did, he'd lose him. If he lost Linc, he wasn't sure he could get through the minefield of the next five months. He bit down on the inside of his cheek until it bled, letting his tongue play with the jagged cut, finding some solace in the taste of copper flooding his mouth. He wrapped the razor blade back in its paper but couldn't salvage the tape, so he slipped it on top of the medicine cabinet and went back to the bedroom.

Linc's concerned look made Wyatt flush, something

withering inside him. He'd almost betrayed him. He still wanted to, even now. His stomach churned, his brain firing, like he'd had too much caffeine and not enough sleep. He needed a distraction, something to ward off the voice in his head telling him that nothing would be okay again until he gave in and pressed the blade to his skin.

"You okay?" Linc asked as Wyatt crawled in beside him.

Wyatt didn't answer, just shoved at Linc until he rolled onto his back and Wyatt could straddle his hips, capturing his mouth in a dirty kiss.

Linc tore his mouth away, narrowing his eyes at Wyatt. "Why do you taste like blood?"

"I bit my cheek," Wyatt said, hooking his mouth with his finger to show Linc the gash on the inside of his cheek.

"Be more careful," Linc admonished, pulling Wyatt back down.

"Okay, Daddy," Wyatt sighed into Linc's open mouth.

Linc groaned, gripping Wyatt's hips, pulling down as he thrust upward, grinding their cocks together. "Oh, it's Daddy now, is it? You trying to tell me something?"

"I want you," Wyatt said between kisses. He wasn't

*intoxicating*

lying. He wanted Linc. He wanted Linc almost more than he wanted to cut. Maybe more.

"What do you want, sweet boy?"

Wyatt wanted Linc to fuck him, to hold him down and use him until he didn't feel so empty inside. He glanced over at the side table. The lube remained, but the condoms had disappeared. In the drawer, maybe? Wyatt couldn't bring himself to ask, instead saying, "Use me, Daddy. Fuck my mouth until you come down my throat. Make me take it all."

Wyatt's cock hardened as Linc's pupils dilated, his heated gaze feral as he flipped Wyatt onto his back and rose onto his knees above him. The knot in Wyatt's chest loosened. This he could do. There was more than one way for Linc to fill him up, and Wyatt intended to try them all. Something had to work eventually.

## twenty-three

### LINCOLN

WYATT WAS INSATIABLE.

It was like somebody had flipped a switch. In the seven days since his run-in with that Victor guy, Wyatt had gone out of his way to push Linc's buttons until he either punished him or got him off, usually both, and Wyatt didn't seem to care how it happened. No punishment seemed brutal enough, no orgasm seemed hard enough to satisfy him. Linc found it unsettling, but he had no fucking clue what to do about it, and even if it made him a terrible person, it didn't stop him from giving Wyatt what he craved.

Even now, they sat in Wyatt's bed, the boy riding

*intoxicating*

Linc's two fingers like it was his cock, his head thrown back as he chased his fourth orgasm in the last twenty-four hours.

"Please, Daddy," Wyatt cried. "Please. I've been so good. I just…" His voice tripped on a sob. "I need it. I need you. All of you."

The 'it' he referred to was Linc's cock. He was desperate for it. He told Linc so every time he was naked beneath him, but still, Linc hesitated. Since that confrontation with Victor, it was like the guy was a ghost in their bed, and Linc couldn't shake the feeling Wyatt did all this for him. To prove to that sick fuck that he hadn't broken something in him.

But each day that passed it became clearer to Linc that something was broken in Wyatt, something his dick couldn't fix. Sometimes, Linc thought he should shut the whole thing down for Wyatt's sake…but he knew he never would. Maybe that made Linc an asshole, but if Wyatt needed to get off, needed to be punished and used, then Linc would do it because some part of him feared Wyatt might go looking for his pain elsewhere with somebody who didn't care as much as Linc. But he wouldn't fuck him until he knew it was about them and not proving something to the man who'd abused him. That was his line in the sand. He didn't know why it mattered—his fingers, his cock, his tongue…they were just body parts—but it did. It mattered to Linc, and he wouldn't waver on this, no matter how much Wyatt begged. Not until Linc was sure.

"Fuck me, Daddy. Please. I want it so bad. Your fingers feel good—so good—but your dick would be better. I know it would. Please, I'm ready."

"You're not ready," Linc managed, crooking his fingers inside the tight heat of Wyatt's body, working his prostate until Wyatt sobbed, his cock leaking as he slammed himself down on Linc's fingers.

Wyatt pinned Linc with his stare, pupils so blown his eyes looked almost black. "Please. Please. I *need* this."

Linc fisted his free hand in Wyatt's hair, gripping it tight enough to get the boy's attention. "Why? Tell me why you need it."

Wyatt froze, staring at Linc like he was coming out of a trance. "What?"

"Why do you need it? Need me? Why do you need more than this?"

Wyatt flushed, a hundred emotions playing over his beautiful face: shock, confusion, betrayal. Anger contorted Wyatt's features, tears brimming in the darkness. "Fuck you, Linc."

He slid off Linc's fingers and out of bed.

"Where are you going?" Linc asked.

*intoxicating*

He shot Linc a sullen look. "Bathroom. Do I need your permission for that too?" Wyatt asked, not waiting for an answer before he disappeared inside the darkened room.

Linc sighed, staring up at Wyatt's wobbly ceiling fan. "Nice job, dickhead."

He had no idea what was going on in that kid's brain, but the last thing he'd needed was Linc grilling him about his motivations in the middle of sex. This was supposed to be a casual fuck. A fling. Charlie had even said they'd be sick of each other in no time. But Linc never tired of Wyatt's face, hearing his voice, his laugh. Even his subconscious mind seemed at ease when Wyatt was near. He had fewer nightmares when in Wyatt's bed and he never tired of waking up with Wyatt curled against him. Linc had had more than his fair share of casual hookups. This didn't feel like a fling. It felt heavy and personal and way too real, and it was fucking up Linc's life in every way.

This should have been the easiest fucking job he'd ever had. Babysit the kid, collect a huge paycheck and get his sister free of their father, and then go back to the desert where he belonged, far away from all the people he could hurt. All he'd had to do was keep his head down and stay out of trouble and mind his own business. Now, he was in it up to his fucking eyeballs.

He'd fought a war in the desert against insurgents hell-bent on killing him. He'd witnessed countless deaths and things so horrific he couldn't even utter them out loud to another living soul, but Wyatt scared him more than any of those things. This fucked-up kid with his fucked-up life and his fucked-up family and his permanently crossed wires had somehow wormed his way into Linc's head and made himself at home, and now, it wasn't just a job and it wasn't just sex… Fuck, Linc didn't know what it was, but he wasn't giving it up. He wasn't giving Wyatt up.

Not yet.

Minutes stretched, but Wyatt didn't return. Linc's mind drifted back to the last time he'd found him in the bathroom, some girl slicing into his flesh with a razor. He was up and moving before he even fully comprehended it. The bathroom door wasn't closed all the way. Linc pushed it open, heart stopping when he saw Wyatt sitting in the bathtub just like last time. He flipped on the light, blinking until his eyes adjusted.

Wyatt cut his eyes toward him, glowering at the intrusion. Linc didn't apologize, examining Wyatt for any sign of injury from where he stood in the doorway. The boy seemed fine, the only bruises the ones Linc himself had applied. Wyatt sat in the empty tub, curls snarled and knotted, green eyes luminescent

*intoxicating*

under swollen, puffy eyelids. He'd clearly been crying. Linc sighed, kneeling beside the tub and pushing the stopper into place before turning on the water.

When the temperature was acceptable, Linc grabbed the soap from the shower and a clean washcloth and stepped into the large tub, sliding Wyatt forward to slip in behind him. Wyatt didn't relax against him, just hunched himself over, wrapping his arms around his legs.

"Come here," Linc said, pulling back on Wyatt's shoulders. He resisted at first before reclining stiffly, his head resting against Linc's chest.

Linc didn't talk to him. It was clear Wyatt was still upset. He soaped up the washcloth, gliding it over the boy's chest and stomach, not worried as much about cleaning him as he was about soothing the rough edges of Wyatt's hurt.

Wyatt relaxed in increments, eventually sinking back against Linc. He used his foot to turn off the water before saying, "Talk to me. What's going on with you?"

Wyatt huffed out a breath. "What's going on with me? What's going on with you? I'm literally begging you to fuck me and you keep rejecting me," he shot back, voice cracking.

Linc shook his head even though Wyatt couldn't see

the gesture. "Rejecting you? How many times have you come today? This week? The last twenty days?"

"You know what I mean. It's not the same thing. Why won't you fuck me?" Wyatt's voice was thick like he was choking on his words. "Is it 'cause I'm, like… damaged goods?"

Linc's mouth fell open, grateful Wyatt wasn't looking at him. "What the fuck are you talking about? Damaged…what?"

His words went stony, distant. "It's 'cause you know what he did, don't you? You saw how he looked at me. What he wanted. You know he did things to me, a lot of things…and that I…liked it sometimes… and now, you don't want me that way."

Rage swelled behind Linc's ribcage until he was certain it would burst free of his chest, its own living entity. His pulse throbbed in his ears. He'd suspected that Victor fuck was using his little conversion camp to bilk rich guys out of their money, and he figured the guy was probably a closet case, like most of those sanctimonious pricks…but he hadn't understood the full extent of what Wyatt was getting at the other night. Maybe he should have. The trauma necessary for a person's body to physically shut down at the idea of reliving a past injury, to protect itself even when Wyatt's conscious brain wanted otherwise…it

*intoxicating*

had to be bad. Linc still didn't know the specifics, but it must have been awful enough to leave a permanent scar in Wyatt's head and on his heart.

"Whatever," Wyatt muttered, trying to stand.

Linc wrapped both arms around Wyatt's chest, barring him from moving. "Jesus, Wyatt. No. That's... no. How could you ever fucking think that? Whatever he did to you, that's on him. That's his burden, his fucking sin that he'll have to pay for eventually." At least, if Linc had anything to say about it. "You did nothing wrong. Even if your body responded, you did nothing wrong. None of this was your fault. That's not what this is about."

"Then what is it about?" Wyatt asked, clearly bewildered.

Fuck. Linc couldn't unload all his conflicted feelings on Wyatt, not when he was this raw and vulnerable. But he couldn't lie to him. He focused on Wyatt's specific question. "I'm worried about you...about what that step might do to you," Linc answered honestly.

Wyatt's nostrils flared. "Do to me? Do to me?" Wyatt gave a jagged laugh. "Your dick is pretty fucking impressive, Linc, but I don't think it will change me as a person."

Linc smiled despite himself but didn't acknowledge the jab. "You haven't been the same since your father's campaign dinner. Something about seeing—"

"Don't. Don't say his name again," Wyatt interjected.

"That's what I mean. Ten days ago, you broke out in a cold sweat if my hands went anywhere near your ass. Now, it's like you can't come without my fingers inside you even if it means hurting yourself. It's like you're trying to prove something…to him, to yourself… I don't know, but I don't want you to look back and regret this. To regret us."

Wyatt broke free of Linc's arms to spin around, sloshing water over the sides of the tub. "I finally manage to do something for myself. I manage to…get past this mental fuckery…and now, you're making me feel bad about liking your fingers inside me? About me wanting to be with you in every way? Like, you have to know I wanted to fuck you the day we met, but my body just wouldn't let me. Now that I'm over that, you're using it against me. What the fuck?"

Linc shook his head. "That's not what I'm saying—"

"Then what the fuck are you saying? Because it sounds like you're saying you only want me when I'm broken and not when I'm getting better."

Linc's brows shot upward. "That's not true at all and you know it. I don't think you are getting better. I think you've just found a new way to bury your trauma."

Wyatt scoffed. "I'm not the one who tried to strangle

somebody in their sleep. Worry about your own trauma, G.I. Joe."

Well, this was going well. Maybe Linc should have just kept his mouth shut. "Tell me why you want me inside you."

Wyatt's whole face turned scarlet. "I think the reason should be obvious."

"Then tell me."

He turned away from Linc, crossing his arms over his chest. "Because I do."

Linc dropped a kiss on the top of his head. "I'll ask an easier question. We have months until I leave. Why are you so obsessed with doing this right now?"

Wyatt shook his head. "Time is flying by. It's going so fast I feel like I'm missing everything. I'm going to blink, and you'll be gone, and I'll be back to living my father's life, and it will all be over."

Linc closed his eyes, pressing his chin to Wyatt's hair. "I know it doesn't seem like it, but I'm doing this to protect you."

"I don't need your protection," Wyatt snapped.

Linc pressed his lips to Wyatt's ear. "No? Then why call me Daddy? Isn't it my job to protect you, to take care of you, to know what you need even if it's not what you want? To reward you for being good and discipline you when you're bad?"

Wyatt released a shuddery sigh, his hands running along Linc's arms. "Yes."

"Yes, what?" Linc growled. "Say it."

Wyatt melted against him. "Yes, Daddy."

"Then stop fighting me. Trust me to know when you're ready. Let me take care of you."

"Will you take care of me now?" Wyatt whispered, taking Linc's hand and placing it on his half-hard cock.

Something behind Linc's ribs unknotted just the slightest bit. This conversation had healed nothing but maybe it had stopped the bleeding just a little. He could give Wyatt this. He wanted nothing more. This was easy. This was what he knew.

"Yes, baby, but first let's finish getting you cleaned up. I want you to come with my tongue inside you."

"Yes, Daddy."

## twenty-four

### WYATT

WYATT COULDN'T SLEEP. TWO DAYS HAD PASSED since his fight with Linc, and even though they'd fallen back into a comfortable routine, Wyatt couldn't shake the feeling they weren't okay. The thought left him restless, his mind racing with fatalistic fantasies. It was like he could feel every moment race by, and soon, Linc would be gone and Wyatt would be left alone to deal with reality once more.

Linc's chest rose and fell beneath Wyatt's head, his heartbeat as steady as a metronome. Wyatt might have found it hypnotic if not for the ungodly noise emanating from Linc's face. *He* was clearly not having trouble sleeping. Wyatt worried he might have trouble breathing. Was forty too young for that sleeping disorder that required people to wear masks like Bane in the Batman movies?

Wyatt wouldn't find Linc less attractive in one of those weird masks, he supposed. It'd probably become another odd kink. Honestly, he was grateful Linc seemed to be sleeping so soundly. The last two nights, he'd been plagued with nightmares, crying out in his sleep, kicking off the covers, once even sobbing into his pillow. Wyatt had taken to the internet, looking for any way to help Linc with his episodes, but the articles all said the same thing: leave him be. So, that's what Wyatt would do. He'd take his blanket and curl up in the chair and wait for Linc to settle once more. Neither of them would mention it in the morning.

Tonight, however, Linc was sleeping far deeper than usual. Wyatt shook with laughter as Linc's snores only grew louder, a crescendo in the world's worst orchestra. It just didn't seem possible that somebody that hot could make a noise so unattractive, like a chainsaw being put through a woodchipper. It was kind of adorable. A thought he'd never share with another living soul.

Something about Linc's snoring made him seem more real, more human and less superhero. It didn't

*intoxicating*

happen every night, only the nights when Linc slept hard. And it wasn't his snoring that kept Wyatt up, just his own intrusive thoughts. He could literally sleep through anything. His mother loved to tell the story of how he once slept through an entire brass band performance at his father's rally.

He rolled away from Linc, snagging his phone from the side table and clicking his text app, pulling up the only other person he still associated with who would be up at that hour.

**Whatcha doing?**

Three dots bounced for what seemed like forever before her response appeared. **About to seal the deal with an Olympic skier and his perky-breasted ice-skater girlfriend.**

After a moment, a picture appeared. Charlie sat in a smoke-filled night club, backlit by multicolored lasers. She wore some kind of silk romper that plunged to her belly button and khaki boots that went over the knee. She sat in the lap of a guy, who looked like he should be on the cover of Viking Monthly, while some tiny pale redhead bit down on her earlobe. Charlie was right. The girl did have perky breasts. He sighed.

**Wyatt: I'm bored. Call me. Better yet. Come over.**

**Charlie: No can do. These two are locked and loaded and we have a suite booked upstairs. I love**

**you but I'm not wasting this Molly on you. Where's Father Time?**

**Sleeping. I think I wore him out.** Wyatt rolled back over, nestling his head next to Linc's before snapping a pic. Wyatt looked mussed. Linc looked like he'd died in his sleep. Wyatt snickered and sent it. **Delete that and never tell him I sent it.**

**Charlie: Well, you two look downright fucking domestic. Sorry you're bored. It's the hazard of banging geriatrics, boo. But I gotta run.**

**Wyatt: Noooo. Don't leave meeeee...**

**Charlie: Hey, don't be mad at me that your man can't keep up with your twenty-two-year-old libido. Go watch porn and jerk off.**

The idea had merit, but there was only one problem. **I'm not allowed to do that without permission. And I'm not waking him up for that. He needs his rest.**

**Charlie: OMG. You kinky little fucks. I can't help you, young Padawan. Go play one of your dumb video games you love so much. Just not Fallout 'cause I like to watch you play that one and we were in the middle of a game. Now stop bothering me so I can go get laid. Byeeeeee.**

*Bitch,* he thought to himself before setting down his phone and sitting up. He poked Linc twice in the chest to see if it would disturb him. Linc made

*intoxicating*

a strange guttural noise, rubbing his forearm over his face before throwing it over his head, the other hand twitching where it lay on his belly. There was a moment of silence, and then Linc's snores went nuclear, the sounds falling from his lips causing Wyatt to collapse with laughter. He considered recording Linc's snores for Charlie but then thought better of it.

He snagged his shorts from the floor where he'd dropped them earlier, closing the door behind him before padding barefoot into the living room. He flipped on the television, cueing up his PS4 and flopping onto the sofa, tucking his legs beneath him as he waited for it to boot up. The title page faded into view. *Call of Duty 4*. He hadn't played in weeks.

Wyatt's finger hovered over the button as he gazed toward the hallway. He'd avoided his games for a reason. There were bombs and grenades and machine gun fire. He didn't want to trigger another of Linc's attacks. Wyatt chewed on his bottom lip. Linc was sleeping, dead to the world for all intents and purposes. Wyatt would just keep the sound low.

He adjusted the volume and settled in, losing himself in the game. It was easy to free his mind when he had a mission with specific tasks to complete. It quieted the voices in his head, helped loosen the knot that seemed to live in his throat.

He wasn't sure how long he'd been playing when he caught something out of the corner of his eye. He sucked in a startled breath at the sight of Linc silhouetted by the dim light of the hallway. He jabbed his finger down on the pause button, jerking to his feet. "Hey, sorry if I woke you."

Linc said nothing, didn't acknowledge Wyatt, just stood with his hands fisted at his side, motionless. Wyatt's heartbeat skyrocketed as he crept toward Linc, stomach churning. How long had he just been standing there?

"Linc?"

Wyatt stood beside him but far enough away he could avoid his reach if he had to. Linc didn't seem to even see him at first, his sharp gaze darting around the room, like he was scanning for something in the distance, seeing something Wyatt couldn't.

"Linc?" Wyatt said for what felt like the hundredth time.

Linc's gaze snapped to him. "Keller. Where's Robins? Where's Martinez? We gotta move. We gotta get out of here," he said in a harsh whisper. He pointed upward. "They're on the roof. Stay with me, and stay quiet."

Wyatt could do this. He'd read about this. He just had to remind Linc where he was, remind him it wasn't real. "Linc. It's me. It's Wyatt. We're at the penthouse. Remember? Can you hear me?"

Linc snagged his upper arm. "There are too many windows. Fuck, they've got us pinned down. Let's go. Let's go," he muttered.

Wyatt allowed Linc to drag him deeper into the hallway, away from the sliding glass doors. A sheen of sweat coated Linc's skin as he scanned his surroundings once again with glassy eyes. Wyatt could only try again. "Linc. It's me. It's Wyatt. We're at the penthouse. Do you remember? Can you hear me, baby? Please, can you hear me?"

Wyatt racked his brain, trying to recall every word, every article, anything he'd read that could bring Linc back to him. There was so much information on Google, he couldn't know what was true, so he stuck with the information that overlapped. Say his name. Orient him to where he was. Do it as many times as necessary. So, that's what he did. He reminded Linc over and over until his voice sounded hoarse and the words made little sense. Linc still had a death grip on Wyatt's arm. It would definitely leave more bruises tomorrow, but Wyatt didn't try to pull away. He gripped Linc's wrist, startled to feel the rapid, uneven pulse beneath his fingers.

Suddenly, Linc's face crumpled, eyes wide with

horror. "Oh, fuck. No. Is that…is that Robins? Oh, fuck. He's… Jesus. No. He was…" Linc dropped suddenly, yanking Wyatt down with him. "Oh, fuck. Martinez was with Robins. Where *the fuck* is Martinez? Shit. Are they all dead?"

Linc wasn't talking to him or even Keller, whoever that was. Linc was talking to himself, some kind of running monologue in his head. He was drenched with sweat now, his hands shaking as he pulled his knees to his chest, dropping his head into his hands.

"What am I going to tell his father? Shit. Shit. Shit."

Now free, Wyatt knelt before Linc, doing something the articles said never to do. He grabbed his head, forcing Linc to meet his gaze. "Linc. Please. It's me. It's Wyatt. We're at the penthouse. Okay? Okay?" A sob escaped, but he bit down on his lip. He couldn't afford to fall apart. This was about Linc, not him. He had to be strong for Linc. "Can you hear me? We're at the penthouse. You're okay. We're okay. You're here with me. Fuck. Come back to me. I'm right here. Just…just come back. Okay? I don't want to do this shit without you. Okay?"

Wyatt wasn't sure how long he sat there, repeating those words and phrases in various forms. It felt like hours, but it was probably only minutes. "Wyatt?" Linc's voice was raw, steeped in confusion.

*intoxicating*

Wyatt smiled at him, gripping his face. "Hi. Hey, you're okay. You just... I think you had a flashback. You're safe." Linc blinked the sweat and tears from his eyes, staring at a spot over Wyatt's shoulder like he was waiting for his brain to come back online. "Can...can I touch you?" Wyatt asked.

Linc gave a wobbly smile, gaze meeting his. "You are touching me."

Wyatt dropped his hands. "The stuff I read online said you're only supposed to touch somebody in crisis with their permission, but I didn't know what else to do. I'm sorry. I wasn't trying to...violate your space or whatever."

Linc yanked Wyatt against him, hugging him tight like he was his own personal security blanket. "I'm sorry, baby," Linc whispered against Wyatt's hair. "Did I hurt you? Are you okay?"

"I'm fine. You didn't hurt me." Linc clearly didn't believe him. He thrust Wyatt away from him to run his hands over Wyatt's throat and arms, zeroing in on the red handprint on his bicep, his nostrils flaring. Wyatt shook his head. "I swear, I'm fine. It's nowhere near the bruises I've begged for. You didn't hurt me."

"I could have. Jesus, Wyatt. I could have killed you."

Wyatt shook his head, steeling himself for whatever came next. "This is my fault. I shouldn't have been playing that game. I knew the gunfire could trigger you, but you were snoring so loud and I had closed the bedroom door. I just didn't think you might wake up and come looking for me. I'm so sorry."

"Don't apologize," Linc grunted, cradling Wyatt against him in an iron-like embrace. "This is on me."

Wyatt couldn't let Linc take the blame for this too. "No, I knew better. All the articles I read, the videos… everything said that things like loud noises and fireworks could cause an attack… I knew better and I did it anyway because I was selfish and I was bored and I knew I wasn't allowed to jerk off."

Linc snorted out a laugh as Wyatt's cheeks turned pink. "Please. Stop."

Wyatt snapped his mouth shut, waiting for Linc to say more, but he didn't. Wyatt pressed his ear to Linc's chest. His heart was still a drum, but no longer a frantic rhythm, just a dull, heavy throb.

"You read up on PTSD?" Linc finally asked, voice thick, his chest vibrating below Wyatt's ear.

Wyatt flushed, grateful Linc couldn't see his face. "Well, yeah. After the last time, I worried it might happen again, and I didn't know how to help you. Sometimes, you have nightmares, and I wanted to make sure I knew what to do. I felt so stupid, especially since I turned it into a sex thing last time."

*intoxicating*

Linc laughed low. "Lots of people turn their trauma into sex things. It's just sort of the human condition. Besides, I was there too, you know. I could have stopped you. Probably should have, even. I don't think the proper apology for attempted murder is mutual orgasms. I wanted what happened that night, minus almost killing you." He pressed a lingering kiss to Wyatt's temple.

It was a strangely intimate and entirely unfamiliar gesture, like something a boyfriend would do. It tightened something deep inside, intensifying that oozy feeling in his belly. His chaotic thoughts tumbled from his lips. "I did too…want it, I mean. Even your hands on my neck, just you know, with you awake," Wyatt finished lamely, at a loss for what came next.

"Yes, I definitely prefer to be awake enough to enjoy my hands on you," Linc assured him. "Let's go back to bed. I'm exhausted, and you must be too after all this."

Linc got them both on their feet in one graceful move. He threaded his fingers with Wyatt's, drawing him back toward their room. The thought had Wyatt tripping over his feet. When had he started thinking of his room as their room? He shook the thought away before it could grow roots. None of it mattered.

He let Linc take charge, let him strip his shorts off and pull back his covers. Once he was on his side, Linc slipped in behind him, wrapping his arms around him from behind. Wyatt closed his eyes, the tension finally leaving him. "Shouldn't I be spooning you?" Wyatt asked, only half joking. "You're the one who had a rough night."

Linc was quiet for so long, Wyatt thought he wasn't going to answer him. "I need to hold you. Holding you makes me feel safe. Like you still trust me to take care of things…of you."

Wyatt's heart felt like it exploded in his chest. He twisted, wiggling in Linc's arms until they were nose to nose. Linc looked worn down. Wyatt's breath caught in his chest as he cupped his cheek. "Don't be stupid. Nobody takes better care of me than you do. Nobody but Charlie has ever even tried." Wyatt kissed Linc. "Nothing you do will ever change that."

# twenty-five

## LINCOLN

LINC OPENED BLEARY EYES, FEELING LIKE HE'D BEEN hit by a truck. Without looking, he knew Wyatt wasn't beside him. The bed felt empty. He sat up, noting the setting sun as his hand searched the side table blindly.

"If you're looking for your phone, it's charging in your room," Wyatt said. He sat in the chair in front of his lighted vanity table, which was scattered with colorful tubes and bottles of makeup. Wyatt was covered in makeup too and watching Linc in the mirror's reflection.

"What time is it?" Linc asked, voice raw.

Wyatt swiped a small plastic applicator over his

lips. "Almost seven."

"At night? How…"

He smacked his lips together. "You had a rough night. You needed rest. I put your phone in your room. I texted Charlie and Graciela not to come by today and I made sure my father was still out of town. I knew nobody else would bother us. I've been checking your phone though, just in case Ellie called about your dad."

Linc grunted, digging his fingers into his eyes before stumbling naked into the bathroom to relieve himself and splash some water on his face. He felt hungover. He'd never had a flashback while he was awake. Just nightmares while he slept. Maybe he'd been sleepwalking. He just couldn't remember, and that thought left his insides cold. What if he'd hurt Wyatt again?

*Wyatt.* His name was like a grenade detonating in Linc's chest, leaving him scattered and destroyed in its wake. This kid…he was constantly surprising Linc. Wyatt had taken care of him last night. He'd researched how to deal with Linc's flashbacks, had sat there for who knew how long waiting for Linc to come back to him. He'd protected him last night, watched over him all day, and even kept the other people in their lives at a distance…all for Linc. He'd thought of everything, even Ellie and his dad. Shit. Linc didn't know what the fuck to do with that information. He ran a hand over his scruffy face, suddenly feeling a hundred years old and more confused than ever.

When he returned to the bedroom, he wandered over to Wyatt, who wore a bright pink hoodie and a pair of short white shorts that left his long legs exposed. He leered at Linc's naked body in the mirror, a smirk on his face. "Hey, Daddy," he said in a singsong voice, clearly amused with himself.

The way Linc's dick responded to that word falling from Wyatt's lips was Pavlovian, his blood rushing south. He slowly spun the boy's chair away from the mirror, pressing a lingering kiss to Wyatt's mouth. He tasted like strawberries but smelled like suntan lotion, and Linc wanted to bury himself in his scent. He wanted to bury himself in Wyatt.

Wyatt's expression morphed into concern, narrowing his eyes at Linc. "How do you feel?" he asked, running his soft hands along Linc's scruffy jaw.

Wyatt's worry had a knot forming in Linc's chest. That was a loaded question, one Linc didn't want to deal with, so he just pulled Wyatt in for another kiss, dirtier this time, letting his tongue explore as he guided Wyatt's hand to his half-hard cock. "How do you think I feel?"

Wyatt moaned against his lips, tightening his warm

fist around Linc's arousal. "Good, so fucking good."

Linc pulled back enough to cup Wyatt's face. He'd clearly spent the day playing with his makeup. He'd pinned his curls off his face with a chunky black clip, and his already perfect creamy skin now shimmered like a prism when the light hit it. He'd painted his eyelids a glittery silver-blue and his full lips a frosty pink. He looked like some virginal sprite from a faraway land, and Linc wanted nothing more than to dirty him up. He unclipped Wyatt's hair, mussing his curls. "You've got your war paint on," Linc whispered, biting down on Wyatt's lower lip. "Feeling brave?"

Wyatt's cheeks flushed, and he glanced away. "I can take it off," he muttered.

Linc hated that look, the shame somebody—probably his fucking father—had drilled into him over something Wyatt clearly loved. Linc caught him under the chin, forcing him to meet his gaze. "Oh, no. No way. Daddy's got big plans for you. I want to see those pretty pink lips wrapped around my cock." Wyatt's pupils dilated, his tongue darting out to lick over his lower lip. "Get me hard, baby… I wanna fuck you."

Wyatt stared at Linc, like he worried Linc was teasing him. He wasn't. Linc didn't know when he'd made the decision to give them what they both wanted, but as soon as the words left his mouth, he knew it was true. He needed to be inside Wyatt, needed to possess every part of him.

Wyatt slipped from his chair and slid to his knees, his eyes locked on Linc as he took his cock to the back of his throat and swallowed. "Jesus. Yeah, that's it," Linc muttered as Wyatt's muscles constricted around him. Wyatt still had no technique, just sloppy enthusiasm and no fear... *Oh, fuck.* And no gag reflex. His boy had zero gag reflex. "You look so good on your knees for me. So pretty with my cock in your mouth."

Wyatt pulled off with a pop, his gaze searing into Linc's soul. "Imagine how pretty I'll look with your cock in my ass," he teased before hastily adding, "Daddy."

Linc laughed, shaking his head. Wyatt made a move like he was going to swallow Linc down once more, but Linc gripped his hair, pressing the head of his cock against Wyatt's lips. "Open."

Wyatt complied, moaning as Linc ran his length along the velvet softness of Wyatt's tongue.

"So fucking perfect. God, you were born for this."

Wyatt's lips closed around him, sucking hard, his hands gripping Linc's ass, urging him deeper. He gave his boy what he wanted, fucking into the wet heat of Wyatt's mouth, only stopping to hold himself deep inside until Wyatt choked, tears streaming from his eyes, causing black tracks to run down his otherwise beautiful face. It shouldn't have been so hot but it was.

He pulled out, tugging Wyatt to his feet before giving him a filthy open-mouthed kiss. "Who do you belong to?"

"You, Daddy," Wyatt promised, his shimmery pink lips wet and swollen, dirty face flushed and his eyes bright with tears.

Linc stroked his cock, pushing Wyatt toward the bed. "Who makes the rules?"

Wyatt stumbled as he rushed to comply. "You do, Daddy."

Linc turned Wyatt away from him, his voice a low rumble. "You going to be good for me?"

Wyatt's head bobbed. "So good, Daddy."

"Good boy. Arms up." Wyatt complied, allowing Linc to pull his hoodie off and toss it away. He pressed between his shoulder blades. "Bend over," Linc murmured.

Wyatt folded himself onto the mattress, burying his face in the comforter, already panting. Linc peeled Wyatt's shorts down to mid-thigh but left them in place, nudging Wyatt's legs apart and fondling his hard cock. Wyatt gave a startled cry, knees buckling.

"Uh-uh. Get that ass in the air where it belongs," he chided, spanking his bottom hard enough to leave one

*intoxicating*

perfect handprint.

He wished he could photograph Wyatt like this, show him the beautifully debauched picture he made. He shook the thought away, turning to flip on the light in the darkening room and grab the lube and condoms he'd stashed in Wyatt's drawer. The boy's gaze followed him now as he moved around the room, but Linc pretended not to notice. He dropped the supplies within reach.

"Daddy," Wyatt moaned, rocking his hips against the sheets. Linc slapped his ass once more, harder this time. "Ow," Wyatt whimpered, breathless.

"Behave."

Wyatt made a frustrated noise. Linc laughed low, but he wasn't faring much better. He was hard enough to hammer a nail through a board. He just wanted to forget all the foreplay and drive himself into Wyatt's willing, hot little body until he was painting his insides, but they weren't there yet. Wyatt needed attention.

"Please, Daddy."

Linc yanked Wyatt's head back, sealing their mouths together for a quick kiss. When he pulled back, Wyatt chased his lips. Linc shook his head. "I love it when you beg. But I'm just getting started, baby boy. Color?"

"Green. Green. Green," Wyatt chanted, dropping his forehead to his folded hands.

This time, it was Linc's turn on his knees. He spread Wyatt's ass, cock leaking at the sight of his slightly puffy hole. Wyatt loved to fuck himself hard on Linc's fingers, sometimes too hard. Fuck, someday soon, he'd make Wyatt ride his cock with the same eagerness. But not tonight. He leaned forward and swept his tongue across Wyatt's entrance.

"Oh, fuck."

Linc smiled, spreading him wider. He licked and sucked at Wyatt's tight pucker, loosening him up one swipe at a time until he could spear his tongue inside. Wyatt was a sobbing mess of half-bitten-off moans and half-formed sentences as he babbled nonsense.

"Daddy... Daddy... Please... I can't... You have... You... Fuck, please... Oh, God. Oh, fuck. Deeper. Oh, you feel so good."

Linc reached for the lube, coating his fingers and rubbing over Wyatt's hole before pressing his index finger inside. Linc bit off a groan as the tight suction of Wyatt's body pulled him deeper into the soft heat. Fuck. He squeezed his cock, trying to stave off the orgasm that was already way too close for them having done next to nothing. Just listening to Wyatt lose his mind was almost enough to get Linc off.

"More. We've done this before. I can take it. Please," Wyatt begged through ragged breaths, fucking himself on Linc's finger.

Linc added a second and eventually a third, working both in and out, massaging Wyatt's prostate on every other pass until he was grinding himself back on Linc and fucking himself against the sheets. Linc used his free hand to spank him. "Stop that," he growled, pulling free of Wyatt's body and wiping his hand on the comforter. "On the bed."

Wyatt crawled onto the mattress and collapsed on his stomach, burying his face in the pillow.

Linc followed, pulling the boy's shorts down and off. "Roll over on your back. I want to look at you."

The command seemed to shake Wyatt, freezing him in place for a split second before he rolled over. He placed his feet flat on the mattress, knees bent, his hand migrating toward his cock. "Don't even think about it," Linc warned. "The only way you're coming is with me buried inside you."

Wyatt's gaze went hazy, his hand falling to his side. Linc sat between Wyatt's knees, his legs framing Wyatt's body. He leaned forward, pressing a reassuring kiss against Wyatt's lips before pulling his lower body onto his lap and rubbing his hands over the petal-soft skin of his abdomen. He slid the condom on and slicked himself with lube, rubbing his cock between Wyatt's cheeks until the head was snug against his entrance.

"Are you sure?" Linc asked one last time.

Wyatt stared at Linc incredulously. "Yes. A thousand times yes. Consent given. Green means go. Fuck me. Fuck. Do it. Just make me yours for real. Please."

Linc pressed forward before Wyatt quit talking, breaching past the first ring of muscle and sinking into the tightest heat he'd ever known. In his head, Linc recited the Military Articles of Conduct, trying to get a grip on himself. He was only at article two when he felt Wyatt's body seize around him.

## twenty-six

### WYATT

WYATT SQUEEZED HIS EYES SHUT, HIS HANDS FISTING in the sheets as his body betrayed him, and the searing burn forced tears from his eyes. *No. No. No. No. No. Please, not now.* He wanted this, wanted Linc. More than he could ever put into words. Frustration stole his breath like a lead weight on his chest. This wasn't fair. It just wasn't. Why did this keep happening to him? It didn't make any sense. He pushed heavy breaths out through his nose, trying to force his body to relax, to accept Linc's invasion, but he couldn't stop trembling.

"Wyatt?"

The concern in Linc's voice only increased the weight

on his chest, making it harder to breathe. He shook his head, swiping at the tears on his cheeks. "I'm fine, okay? Look, you know it hurts but don't stop. Please." Linc's brows collapsed as he examined Wyatt's face. After a moment, he shifted. Wyatt snatched at his arms. "No! Please, don't leave. I can do this. I can. I swear it."

Wyatt hated the desperation in his voice, the way his words caught on a sob, but he was all in now. If he didn't follow through with this, he'd never risk it again. He needed to work through it, not around it. Between his runny makeup, his tears, and the cold sweat breaking along his skin, he was sure he looked like a horror movie. This was not sexy and not at all what Linc had signed on for. Jesus. He wanted to pull the pillow up over his face and just die. Why would anybody want to deal with all this?

Linc rubbed soothing circles on Wyatt's thighs. "Hey. I'm not leaving you. I'm just getting into a more comfortable position…for both of us…okay?"

Linc talked to him like a negotiator trying to talk a person off a ledge. If there was a god, the bed would just open and swallow him whole. Linc was likely regretting every life choice that had led him to that moment. He sucked in a pained breath as Linc's movement jostled them both, forcing him deeper inside. Then the reassuring weight of Linc's body pressed Wyatt into the mattress, his elbows bracketing either side of Wyatt's head.

Wyatt couldn't bring himself to look at Linc. He stared at the dead center of his chest, like it held the secret to all of life's mysteries. He was too afraid of what he'd see when he looked at Linc's face. But as the seconds ticked on, morbid curiosity had him dragging his eyes upward.

Linc gave him a soft smile. "Hi."

Wyatt swallowed hard, staring up into eyes the color of warm honey. "Hey."

"So, how are you enjoying your first time so far? I think we're killing it, no?" His tone was light, almost conversational.

Wyatt gave a wet laugh then winced at the sharp pain in his ass. His smile slipped as disappointment spread through him. He buried his head against Linc's throat. "I'm so sorry."

"Hey, look at me." Meeting Linc's gaze took a Herculean effort. "Forget everything else, okay? Just kiss me. You can do that, right?"

Wyatt lifted his head, barely brushing his lips across Linc's, feeling timid. Linc slanted his mouth over his, his tongue slipping inside. They'd kissed a thousand times but never like that, never slow, methodical, like there was no other agenda other than to just connect somehow. Wyatt had never kissed anybody like that, and it set a whole fleet of butterflies loose in his belly.

He'd never considered sex intimate, more a simple exchange. It was about need. Get off and get out, hope nobody recognized his face. Even with Linc, it was only temporary. *They* were only temporary. But it didn't feel temporary. Linc's whole body covered him with this perfect pressure. They fit together like puzzle pieces, two halves of the same whole somehow just existing in each other's space, the only sound the quiet huffs of their breathing and their lips meeting and parting again and again. It felt intimate and real…

It felt like forever.

Soft kisses grew urgent. Wyatt's heart beat faster, his breath coming in ragged pants, his cock fully back on board with the pain of Linc's invasion, now just a dull ache. He shifted his hips, sucking in a sharp breath.

"You okay?"

Wyatt paused, considering the question, rocking his hips forward just slightly to test his body. "Yeah, I think so. Can…can we try again?"

Linc's breath rushed out through his nose. "Yeah, most definitely."

Linc sat back on his knees, his cock slipping free of Wyatt.

Wyatt panicked. "What are you doing?"

*intoxicating*

Linc leaned forward, smacking a kiss on Wyatt's open mouth. "Trust me."

He reached for the lube, reapplying it to the condom and smearing it across Wyatt's hole once more before the blunt pressure was back. His heartbeat skipped as Linc pressed inside, his hands reaching out to grip Linc's shoulders.

"Linc." He hated the panic in his voice.

"Listen, we can stop anytime you want, just say the word. Otherwise, just focus on me." Linc brushed his lips across his forehead. "On this. It's just you and me."

Wyatt had the overwhelming urge to cry. He stuffed it down. Linc looked at Wyatt like he wasn't broken. He took care of him, made sure he ate, made sure he drank enough water, watched over him. It was why Wyatt had chosen him, why Wyatt trusted only him. It was why he was pretty sure he was in love with him. Just a bit.

Linc pressed forward. "Am I hurting you?" he asked, his jaw clenched.

Did it hurt? It stung a bit, but in a good way. Mostly, he just felt full, overwhelmed…wanted. Having Linc buried inside him made any pain worth it. He'd spent days wanting this, wanting Linc to fill him up, possess him in every way, use his body for his own pleasure. He'd needed to be Linc's in every way, and now, he was. "No. I'm good… It's good. Don't stop."

Linc rolled his hips once and then a second time before he stopped again, dropping his head to Wyatt's shoulder, his back rising and falling with heavy breaths, his limbs quaking just a bit. It was probably adrenaline, but Wyatt hoped, maybe, it was just a little overwhelming for Linc, too.

As the seconds ticked by, Wyatt rubbed his cheek against Linc's, reveling in the burn of Linc's stubble against his skin. "I'm good. You can move now."

Linc made a gruff noise. "Oh, I'm not lying here for you. Do you have any idea how good you feel?" He shifted his hips, and Wyatt moaned. "You're so hot and tight and perfect. Fuck, your body is just… I just…I just need a minute."

The weight on Wyatt's chest lifted, and the sudden lightness made him almost dizzy. Linc was close to losing it. Wyatt had done that. "It's okay if it doesn't last long," he reassured him. "I'm probably already going to feel like you took a battering ram to my ass tomorrow as it is."

"That's romantic," Linc said around a soft laugh. He pulled back enough to look Wyatt in the eye. "Are you sure you're okay?"

"I've never been better. I promise." When Linc looked unsure, Wyatt pulled out the only weapon

*intoxicating*

in his arsenal. He gave Linc his best pout. "Fuck me, Daddy. I need it." It wasn't a lie.

"Christ. You don't fight fair, kid." He threaded his fingers in Wyatt's hair, their mouths meeting as he rocked into Wyatt. With each thrust, his body relaxed a little more, opening for Linc, and soon, Wyatt's hands were fisting in the sheets, his hips driving up to meet Linc. But it wasn't enough. No matter how deep Linc went, it just wasn't enough. He needed more.

Linc shifted above him, pushing Wyatt's knees higher. On the next thrust, bursts of lightning shot along his spine. "Oh, God. Oh, fuck. Do that again," he begged.

"Yeah? You like that, baby?" Linc growled. "You want more?"

Linc's words had Wyatt's cock throbbing. "Yes, Daddy. Please."

Linc sat back on his knees, dragging Wyatt's hips closer, practically folding him in half before fucking into him once more. Wyatt's brain fell offline. He couldn't think, couldn't form a complete sentence. Each time Linc found Wyatt's prostate, it dragged animalistic sounds from him until his cock leaked with every thrust.

"Daddy, I need…more. I want more."

Wyatt wasn't sure what more he wanted. He didn't

know what to ask for, but Linc clearly did. He slung his hips faster, driving impossibly deeper, hitting Wyatt just right. Wyatt felt like he was hurtling toward a cliff.

Wyatt sobbed when Linc's hand finally closed around his neglected cock. "Yes, please. Please."

Linc's grip was tight, his only lube Wyatt's own fluids. It was just this side of painful as Linc's strokes kept time with his thrusts. It was so much, too much, but not enough. The fullness in his ass and Linc's unforgiving pace as he worked his cock made him feel close. So close. "Can I come, Daddy? Please… Oh, God. I'm gonna… Please, say it's okay. Please, say it's okay."

Linc growled low. "Come for me."

Light exploded behind Wyatt's eyes as pleasure flung him over the edge, and he came hard, painting his abs and chest with his release.

Linc drove into Wyatt once more, his body going rigid as he came with a guttural shout. He dropped his head to Wyatt's shoulder, his body shivering through the aftershocks.

"Are you okay?" Linc breathed against his ear.

"I'm more than okay. I'm amazing," Wyatt answered honestly. "I'm pretty sure I can hear color now. That was…wow."

Linc smiled, pressing another kiss to Wyatt's forehead before he slipped from Wyatt's body. He removed the condom, tying it off before dropping it in the trash beside Wyatt's bed.

"I'll be right back."

The bed felt empty with his exit. Wyatt watched Linc pad naked to the bathroom. He returned with a wet washcloth, cleaning Wyatt up before tossing the cloth on the floor. "We'll take a shower in a while," Linc declared, dropping back into bed and pulling Wyatt against him.

"I don't think my legs will hold me up yet," Wyatt said around a huge yawn.

Linc reached over and switched off the lamp. A thin sliver of moonlight cut a path across the floor, stopping just short of the bed. Wyatt stared at it until he grew cross-eyed, waiting for the panic to set in. But, for the moment, it seemed all his demons were sleeping. Maybe Linc had worn them out too. The thought made him smile.

"I like when you smile. You should do it more often."

Wyatt looked up to find Linc studying him. He couldn't imagine what he looked like after all this. His makeup was likely long gone, except for his mascara. He probably looked like he'd escaped from a goth band. There was nothing he could do about it. He just shook his head. "I smile all the time."

Linc scoffed. "No, you smirk, like the bratty little shit you are, but you rarely just smile."

Wyatt shrugged, looking away. "I smile when I'm happy. There's just not usually much to smile about."

Linc fisted his hand in Wyatt's hair, tugging his gaze back to him. "But you're happy now?"

Heat flooded Wyatt's cheeks, and he was grateful the lights were off. "Yeah, I think I am."

"Good," Linc grunted.

The words slipped out before he could stop them. "Are you?"

Wyatt's heart sank when Linc fell silent, but then he pulled him closer, tucking Wyatt's head under his chin. "Yeah, kid. I think I am too."

"Good."

It wasn't good. It was a disaster, but Wyatt would deal with that later… Much later. What was the harm in pretending, just for a little while, that he could have a happy ending?

## twenty-seven

### LINCOLN

LINC DISLIKED MANY THINGS—MIAMI TRAFFIC, homophobes, people who used their hazard lights in the rain—but there were three things he truly hated: unanswered questions, sugary breakfast cereal, and fucking cartoons. This morning, all three things were assaulting him at once, making his left eye throb.

Beside him, Wyatt sat with his pajama-clad legs tucked beneath him, his mouth full of cereal as he laughed at a sentient sponge wearing pants. Linc usually didn't allow Wyatt junk food first thing in the morning, but yesterday, he'd promised the boy anything he wanted if he made it through his father's charity luncheon without incident. Wyatt had chosen morning blow jobs and Lucky Charms, and Linc was a man of his word.

He was all about reinforcing good behavior, and he didn't think he'd ever grow tired of blowing Wyatt, but the smell of soggy marshmallows and sugary milk set his teeth on edge as much as the cartoon blaring from the television. The cartoons weren't as much a part of the original negotiations so much as an addendum Wyatt had proposed a split second before he'd maneuvered himself down on Linc's cock an hour ago. He'd pled and pouted and called him Daddy all while staring up at him with those big green eyes and enthusiastically pleading his case. Wyatt had ridden his Daddy's cock like a boy who really wanted to watch cartoons, which was how Linc, now showered and shaved, sat on the sofa, listening to Wyatt snort with laughter as the carefully constructed walls he'd built around his dysfunctional childhood crumbled.

In the Hudson household, cartoons and cereal were more than pantry staples. Linc grew up in seedy pay-by-the-hour motels where the dirty carpets would leave your feet black, the linens always held suspicious stains, and there were never any kitchens. There were weeks when he and his sister had lived on nothing but knock-off brand dry cereal bought with

*intoxicating*

change scrounged from couch cushions and mined from the sea of unwrapped candy and loose tobacco always floating in the bottom of his mother's purse.

His mother would often disappear for days, leaving Ellie to figure out how to get them to school and home—when their mother had remembered to register them for school. Late at night, his sister would stick VHS tapes of *Bugs Bunny* or *Tom and Jerry* into the VCR so they didn't have to listen to the sounds of sirens, drunken brawls, or the prostitutes conducting business in the rooms next door. Cartoons were the background music to every bad thing in Linc's life until his mom died and he escaped to the military. All these years later, they still made his skin crawl.

Despite all this, Linc let Wyatt have his cereal and his cartoons because, for the first time in almost a week, he seemed to be enjoying himself. Which led to the third thing Linc hated: unanswered questions. Something had changed in Wyatt since Linc had fucked him. It wasn't an obvious change, more a tension in his face, the anxious look in his eyes when Linc wasn't punishing him or buried inside him. When Wyatt didn't have something to distract him, he grew restless, agitated, like a caged animal, but whenever Linc asked if something was wrong, Wyatt would smile and say he was fine.

The front door slammed wide, and Wyatt jumped, lurching to the other side of the couch on instinct, glaring at Charlie as she dropped her oversized handbag on the counter.

She shrugged. "What? If the deadbolt was in place, I wouldn't be standing here right now. You two should be more careful."

She plopped down between them on the sofa, swinging her sandaled feet into Wyatt's lap as she dropped her head onto Linc's thigh. "Dude, you didn't tell me your sister was such a smoke show."

"Excuse me?" Linc asked, the throbbing in his head increasing.

She turned her phone screen toward him, showing him his sister's smiling face. Ellie *was* beautiful, he conceded, studying the picture. She stood on a dune, her tawny hair blowing in the wind, her hazel eyes appearing more green than brown in the sunlight. His heart twisted. Ellie belonged on that California beach, not trapped in a small shithole apartment taking care of some demented old man.

He shook his head. He needed to call her. He'd spent so many days caught up with Wyatt, he'd neglected Ellie. He was really failing on all fronts.

"Seriously, dude. She's so hot. I can't believe she's your older sister. Like, she doesn't even look thirty."

*intoxicating*

She spun the phone around to show Wyatt, who nodded in agreement before spooning in another mouthful of cereal.

"Why are you stalking my sister?"

"How else am I supposed to find out if you're some secret psycho killer?" she asked as if it were obvious. "Your social media profile is nonexistent. No Insta. No Twitter. Just your old man Facebook account with,, like ten pictures of you standing in front of various desert backdrops, like the world's most boring school photos."

"I'm sorry I couldn't capture some of my more exciting moments for you, but the government frowns on us recording ourselves when we're deployed. We don't like to just hand the enemy our location."

She made a distracted 'hmm' noise, like she'd already dismissed him. He allowed himself a moment to contemplate rolling her onto the floor.

"Did you come over here to shame me about my internet usage or did you have some ulterior motive?"

"Uh-uh. I came here to talk to Wyatt about the gala and to ask you about him."

She turned the phone toward Linc once more. It was a photo of him and Jackson against said boring desert backdrop wearing their fatigues. Jackson had a black bandana around his head to protect his bare scalp from the scorching heat and was mean mugging for the camera. "What about him?" Linc managed.

She tsked, shaking her head. "Who is he? Is he single? Is *he* a serial killer?"

"Do you have some kind of murder fetish?" Linc deadpanned, earning a snort from Wyatt.

Charlie arched one perfectly manicured brow. "Wouldn't be any weirder than your kinks, would it, perv? Now, spill. Who is he?"

Linc sighed, digging his thumb into his left eye. "At the moment? He's my boss."

"Oh, God. He's not as old as you, is he?" she asked, curling her lip in disgust and zooming in on Jackson's face.

Linc gently flicked her nose. "He's not as old as me, no."

She perked up. "Single?"

Linc made a vague gesture. "As far as I know? We haven't really gotten into his dating life."

"Straight?"

She was relentless. He shrugged. "In theory."

Charlie clapped her hands in excitement, her phone muffling the sound. "Excellent. I want to meet him."

Wyatt frowned at that. "Why? Do you even date?"

"Who said I wanted to date him?" Charlie countered.

Linc thought about telling Charlie to back off, but in the short time he'd known her, he'd come to realize pushing her away would only cause her to come back stronger. The girl was a rubber band, and he wouldn't be on the other end when she snapped. "Don't do anything that'll get me fired."

Charlie swung her feet from Wyatt's lap and stood up, swaying. "Oh, head rush." She walked to the counter. "Don't worry about it, Missing Linc, I promise I'll be gentle with him."

*Yeah, right.* "Also, leave my sister alone."

"No can do, Lincoln Log."

"Stop that," Linc grumbled, knowing full well she'd only stop when she'd run out of stupid nicknames for him.

"We're already Facebook friends, and we're going for drinks next time I'm in Orlando, which will be in just three short weeks when I go for that photoshoot thing with Kristiane."

"What could you possibly have in common with Linc's forty-something-year-old sister?" Wyatt asked around a mouthful of cereal.

"Don't talk with your mouth full," Linc muttered.

"Sorry, Da—Sorry," he muttered, face flushing scarlet.

Charlie made a noise like a dying seal. "Freaks," she cackled before saying, "Linc's sis is a badass costume designer and I'm an actress-slash-model-slash-singer.

What don't we have in common? Don't be jelly, boo. You'll always be my number one ride or die, promise."

"You said you needed to talk about the gala?" Linc reminded her.

She nodded. "Yeah, your dad's douchey image consultant had the fucking audacity to send me dresses he'd deemed 'appropriate.'" She air quoted her last word with a flourish. "He also gave me a list of talking points and topics I was not to discuss under any circumstances because this is the most important fundraiser of the season."

"Sounds like Dad's worried about something. Maybe the campaign isn't going as well as he thought it would?" Wyatt said, perking up.

"Just wanted to let you know I plan on ignoring the dresses and will use the list of banned topics as my personal to-do list."

"It would disappoint me if you didn't," Wyatt said.

She dropped a sloppy kiss on Linc's forehead and then Wyatt's before sauntering toward the door. "Oh, and B.T. dubs, I'm pretty sure there's a private investigator lurking in your lobby. Just so you know."

Linc went rigid at her casual statement. "Why do you think they're a PI?"

"Because he's wearing a hat and sunglasses inside and he was talking to the front desk guy all shady

*intoxicating*

like. Also, I'm pretty sure he was filming me getting on the elevator." She checked her phone before setting it down and shoving both hands in her hair until it looked disheveled. She untucked half her shirt and smeared her shell-pink lipstick.

"What the hell are you doing, you freak?" Wyatt asked, spoon paused in midair.

"I just told you there's a private investigator in the lobby. I'm making it look like I just came over here for a quickie. *You're welcome.* God, I have to do all the mental heavy lifting around here." She snagged her purse and gave a little wave. "Bye, boys. See you tomorrow night."

Linc waited fifteen minutes before heading down to the lobby. Charlie was right. Sitting in a plush green chair was a man in a pink polo shirt wearing aviators and a baseball cap. While he didn't have a camera, he'd set himself up so his phone pointed toward the elevators.

The usual morning crew stood behind the desk, their eyes darting between the man and Linc as he approached. The boy working wasn't much older than Wyatt. He had rich copper skin and a close-cropped fade and eyes so dark brown they appeared almost black. His name was Reggie. He and Linc had made small talk and exchanged pleasantries a hundred times over the course of Linc's employment, and when he approached, Reggie gave a half-hearted wave.

"Hey, Linc."

"Hey. How's it going?"

The boy's gaze once more slid to the man in the pink shirt before he leaned in close. "Is Wyatt okay, dude?"

Unease trickled along Linc's spine. "Why do you ask?"

"I just mean, first he doesn't leave his apartment for months, then when he does, you show up and follow him everywhere, and now, his dad's got some PI watching our lobby. Did somebody, like, put a hit out on him or something?"

Linc turned to look at the man. "That guy says he works for Mr. Edgeworth?"

"Yeah."

"Did you call the senator's office to confirm? Why didn't anybody call and ask me?"

Reggie winced, rubbing at the back of his neck. "Linc, man, I just work here. I assume my manager talked to somebody."

"If you see anything else like this or if anybody shows up here asking questions, you call me," Linc said, handing him a card with his number on it.

"Sure. Is Wyatt okay, though?"

That was a great question. Linc had no idea. "Yeah,

*intoxicating*

he's fine. This is all his father's campaign people. He pays them to be paranoid, you know?"

Reggie nodded, though his expression implied he didn't know. Linc turned away, pulling up Jackson's number and hitting the call button.

"Avery," Jackson said by way of greeting.

"What do you know about Edgeworth hiring a PI to sit on our lobby?"

There was a long pause. "There's a PI in the penthouse's lobby?"

"Yeah, the front desk guy says the PI claims Edgeworth hired him to stake out the place. Does that make any sense to you? If he was going to watch the lobby, why not contact you? You handle all his private security, no?"

"I'll call you back."

Twenty minutes crept by before Jackson returned his call. "The image consultant hired the dude."

"What is this fucker's deal? I've never heard of an image consultant or publicist this involved in things. What does this guy need an investigator for?"

"The senator received an email threatening to expose all of his son's sins, claimed they had proof."

The sudden rush of adrenaline caused a sharp pain in Linc's chest. "What sins? What the hell does that even mean? This is that Miranda bitch from the paper.

Can we not get her to back off? Can't you make some phone calls?"

"This is the first I'm hearing of any of it." There was no missing the frustration in Jack's voice. "Listen, until we figure out what's going on, when you two leave that building, you are strictly business. The more pressure Edgeworth feels about this campaign, the worse it gets for all of us. If anybody finds out that there's something going on between you two...we're all fucked."

Linc didn't bother to deny there was anything going on. What the fuck was the point? Everybody in their inner circle already knew. Everybody but Monty Edgeworth. This was an absolute clusterfuck. "Understood."

"Hey, one last thing," Jackson said, hesitation in his voice.

"Yeah?"

"Why is Charlemagne Hastings friend requesting me on Facebook?"

# twenty-eight

## WYATT

LINC HAD BEEN ON THE PHONE FOR HOURS, FIRST with Jackson and now, with his sister. Wyatt wasn't eavesdropping. It wasn't his fault Linc's voice carried from the patio into his bedroom. Sure, he might have been sitting just inside the doorway where the acoustics were better, but the point was, Linc couldn't be mad at Wyatt for listening in.

"I'm sorry, El. I really am. I'll find a new night nurse so you can get some sleep."

Wyatt wasn't sure what Ellie's response was, but there was no missing the strain in Linc's voice or the heavy sighs that punctuated his sentences. Wyatt couldn't imagine caring for somebody twenty-four hours a day, seven days a week, especially not somebody with severe dementia. It sounded exhausting and thankless on the best of days. But to stop your whole life to care for a person who abandoned you to your crazy mom? That went beyond selfless, it seemed borderline masochistic. Not that Wyatt should point fingers. He was always looking for new and creative ways to hurt himself.

"Have you heard from Davis about your old job?" Linc asked before saying, "Ellie, you're just starting to make a name for yourself. This is crazy. Put him in the state home you found in Orlando and go back to California. Go back to your old life. I hate that you're the one bearing the brunt of this."

Wyatt wondered how much it cost for round-the-clock care for a patient with a limited ability to care for themselves. Linc was getting paid six figures just to hang out with Wyatt every day, and all they did was attend boring fundraisers. Wyatt imagined the cost of running a person's entire life, keeping them alive…it had to cost a small fortune. At least as much as Linc's salary. It was why he'd agreed to babysit Wyatt.

The notion twisted something deep inside. Not that Wyatt begrudged Linc the paycheck he would receive. The money Linc made wasn't for sex with Wyatt. In his head, he knew that. But some dark part of him

*intoxicating*

whispered that Wyatt was just a means to an end, a paycheck with benefits, and as soon as that check was in his hands, Wyatt would never hear from Linc again.

Wyatt shook his head. Of course he wouldn't hear from him again. That was the point. They were having a fling. Even if they weren't, what would Wyatt do? His father would never set him free. There was no world where he and Linc could just be together. It just wasn't how his world worked.

The more Wyatt thought about it, the gloomier he became. He wandered into the kitchen, making himself a peanut butter sandwich before stabbing the knife into the jar and leaving it sitting on the counter, like a warning to all the other sandwich spreads not to mess with him. He sat at the counter, tearing the bread into small pieces but not eating them. Instead, he glowered at Linc's retreating figure, dipping his head each time he turned to pace back.

His phone vibrated against the counter, snagging his attention. It was a text from Charlie.

**Did Linc sort out your private investigator downstairs?**

Had he? Wyatt had no idea. Linc had barely said five words to him since he came back. **Sort of. All Linc would say is the guy works for my dad.**

**Charlie: I ruined a perfectly good blowout for**

that? I looked like I'd been through a wind tunnel by the time I met up with Miguel. What a dick. I should send him a bill. Wait. Why would your dad hire a PI?

**Wyatt: Fuck if I know? I wanted to ask Linc, but he's been on the phone for hours. You'd think he could spare five minutes for me, but I guess not.**

Three dots danced before the next text came through, jangling Wyatt's raw nerves. **Oh, boy. Somebody's cranky. What happened? You seemed fine at breakfast.**

Wyatt's stomach soured. Had he? **That was then. This is now.**

**Charlie: Uh-oh. Little Black Rain Cloud Wyatt... My least favorite Wyatt. The Wyatt who makes stupid decisions. You're not planning on doing something stupid, are you? 'Cause if so, maybe you should save it for your dad's super important party tomorrow.**

**Wyatt: What is it about this party that all of a sudden makes it so much more important than the others? A week ago, it was just another event.**

**Charlie: My mom said the press will be there because he's getting an award or something. Whatever kind of award it is, I'm sure he bought it.**

Wyatt couldn't control his rolling eyes, even if there

*intoxicating*

was nobody there to witness it. His father would make himself out to be some hero. He glanced over at Linc, who'd planted himself at the end of one of the lounge chairs at the far end of the porch. Linc pinched the bridge of his nose as he continued to talk to his sister.

**Charlie: Hello?**

**Wyatt: Sorry, I just don't know what to say.**

The phone rang almost instantly, Charlie's name blinking onto his screen.

"Yes?"

A sound like white noise filled his ear before Charlie said, "You're scaring me, Wyatt. What's going on with you?"

"Are you in an Uber?"

"No, I bought a car," she said casually. "Don't change the subject. What's your deal?"

Leave it to Charlie to just buy a car on a whim. "What do you mean? Nothing," he lied, gaze straying outside once more.

"Is it your dad?"

He used his pointer finger to poke holes in the remains of his mutilated sandwich. "No. I mean, no more than usual."

There was a slight pause. "So, it's Linc."

Wyatt ducked his head, his response a harsh whisper, as if Linc might somehow overhear. "I didn't say that."

"You didn't have to. It is, isn't it? Did he do something wrong? You two seemed so cozy this morning."

"That's just it. We were…we *are*. It's just…" he started before falling silent once more.

Charlie sucked in a breath. "Oh, honey. You're falling for him, aren't you?"

His laugh was harsh, jarring even. "Falling? More like fallen. I'm there. I'm in it up to my eyeballs. Not that it matters. But there it is. Figures, I can't even do a fling without fucking it up."

Once more, she hesitated. "Have you talked to Linc about how you feel?"

"What? No! Never. My crazy isn't his problem. I'm sure my psychosis is already way more than he bargained for."

"He's super protective of you. His answer might surprise you."

He hated the pity in her voice, like she was hopefully optimistic but just as leery as he was. "It doesn't matter. It would never work out. Linc is only here long enough to collect his fat check, then he'll be long gone, taking care of his dad, and I'll still be here pretending to be the perfect son. What's the point?"

"The point is, it doesn't have to be this way," she snapped. "You could have a life. You don't owe your father shit. I've told you this a million times. Leave, live your own life. You can come live with me. We can be YouTube famous and live off my parents."

Wyatt's stomach sloshed. Charlie just didn't understand. He couldn't just live off Charlie and her family. Besides, his father was right. He had no marketable skills. He was impulsive, argumentative, unable to do even the simplest household task. Wyatt didn't even know how to write a check. His father would never let him go, anyway. He'd spend the rest of his life harassing Wyatt if he ever dared try to leave. That woman from the press was already fishing around about Wyatt's past. How long before she figured out Wyatt was gay? The thought didn't scare him as much as it once had, but his father's wrath did.

From the corner of his eye, he saw Linc rise and walk toward the house.

"I gotta go." He didn't wait for her answer before ending the call.

Outside, the weather changed as quickly as Wyatt's mood. Black clouds now blotted out the sun, painting the whole sky in shades of gray, gearing up for their daily afternoon thunderstorm. Linc slid the glass door closed behind him just as the first rumbles of thunder rolled across the sky.

Linc frowned when he saw the remnants of Wyatt's

lunch, noting the open jar of peanut butter and the sticky knife. "Clean that up. Graciela does enough around here without having to deal with shit like this. You know better."

Linc wasn't wrong, but Wyatt didn't care. "She's the housekeeper. She gets paid really well to clean up 'shit like this.' It's literally her job," he reminded Linc, tone flippant.

A shiver rolled over Wyatt when Linc's brow shot up, his voice dropping a full octave. "Did I ask for a debate? Clean it up. Now."

"Or what?" Wyatt asked, crossing his arms over his chest like a sulky teenager.

Linc came around the counter, looming over his shoulder. "You know, if you want me to punish you, you could just ask nicely," he murmured against his ear.

Wyatt's cock hardened in response, goosebumps erupting along his skin, but he wasn't done. "It's not always about that," he snapped.

Linc turned the stool until they were face to face. "Then what is it about?"

The weight on Wyatt's chest was back, crushing him. What was he doing? Why was he poking at this? He would never get the answer he wanted. He needed to learn to enjoy what he had now.

*intoxicating*

"Nothing, just forget it."

He could feel Linc's gaze burning a hole in his skin, but he refused to look at him. "I will not forget it. You've been moody for days. What is going on with you? Just talk to me. Whatever's on your mind, just… say it."

"Why do you keep pretending you care about me?" Wyatt wanted to suck the question back the moment it left his lips, but it was too late. Linc froze. Wyatt wasn't sure which one of them looked more horrified.

"Just forget it," he muttered, face in flames.

He slid off the stool, ducking under Linc's arm, moving to do what he'd asked. Wyatt swept the remains of the sandwich into the garbage and wiped down the counter before replacing the peanut butter lid and returning it to the cabinet.

He could feel Linc watching him as he moved, but he refused to look up, refused to even acknowledge he still stood there. He just couldn't. Linc's silence was a knife twisting in his heart. What had he really expected him to say?

It was a testament to Linc's military training that he never heard him coming, never even saw him move, just found himself pressed between Linc's frame and the edge of the countertop now biting uncomfortably against his hips.

Outside, thunder rumbled and lightning lit up a nearly black sky. Linc's hand closed around his throat, his other arm locking around his chest. Wyatt wished Linc's arms didn't feel like home.

"Do you remember the day you flooded the kitchen?" Linc asked huskily.

"Yeah," was all he could manage.

"We were just like this. You were frantic…indignant…acting like the dishwasher had betrayed you. I wanted you even then. You were beautiful. Spoiled. A total brat. You were absolute perfection." His lips skimmed along Wyatt's ear, then his cheek. "I wanted you so badly I contemplated quitting. I couldn't imagine spending the next six months trying to keep my hands off you." Wyatt melted into him, his head resting on Linc's chest, pressing himself back against Linc's half-hard cock. "All I could think about was burying myself inside you. You've been under my skin since day one."

Wyatt sucked in a breath when the hand on his chest plunged beneath the waistband of his pajama pants, roughly gripping his erection and stroking him. He couldn't fight the whimper that escaped.

"I wanted to fuck you just like this, bent over the kitchen counter while you begged me to fill you up, make you mine."

*intoxicating*

"Yes," Wyatt breathed, suddenly wanting that more than anything.

Linc's hand tightened around Wyatt's throat. "Are you mine now?"

"Yes, Daddy," he vowed, breath hitching.

"Only mine," Linc rumbled.

Only ever his. Wyatt couldn't imagine loving somebody else the way he did Linc, no matter how crazy it sounded. "Yes."

Linc squeezed tighter still, cutting off Wyatt's air supply, his heartbeat becoming erratic. "Yes, what?"

"Yes, Daddy," he managed.

Linc allowed him to breathe, massaging his throat. "Say it."

The words felt like a vow. "I'm yours, Daddy."

"Yeah, you are. Just mine. Only mine." He jerked Wyatt a few more times, but then his hand disappeared. "I wish I could fuck you right here."

Wyatt sucked in a breath. He needed Linc inside him now, needed it more than he needed the air he gulped into his lungs. "Yes. Do it. Fuck me. Right here. Show me I'm yours."

"Everything we need is in the bedroom."

"You're a fucking Marine. Improvise," Wyatt reasoned.

"I can improvise lube but not condoms."

Wyatt glanced over his shoulder. "I'm negative. My father had me tested after the cater-waiter. You?"

Linc searched his face for a long moment before he nodded. "Yeah, testing is mandatory in the military."

Wyatt swallowed hard, his tongue darting out to lick over his lower lip. It was fucking stupid, reckless even. But he really was safe, and he trusted Linc was telling the truth. "Then do it. Fuck me. Right here. Come inside me. Mark me. Show me I'm yours in every way."

Linc's only response was a low growl, and then he was shoving Wyatt's pants down. He let his eyes drift shut as Linc bit along the side of his neck and shoulder, letting the pain soothe his ragged edges. Linc hadn't said he cared, but it was close enough, good enough, more than Wyatt deserved.

After a moment, Linc's slick fingers suddenly pressed against his entrance.

Wyatt gave a breathless laugh. "Is that…oil?"

He hissed as two fingers pushed into him. Fuck. He'd never get sick of that feeling.

"That a problem for you?" Linc asked, working his fingers in and out.

Wyatt rocked back, moaning like a whore. "No, Daddy."

Linc chuckled. "I didn't think so."

He worked Wyatt open first with two fingers, then

*intoxicating*

three, but it wasn't enough. "I'm ready, Daddy. Fuck me."

Linc slapped his ass. "I decide when you're ready," he snarled, but the blunt head of his thick cock was already replacing his fingers, and then there was only pressure and fullness and the perfect burn of his body rearranging itself to accommodate Linc's invasion.

Linc didn't wait for Wyatt to adjust, fucking into him hard enough to bring Wyatt onto his tiptoes. Linc drove into him again and again just the way Wyatt liked, like he was there only for Linc's pleasure, like only Wyatt could satiate Linc's need and he'd take it from Wyatt however he saw fit. He needed to be happy with this, needed to appreciate Linc while he still had him, needed to remember every moment.

"Don't go quiet on me now, boy," Linc commanded, gripping Wyatt's hip and changing the angle enough to make Wyatt cry out. "That's better. Let me hear you."

Rain pounded the windows, combining with the sound of their skin connecting and the ragged sounds of their breathing, but Wyatt couldn't find the words. He was lost in the feeling, trying to memorize Linc's scent, the weight of him against his back. They had months to go, but somehow, this just felt like the end.

Condensation formed on the windows, closing them into a cozy pocket that made it feel like more somehow. Something...real. Linc's hand closed around Wyatt's neck again and he stopped thinking, stopped worrying. He focused instead on the steady pressure at his throat and Linc's cock sending jolts of electricity along his spine each time it grazed his prostate. His neglected cock leaked with every thrust, but his hands gripped the counter. Linc hadn't given him permission. "Can I touch myself, Daddy? Please?"

"No," Linc managed through gritted teeth.

Wyatt whined, grinding himself back on Linc. "Please, Daddy. I'm so close."

"I didn't say you can't come. I said you can't touch."

Linc expected him to come untouched?

"I-I don't think..."

"You can. You can, and you will. If you want to come, that is."

Linc released Wyatt's throat, his hand forcing Wyatt's head down to the counter before he gripped his hips, fucking into him with short, rapid thrusts that had Wyatt's eyes rolling back in his head as pleasure ignited along his spine, his balls drawing up tight against his body. "Oh...oh...that's... Oh, God. Yes. More of that. Oh, please. Please. I need to come, Daddy. Please?"

"You can come anytime you want, baby boy, as long as you're not touching yourself."

*intoxicating*

Wyatt sobbed. He couldn't even form words. Linc was hitting him just right, doing everything right. Warmth pooled at the base of his spine, and Linc yanked Wyatt back against him, gripping his throat tight enough to cut off his air supply.

"Come," he growled.

His orgasm slammed into him like a school bus, his knees buckling as he painted the cabinets with his release. Linc kept him upright, his hips pistoning into him relentlessly until it was just this side of too much.

Wyatt barely registered Linc's hoarse shout as he waited for his world to right itself. When Linc kissed between his shoulder blades, Wyatt shivered, knowing Linc's cum filled him up. The thought shouldn't be hot. It shouldn't make him feel safe, seen, cared for, even loved…but it did.

He wished he could get his heart to see this for what it was, but he just didn't know how. When he was in Linc's arms, it didn't feel like a fling.

It felt like love, and it made Wyatt want to cry.

## twenty-nine

### LINCOLN

BY THE TIME LINC GOT WYATT CLEANED UP AND settled on the couch with his dinner, he'd reverted to moody silence. Linc didn't know what he'd thought kitchen sex would accomplish other than driving home the point that Wyatt was just—as Charlie put it—a 'sex thing.' When he'd asked why Linc acted like he cared, he froze. It was a simple fucking question with a complicated fucking answer.

Of course, Linc cared. He cared way too much. Caring about Wyatt was the easiest thing in the world, but caring for Wyatt was a series of landmines. The boy needed a keeper, somebody to look out for him,

*intoxicating*

watch over him, guide him. Linc wanted to be that somebody. He'd meant everything he'd said. Wyatt was perfect just as he was…but he was only twenty-two years old. His life hadn't even started. Linc felt a hundred years old on a good day, and his PTSD was unpredictable. Linc didn't know how to give Wyatt what he needed when both their lives were such equal but opposite disasters. Still, he could have said something more reassuring than "I've wanted to fuck you since I met you," but it was too late now.

Once he finished straightening up the kitchen, he sprawled at the opposite end of the couch, one leg still perched on the floor. Wyatt watched him warily, like he was waiting for something. Jesus, Linc had really fucked this up. "Come here, baby."

Wyatt didn't hesitate, launching himself toward Linc and collapsing on top of him, his body nestled between Linc's thighs and his head on his chest. He buried his hand in Wyatt's curls, dropping a kiss on his head, hoping to convey with actions what he couldn't say with words. Linc could be happy with just Wyatt in his arms. His eyes drifted shut as Wyatt's breathing evened out beneath his palms.

He woke to the sound of the door rattling on the frame as somebody tried to force their way into the penthouse.

"Why the hell is the deadbolt latched?"

Wyatt jolted upright, eyes wide at the sound of his father's voice, his terror clear. The deadbolt in question kept the door from opening wide enough for the senator to see them, but Linc gestured for Wyatt to go to his room, anyway. Wyatt threw one last panicked look toward the door before scrambling to do as Linc asked.

Linc stood, running his fingers through his hair and making sure his clothes didn't look too rumpled. "One moment, sir."

He closed the door in the man's face before releasing the latch and allowing him to enter. Monty straightened his jacket, as if temporarily being denied entrance had caused him physical injury. "Why the hell was the door locked?"

"Because we have a reporter following your son who has gotten past the front desk once already and a private investigator sitting in the lobby. I thought it best to put as many obstacles between them and Wyatt as possible…sir."

The man gave a surprised laugh and clapped Linc on the shoulder. "Yes, of course. That makes perfect sense. Where is my son?"

Linc rubbed the back of his neck. "He just finished eating and went to his room. I think he was on the phone with the girl."

"Ah, yes. Ms. Hastings," the senator replied, mouth drooping at the corners. "I really wish she'd move off to New York or LA with all the other wannabe movie stars so Wyatt can buckle down and focus on his career."

Career? Linc couldn't imagine his Wyatt in some corporate job, no matter how good he looked in a suit. He wasn't meant for that life. He needed to be creative. He was an artist.

Linc just gave him a tight smile before calling out, "Hey, kid, your father is here to see you."

Wyatt appeared in the hallway in shorts and a green t-shirt the same color as his eyes, a toothbrush still in his mouth. "Hey, Pops. What brings you here?" he asked, continuing to scrub his teeth obnoxiously.

"Really, Wyatt," the senator griped. "I'd like to talk to you about tomorrow night."

Wyatt strolled to the kitchen sink and spit before rinsing off his toothbrush and setting it down, giving his father his undivided attention. "I'm listening."

The muscle in Monty's jaw ticked, his nostrils flaring at Wyatt's disrespect. Linc raised his brows at Wyatt from behind his father. Wyatt's lips twitched in an aborted smile. He really loved pushing his father's buttons, but Linc couldn't blame him. Who wouldn't want the chance to torment their tormentor?

"I really need you and that girl to be on your best behavior tomorrow. There will be reporters everywhere, and I cannot have a repeat of last year."

Wyatt snorted. "I'll do my best not to get in a horrific car crash and almost die."

"I'm serious, Wyatt. If you pull another stupid stunt like last year, you'd best finish the job or I'll do it for you."

Wyatt flinched like his father had struck him. Linc clenched his teeth, his hands fisting at his sides. Someday, Linc was going to punch this man in the face, he told himself for the thousandth time. He would make sure this motherfucker paid for every ounce of pain he'd caused Wyatt in his life. "I don't think this is really helping the situation."

Monty jerked his head toward Linc, snapping, "I'm not paying you to think. Mind your own business."

"I'll play along, Dad. Don't worry," Wyatt muttered, now fidgeting with his toothbrush. "I always do."

His father rolled his eyes. "Don't be such a girl. I'm hard on you because you need to toughen up, especially now. Tomorrow night, everything changes for both of us."

Wyatt's gaze jerked to his father. "What does that mean?"

*intoxicating*

His father grinned. "You'll see. Just be on your best behavior, keep that girl in check, and for God's sake, stay off your goddamn knees."

"Wow, real fucking classy, Dad," Wyatt snarked, lip curling. "Is that all?"

His father shook his head, disappointment evident in his expression. "That's it."

As soon as Wyatt's bedroom door slammed, Monty turned on Linc. "I wanted to say thank you, Marine."

Linc kept his face expressionless. "For what, sir?"

"For whatever miracle you've worked on my son. He's still a disrespectful little shit and a freak of nature, but he's done well at each of the family gatherings. Even having that girl there benefits us. They love to have something to gossip about, and if they're gossiping about my son's inappropriate girlfriend, they're not worrying about where he's been for the last several months or whether he's secretly a sodomite."

*I'll kill him later. I'll kill him later.* Linc just muttered the phrase over and over in his head as Monty spoke, trying to quell the murderous impulse flooding his system and leaving a metallic taste in his mouth.

"I am not sure what part I've had to play in that... sir, but as long as you are satisfied with my job performance."

Monty chuckled. "Don't be modest. I think your

military discipline is exactly what my son needed. I'm grateful."

Linc bit down on the inside of his cheek as thoughts of Wyatt's many discipline sessions filled his head. "Happy to do my part, sir. Your son responds very well to a firm hand and hard limits."

Wyatt made a choking sound from somewhere in the recesses of his room. The little shit was eavesdropping...again. He was always listening. Linc fought the urge to smile as Monty's forehead collapsed into a frown, like he was uncertain how to respond.

"Well, yes, I suppose he does. Just...keep up the good work, and maybe there'll even be a bonus for you when this is over."

Linc gave a single nod and walked the senator to the door. The man turned back as if to say something but Linc shut the door in his face and secured the lock and the latch. That was enough visitors for one day.

FOR A NIGHT MEANT TO CHANGE LIVES, IT FELT JUST like every other boring fundraiser Linc had been forced to attend since taking this job. It was the same rubbery chicken and canned laughter. The same inappropriate jokes made at the expense of the less

*intoxicating*

fortunate and tolerating old women who groped the boy who rightfully belonged to Linc. Even the same terrible music filled the ballroom. If Linc had to hear one more eighties power ballad played by an orchestra, he might wrestle the bow from the violinist and slit his own throat with it.

Linc had changed up their routine somewhat to thwart the horde of reporters. They'd taken Charlie's new Land Rover and Linc had brought them in through the service entrance. They'd arrived just before dinner to minimize Wyatt's interaction with others. The boy wasn't doing well. If he was sullen before his father's visit, he was now downright maudlin. He'd spent hours in the bathroom before they left, just sitting in the empty bathtub staring at the wall. Linc had no idea how to help him.

There was nothing he could do now that they were there in front of all those prying eyes. Since the senator had invited the press, they sat scattered among the others in their finest clothes, making it impossible for Linc to know who they were... All except one. The reporter from the Miami Sun sat dead center of the group, and she had eyes only for Wyatt.

Linc could only stand with his back to the wall with the other security staff, his gaze glued to Wyatt, who looked like he was about to puke into his beet salad.

Beside him, Charlie split her time between making inflammatory comments to the rest of their table and casting worried looks in Wyatt's direction.

He wasn't even attempting to play his father's games. Gone was the Wyatt who would smirk and joke and even flirt with harmless old ladies. His father's comments yesterday had broken something in Wyatt. Something Linc wasn't sure anybody could fix.

He winced along with the others as feedback filtered through the overhead speakers followed by a loud tap on the microphone. A woman cleared her throat, and people turned in their seats to give her their attention. Linc had never seen the woman before. She was a petite brunette, with glossy chestnut hair and a big fake smile, wearing a high-necked purple gown that hugged her tiny figure. "Excuse me, y'all. If I might have your attention for just a moment? Thank you."

Once everybody had quieted, she continued, introducing herself to the audience as Calliope Jenner, the personal assistant of Senator Edgeworth himself, before droning on at length about all the good Monty had done for the state of Florida and how she couldn't be prouder to work for him. The man of the hour sat at the table at the front of the stage, beaming at the girl. Wyatt's mother didn't seem as fond.

"But enough of me, please help me give a warm

*intoxicating*

welcome to the man himself, Senator Montgomery Edgeworth."

She clapped enthusiastically, a deranged smile on her face, until a smattering of others joined in. Monty rose, waving like a beauty queen before taking the stage. Wyatt had said the man would receive some kind of award tonight, though Linc couldn't imagine what for. Did they have a World's Biggest Asshole award? Most of the state hated the man's guts.

"Thank you. Thank you. It's great to see everybody here tonight. Especially you, Ted. You still owe me a hundred bucks off our last golf game. I hope you brought your checkbook." Everybody tittered at his lame joke. "Y'all think I'm kidding. He's a terrible golfer." His smile slipped away. "No, but seriously, folks. I'm afraid I've brought you here under false pretenses. I know you think this is just another fundraiser for me—which it is—but tonight, we're gathering for another reason, to honor my dear friend, Victor Osborne, and celebrate all the contributions he's made to making Florida great again, the kind of state that embodies our ideals and our vision of the future. So, please join me in welcoming him to the stage to receive the 2019 Florida Visionary Award."

This time, the applause was thunderous. The blood drained from Wyatt's face. Charlie's eyes cut to Linc, her hand settling between Wyatt's tight shoulders. Linc's blood rushed in his ears as he stared down Wyatt's rapist, smiling and waving from the stage. That's what he was. A fucking rapist, and if Linc got five seconds alone with the man, he'd rip his throat out without a second thought.

The man gestured for everybody to quiet down. "Thank you. Thank you, everybody, so much. While tonight is about the good senator and doing everything in our power to get him re-elected and keep that hippie out of office, I want to share some exciting news. Light of God Ministries has truly received a multitude of blessings this year. You, and others like you, have opened your hearts and your wallets, and thanks to your generous donations, we are honored to announce we are expanding our campuses to include Northern Florida, Georgia, Tennessee, and the Carolinas. Children and teens all across the nation will now come and learn of His word, receive the discipline and attention they need to turn away from the sins of the secular world, and grow to be good God-fearing Christian men and women."

There was a smattering of applause, but Victor was scanning the crowd as if looking for someone. Linc's stomach dropped.

Wyatt.

When he found Wyatt, ghost white and sweating,

*intoxicating*

he gave a slippery smile that made Linc's skin crawl and sent his heart rate through the roof.

"Wyatt, stand up, please."

Wyatt looked around in confusion, his gaze locking on his father who stood in the shadows of the stage. One look from his father had him lurching to his feet. Charlie gripped his hand, linking their fingers to hide his trembling.

Victor raised his hand to block the stage lights, narrowing his beady eyes at Wyatt. "There he is. Many of you don't know this, but Wyatt spent every summer at the ministry throughout high school, worked closely with me as not only a devoted student but an intern of sorts, working the programs just as the other students did. It seems only fitting now that he help me expand our reach. I look forward to working closely with you in the future."

Wyatt stood paralyzed long enough for Victor to raise his glass in a toast and for the others to follow suit, but as soon as Victor left the stage, Wyatt wrenched his hand from Charlie's grasp and stumbled toward the doors of the ballroom.

Charlie watched him go, lost as to what had just happened. "Guess it wasn't Monty's award after all," she muttered as she reached Linc's side. "What the fuck am I missing? What's going on?"

"I don't know, but I need to find him. Can you try to run interference with his father?"

"Done."

# thirty

## WYATT

WYATT SNAGGED A GLASS OF CHAMPAGNE FROM THE server as she passed, downing it before snagging another from a different server, a man with dark curly hair who smiled at him as he took his empty glass. Wyatt didn't smile back. He kept his head on a swivel, trying to find the closest bathroom. He should have seen this coming. He should have kept his guard up, but he was just too fucking tired. He was tired of the games and tired of hurting. It was all too much.

He located the sign pointing toward the restroom, flagging down another server as he passed, gulping down his third glass. He wasn't wasted enough to deal with any of this. He was halfway to the restaurant when he spotted Miranda speed-walking toward him in a black cocktail dress and sky-high stilettos. *Not fucking now.* "No comment," he snapped, attempting to side-step the reporter.

She tilted her head, looking confused. "I really don't get you. I would think you'd love the free publicity. I'm certain your father and Victor Osborne would. Your father just handed you the keys to a kingdom, but you look like somebody shot your puppy."

"Just leave me alone, lady. Don't you have better things to do than worry about my life?" He pressed forward, leaving her behind.

"Seems like an awfully big responsibility for a twenty-two-year-old with a record, but I guess when your daddy's a senator, things like that get swept under the rug."

Wyatt stopped short at her words, turning around. "So, you know?"

She smirked at him, raising one perfectly manicured brow. "About your multiple DUIs? Your house arrest? About how, somehow, your father managed to get it buried? Yeah, I know. We have private investigators, too."

Wyatt shook his head, feeling trapped. "Why are you doing this? Why are you so concerned with my

*intoxicating*

life? What did I ever do to you?"

Miranda scoffed. "What did you do? You rich white men get to wear your privilege like it's Teflon armor. Nothing ever sticks to guys like you and your father. His barbaric policies never touch people like you... they only affect people like me. People of color. The LGBT community. Women. Guys like you always have daddies who buy your way out of DUIs and get you fancy jobs you're not qualified for. Nobody feels sorry for you."

"Fuck you, lady," was all that Wyatt could manage.

Once in the restroom, he locked himself in the very last stall, pressing his head against the coolness of the door. He slipped his hand into his pocket, closing it around that tiny piece of paper he'd taken from above the medicine cabinet before he'd left home. He pulled his suit jacket off and dropped it to the floor, shoving up the sleeve of his left arm. He unwrapped the blade, blinking through sweat and tears. He just needed one cut. Just one, just enough to relieve the ache, to get the poison out of him and make the pressure go away.

"Wyatt?" Victor.

Wyatt's stomach lurched. Had Victor followed him? He moved deeper within the stall, needing as much distance between them as possible. Maybe if Wyatt stayed quiet, he'd just leave.

"Don't be shy. I saw you come in here. I wanted to see if you were okay. You didn't look so good. Have a little too much to drink?" he asked.

"I'm fine," he muttered even as his stomach churned and his grip on the safe side of the blade tightened.

He was just outside the stall now. Wyatt could see his black loafers peeking under the door. "Did you like my surprise? It took some convincing—and a very large donation—for your father to see the logic of my choice, but I've always known how special you are. Always."

It was Victor's idea? Victor had literally bought him from his father. His father had no idea what Victor really wanted, but he wasn't even sure it would have mattered. Wyatt sucked deep breaths in through his nose to keep from throwing up. He wouldn't do it. He'd never help subject kids to the shit he went through. He'd die first. But Wyatt said none of that. He couldn't say anything at all. He just stood there, shaking. His skin was in flames, but he was freezing.

"I thought you'd be excited to come back to me. You were always such a devoted student. So eager. You were always my favorite." He laughed despite Wyatt's silence. "I know, I'm not supposed to have favorites, but I do."

Do. Present tense. He was doing the same things to other kids that he did to Wyatt. "You're fucking sick.

*intoxicating*

How the fuck do you live with yourself? Your torture sessions don't work. They never have," Wyatt spat, forcing down the sob threatening to bubble up.

Victor sounded delighted that he'd elicited a response. "Well, now, that's just not true. Look at you. You have a beautiful girlfriend. You're about to have a lucrative career. Your father is about to be re-elected. Everything is working out for you. I'd like to think I played a part in that."

Wyatt's heart pounded against his ribs, his blood rushing in his ears. "Do you think the things you did to me...the things you made me do...do you think that somehow changed who I was? Prayer didn't change me. The fucking sick shit you did to me... the shit you're probably still doing to other boys like me...it didn't change me. God couldn't make me not gay any more than he could make you any less of a fucking monster."

The door rattled as Victor leaned against it. "Don't be jealous. I never touched those other boys. They were nothing like you... It was only you I couldn't resist. Don't pretend you didn't like it. You came back again and again. What we had was special. We could still have it. Nobody would ever have to know."

Wyatt slammed his fist against the stall door. "Get the fuck away from me."

The door to the restroom opened. "Wyatt?"

"Linc?" he managed, relief flooding his system until he was woozy.

"We're in the middle of a conversation," Victor said.

"And now, you're not," Linc said. "Come on, Wyatt."

Wyatt looked down at the razor in his hand, carefully folding it back into the paper and slipping it into his pocket. He left his jacket on the bathroom floor, needing to get as far away from Victor as possible.

Linc gripped his upper arm, pulling him toward the door. Victor snagged his other arm. Wyatt sucked in a startled breath.

Linc turned, his gaze falling to Victor's hand on Wyatt's arm. "You have two seconds to get your hand off him before I tear it off your fucking body and beat you to death with it."

The older man paled, freeing Wyatt instantly.

Linc took his arm once more, pulling him through the lobby and dragging him into a small, deserted conference room just before the fire exit. As soon as the door slammed shut, Wyatt's back hit the wall and he slid down it, bracing his elbows on his knees. "I can't do this anymore, Linc. I can't. I can't work for that man. That reporter, she knows about my DUIs. She's going to expose me, tell everybody what I did, and I don't even care. I'm just so fucking tired. I'm so tired of all of this."

Linc knelt beside him, taking his face between his hands. "Say the word and it's done, baby. We can walk away right now. I'll find Charlie, and it'll all be over."

Wyatt shook his head. Linc couldn't be serious. "I won't do that to you. You need this money. You and Ellie need it for your dad. I just need a minute. I'll be fine. I just need to breathe. Why is it so hard to breathe?"

"Because you're having a panic attack. I'll find another way to pay for my father's care. I'm not letting you stay here. Not at the risk of your health…your sanity. Jesus, Wyatt. You're not going to work for the man who raped you for years. That's crazy. I'll have Jackson find me another job."

Wyatt's breath caught on a sob, and he shook his head. "I'm not worth this headache, Linc. I'm not. Believe me. I'm never not going to be fucked up. It's just a part of who I am now. I'm just a mess. I will always be this huge mess. I'm a bad investment."

Wyatt's heart sank as Linc stood.

"Stand up."

Wyatt's gaze jerked upward. "What?"

"I gave you an order. Stand. Up."

Wyatt did as Linc commanded, even though his knees wobbled.

Linc pushed Wyatt's hair back off his face. "Who do

you belong to?"

A strange calm washed over Wyatt, his lids slipping half-closed. "You, Daddy."

"Who makes the rules?"

"You do, Daddy."

"That's right. I make the rules. I worry about the big things. Don't I always take care of you?"

He did. Linc was always there. He took care of everything. "Yes, Daddy."

"That's right. Always. I'll always take care of you. If you're fucked up, I'm fucked up, too. But I'm here. I'm here, and I'm not going anywhere. I won't let anybody hurt you."

"I love you," Wyatt blurted before slapping his hand over his mouth.

Linc pulled Wyatt's hand away, kissing him until he was breathless.

Did people get to be happy in real life? Could Wyatt be happy? Could he just walk away from his father and his money and live a life with Linc? A life free of his father's demands and his insinuations? *"Stay off your knees."* That's what he'd said last night. As if the only conceivable outcome was Wyatt on his knees.

Fuck him.

He dropped down before Linc, looking up at him like he'd done so many times before, his hands deftly opening Linc's pants.

"Wyatt—" Linc started, but then he groaned as Wyatt's lips sealed around his cock. "Fuck, this is not a good idea."

Wyatt closed his eyes, concentrating only on that salty tang of Linc's skin and the heavy weight of his cock as he hardened for Wyatt.

Metal scraped as the heavy conference room door pushed open. "That reporter said you were in here. People are look—Jesus Christ, Wyatt. What the fuck?"

Linc jerked Wyatt to his feet, hastily zipping up his pants before turning to Wyatt's father. Monty looked back and forth between the two. "Have you...have you been violating my son in my fucking house? While I paid you? Are you... But you're a Marine? A decorated war vet? How... Did my son seduce you?"

Wyatt couldn't help the gasp that escaped. "Seriously, Dad? Do you really think that's how all this works?"

Linc pushed Wyatt behind him. "Wyatt didn't seduce me. I seduced him," Linc told the senator, crossing his arms over his chest, like he dared the senator to say otherwise.

"You. You're fucking fired. Get the hell out of here. And don't think you'll get a penny from me now."

"Dad, you can't do that. He needs that money."

"Then he should have thought of that before he turned my home into Sodom and Gomorrah." He looked to Linc. "Get the fuck out of here. Go get your shit out of my home and don't come back."

Linc's jaw tightened, his eyes steely. "I'm not leaving without Wyatt."

Monty looked confused by Linc's statement. "Oh, I get it. You think that you can use my son for his inheritance. That will never happen. My son will never see a penny of his trust fund if he doesn't fall in line."

Wyatt exploded. He just couldn't fucking listen to one more word. "I don't want your fucking money, Dad. I've never given a shit about that. I just wanted you to fucking accept me, to love me. How can you not get that? I didn't choose the way I am, I just am. You can't guilt it out of me. You can't beat it out of me. Hell, your friend Victor couldn't even torture it out of me. Can't you just love me? I'm your son." He hated the way his voice cracked, that tears slipped from his eyes. His father didn't deserve his pain.

"Love you? You're not worthy of my love. You refuse to turn away from this sinful lifestyle. I'll never accept that. I will not waste my time loving a son I'll never see in the hereafter. You are spitting in God's face. What you're doing is…immoral. Unnatural. It's just wrong."

Wyatt hadn't thought he could feel any worse than

*intoxicating*

he did, but his father knew just where to aim to inflict the most damage. Wyatt's ears filled with the sound of his own heart breaking. His father really never would love him. Never.

"Let's go, Linc."

Linc took his hand and led him to the door. Wyatt turned around just as Linc opened the door, an idea forming. "You'll pay Linc every penny of his salary or I'll go public."

"You're leaving here holding hands with him. How else could you possibly humiliate me further?"

"The abuse?"

"Abuse? Please, you needed to toughen up."

"Do you really think that's how it will play out in the press?" Wyatt asked.

He scoffed. "Nobody will believe you."

"Charlie is an excellent photographer. I bet that reporter would love to see those pictures. She'd love to show the world who you really are," Wyatt lied. There were no pictures.

His father's face went white. "You wouldn't dare."

"Fucking try me," Wyatt shot back.

His father advanced on him. Wyatt took a step back, but then Linc was there. "Give me a fucking reason to kick your ass. Just give me a reason."

Wyatt shivered at the malice in Linc's tone. Monty

stumbled back, clearly taking Linc at his word.

Linc took Wyatt's hand, leading him back into the lobby. He reached into his pocket and pulled out Charlie's keys. "Go out the service entrance, just the way we came in. I'll find Charlie, and we'll get the fuck out of here. Okay?"

Wyatt gave a jerky nod, staring at the keys like he'd never seen them before. He watched Linc disappear into the crowded ballroom, his gaze snagging on the reporter from earlier. Miranda.

She studied Wyatt, her eyes less accusatory now, more…something else. Confused, maybe?

Wyatt couldn't worry about her now. He made his way through the back passages that ran behind the kitchens, pushing open the door and walking into the oppressive heat of the night. It hit him like a wet blanket. Adrenaline surged through him as the events of the night swirled in his head. He fumbled for the key fob as he found Charlie's car right up front.

Wyatt opened the driver's side door, pushing the button to turn over the engine. He sighed at the blast of frigid air that hit his overheated body. He closed his eyes, dizziness rushing over him as those three glasses of champagne he downed took hold. What had he just done? Blackmailing his father? Leaving with Linc? What would happen now? He had nothing. He was leaving with nothing.

Only Linc.

Linc was enough. Linc was everything. But was he everything for Linc? Would Linc regret this in a week? A month? A year? His stomach sloshed. He slipped the razor from his pocket. He just needed a release. Just one small cut to get rid of the poison, to dampen the panic stealing the breath from his lungs. He shoved his sleeve up once more, hands shaking as he pressed the blade just under his bicep, close enough to his body to hide the cut.

He hissed as his skin split, hand jumping as a loud noise startled him. He barked out a laugh as he realized his elbow had hit the horn but frowned as crimson arced through the air, splashing over Charlie's white leather interior once, then again. He blinked stupidly at the gash in his arm and the blood spurting from it, like a horror movie. He slapped his hand over it, but it didn't help.

Almost instantly, his chest hurt and his vision grew fuzzy, like he looked at the world through the bottom of a well. He tried to get out of the seat, to find Linc, yell for help, but he slipped, his body slamming into the asphalt, his head bouncing off the ground below. That would hurt later. He stared up at the streetlight as the world began to slip away.

"Wyatt? Oh, God. Call 911!" Linc. Linc was there. Linc would make it better. Wyatt felt himself being pulled and tugged, and then something squeezed his arm so tight he thought maybe it was being ripped off.

Charlie's panicked voice filled his ears. "We need an ambulance. Please. Hurry! We're at…"

He was fading. "Wyatt, stay with me. What have you done? Oh, God. Oh, fuck. Baby. Stay with me. What did you do? I love you. Stay with me."

Was Linc crying? It must be terrible if Linc was crying.

"Wyatt!" Why was Charlie screaming?

Everything went black.

## thirty-one

### LINCOLN

LINC STARED AT THE BLOOD COATING HIS HANDS. There was just so much of it. It saturated his clothes and even his shoes. Wyatt's blood. Charlie sat beside him on the bench, but she focused her attention on her parents standing a few feet away talking amongst themselves. When she'd called them, they'd dropped everything. They'd brought her a change of clothes and had stayed to make sure Wyatt was okay.

Was he okay? He'd been in surgery for hours. *"Brachial artery laceration. Severe blood loss. Touch and go."* Linc had tried to focus on the doctor's words, but he just kept flashing back to Wyatt lying on the pavement, the life leaching out of him. He'd looked so scared, and he just clung to Linc until he'd lost consciousness. The doctor said he was lucky to be alive...that if they hadn't found him...hadn't used his belt to tourniquet Wyatt's arm...he could have bled out right there on the street. Linc could have lost him for good.

They'd offered Linc scrubs so he could remove his bloody clothes, but he'd refused. He wasn't moving from that spot until they told him Wyatt was okay.

"He has to be okay," Linc muttered under his breath.

"He will be," Charlie promised. "He will be," she said again, like she was trying to convince herself.

The automatic doors of the waiting room slid open, and everybody looked up at the commotion. Linc's nostrils flared. Monty strode toward the desk like he owned the place, the intern in purple hot on his heels as were two men dressed in suits.

Where the fuck had he been this whole time? Charlie had been calling him for hours.

She stood, rushing to meet him. "Wyatt's still in surgery."

"What happened?" he snapped.

Her hands flailed at her sides. "He was bleeding really bad from a cut on his arm."

"Did you make sure they admitted him under a fake name?" he asked, not acknowledging her previous

*intoxicating*

statement.

Charlie stumbled back. "What?"

"A fake name. Did they use an alias so we can keep this quiet?"

Charlie's face contorted, enraged. "Do you even care if he's going to live?"

Monty rolled his eyes. "Oh, please. Don't be a child. We both know he did this to himself," he said, dismissing her and turning back to the woman behind the desk. "Excuse me, young lady. I need to talk to you." The nurse behind the desk flicked her eyes upward when he banged on her desk.

"I'm on the phone," she told him, pointing to the receiver like he was an idiot.

"Do you know who I am?"

"Dr. Levkoff, I'll call you back," she murmured before setting the phone down and smiling at the senator. "Yes, sir. I know exactly who you are. You're the man who got away with stealing a hundred million dollars from the company that owns this hospital. You're the reason half of us didn't get raises and why we're so grossly understaffed. I know exactly who you are."

The man's expression would have made Linc laugh on some other day.

"How dare you? I want to speak to your supervisor."

She glanced down at her badge, pulling it forward

until it was practically resting on his nose. "I am the supervisor, sir."

He sneered. "I need to speak with a physician or administrator, somebody who looks old enough to drink, preferably a man."

The nurse rolled her eyes but left to comply. Moments later, a severe-looking woman with a bun and reading glasses approached the senator. "My name is Angelica Phipps. I'm the administrator. How can I help you?"

"You admitted my son under his real name. We need to get that changed immediately. I also want updates as to his condition at regular intervals. You need to close off this wing of the hospital, and you need to alert security to ensure no press is permitted on the hospital campus."

The woman looked at him over the rims of her glasses. "Senator, I'm not sure exactly where you think you are, but we don't work like that around here. I'll be happy to get you a status update on your son's condition, and I'll talk to our IT people about putting your son under an alias to protect his privacy, but with all due respect, I think that ship has sailed. Perhaps your time would be better spent worrying about him making it through surgery."

She didn't wait for his response, turning to murmur

*intoxicating*

something to the nurse behind the desk before disappearing behind another set of double doors.

"We need to get ahead of this," he told the girl in purple. "Get Gerald on the phone now. We need to put out a press release. We'll call it an accident, say he cut himself on a jagged piece of metal."

She jotted down notes, nodding like a bobblehead. "Should we wait until we know his condition?"

He shook his head. "No, the media is probably already speculating. Honestly, publicity-wise, it would be better for all of us if he didn't make it."

Both the nurse behind the desk and the intern sucked in a startled breath at his callous remark.

Linc didn't remember leaving his seat, he didn't remember how Monty ended up on the ground, but he relished the feel of his fist connecting with his soft doughy face, with his grunts of pain and the satisfying sound of his nose breaking beneath his hand. People pulled at him, trying to free the senator, but they were gnats buzzing around him, more an annoyance than a hindrance. Montgomery Edgeworth deserved all this and more, and Linc would happily add this man's blood to Wyatt's.

Charlie was screaming at him, her fists hitting his shoulders. "Linc, stop! He's not worth it. Oh, my God. You're going to kill him. Stop! This isn't helping Wyatt."

Wyatt. Wyatt was in surgery. Wyatt might die. Fuck.

He stared down at Monty's bloody face, whatever satisfaction he'd felt fading under the reality of the situation. He let the two men pull him away.

Jesus, he couldn't lose Wyatt. He just fucking couldn't. He didn't just care about the kid, he loved him. He was in love with him. He should have fucking told him yesterday. Now, he might never have the chance. Fuck.

The girl in purple rushed to help the senator to his feet, but he shoved her away. "I'm fine!" he shouted, standing and straightening his jacket.

The senator wasn't fine. His nose gushed blood onto his overpriced tuxedo. The nurse behind the desk offered him a snowy white towel, her face equal parts amused and concerned. The administrator pushed back through the doors just in time for Monty to shout, "I want him arrested."

"Come on, Mr. Edgeworth. Can't we just focus on Wyatt?" Charlie asked. "Remember? Your son? The one fighting for his life?"

"Yeah, well, whose fault is that?" he grumbled, holding the towel to his nose.

"I have an update on your son if you're interested?" Ms. Phipps asked, looking at the senator as if he were something stuck to the bottom of her sensible shoe.

*intoxicating*

"Well, go on then," he said, his voice muffled from the fabric.

"Your son is out of surgery. They are taking him to recovery now. He's in stable condition, but it's going to be a long road. The surgeon will be out to speak to you shortly."

"When can I see him?" Linc asked.

"That's not my call," she said, not unkindly, before turning and disappearing once more.

The senator turned on him then, shoving a finger into his face. "You stay the hell away from my son. This is your fault."

Linc snorted, contemplating breaking the man's short, stubby digit. "My fault? You called him a sodomite. You told him he wasn't worthy of your love. You've been breaking his heart his entire life. You wanna have me arrested? Fine. But you won't go anywhere near him without his consent. Do you fucking hear me?"

Monty scoffed at him. "How do you intend to stop me?"

Charlie stepped forward. "My father called our attorney. He'll be here any minute. He's going to file an emergency injunction for a restraining order."

"A restraining order…against me? A senator?" He looked to Charlie's father. "You better control your daughter."

The man shook his head. "Charlemagne showed us the bruises. She's been documenting them for years. They're very compelling. No judge will overlook them. Not with your behavior tonight and certainly not with your family values platform."

Monty looked taken aback. "My behavior? This man just tried to kill me."

"You had it coming," Charlie shouted. "Somebody should've knocked you on your ass years ago."

Charlie's father shook his head, lowering his voice. "You'd be smart to just walk away, Monty. Just let the boy go. You've done enough harm."

"I called Jackson, too," Charlie told Linc.

"You called him? You have his number?" Linc asked.

"What can I say? I work fast," she told him with the barest hint of a smile.

Before anybody could say anything else, a woman appeared in pale blue scrubs. She approached Linc. "He made it through surgery. He's stable. He's in recovery, but he's not awake yet. We had to harvest a vein from his leg to repair the damage to the brachial artery, so he has a rather substantial wound on both his left arm and his right leg. He's got good blood return, so we're hopeful there will be minimal damage, but with this sort of injury, there's always the possibility

*intoxicating*

of amputation."

"My God," Monty muttered.

Linc ignored him. "Will he be able to use his left hand again?"

She gave a gentle shrug. "We aren't sure if there was any nerve damage yet, but right now, our main concern is perfusion, making sure he maintains blood flow to the limb and monitoring for infection."

The knot in Linc's chest loosened. Wyatt was stable; they could get through anything else together. "When can I see him?"

"As soon as we've moved him into a room."

Monty stepped in front of Linc, causing the surgeon to take a step back. "Excuse me. That's my son. I'm his next of kin."

She frowned. "Your son is a grown man. This man is listed as his emergency contact on his phone. His paperwork says fiancé. I'm not sure what to tell you, sir."

Monty looked like he was going to have a stroke at the word fiancé. Linc might have embellished a little on the admission paperwork, but it wouldn't be a lie for long. Wyatt was his. Maybe he was too young or Linc was too old or they were both just too fucked up for a relationship, but it didn't make it any less true. Linc loved Wyatt, needed Wyatt as much as Wyatt needed him. He had no idea what would happen going forward, but whatever it was, they'd deal with it together. As long as Linc didn't end up in prison.

The senator's phone rang, and he moved to the far side of the waiting room to answer it, still holding the towel to his bruised and battered face. Where was Wyatt's mother? His grandmother? Had Monty even told them?

His phone vibrated against his leg. Ellie's name flashed across the screen. "Hello?"

"Charlie texted me. She said Wyatt was hurt. Is he okay? Are you?"

Linc frowned. "What?"

"Relax, Linc. Do you think I couldn't tell you were into him? Did you think Charlie wouldn't give me all the dirty little details as soon as we talked?"

"How long have you two been talking?" he asked, bemused.

She ignored his question. "How bad is it? Is he going to be okay?"

Linc dropped himself into the nearest seat and spent the next hour talking to his sister, trying to explain to her that he didn't know what was happening with the job, with the money, with Wyatt.

"Don't be an idiot, Linc. We'll figure it out. I just want you to be happy. That's all I've ever wanted."

*intoxicating*

Linc leaned back, closed his eyes, and breathed a sigh of relief and just let her talk, her reassuring words soothing the ragged edges of his nerves.

Linc really didn't deserve Ellie, but he was certainly glad he had her.

# thirty-two

## WYATT

OPENING HIS EYES WAS EXHAUSTING. THE DIM LIGHT above scattered the thousand spiders nesting in his head, making his brain buzz like he was being electrocuted. Somebody had wrapped his world in cotton. Everything was fuzzy. Everything hurt. His arm was on fire and somebody had forced it through a block of Swiss cheese. Wyatt blinked in confusion. No, that wasn't right. It was spongy and looked like cheese, but it held his arm propped up, which was swaddled in a thousand bandages.

He slowly looked around, his stomach lurching in protest as the world tilted on its axis. Tiny screens

*intoxicating*

surrounded him, lines jumping and numbers he didn't understand blinking, and six bags of fluid hung from a metal pole over his head, leading to a line in the side of his neck. Machines beeped, pumps whirred, and down the hallway, somebody was shouting. It was all so much. He tried to lift his uninjured hand but found it weighed down…by Linc.

Linc had pulled the reclining chair up to the bed, propping his feet next to Wyatt's, holding his undamaged hand in a death grip. He'd lost the battle for sleep, his head tipped back, mouth hanging open.

Wyatt's eyes filled with tears. Linc had stayed. He swallowed, opening his mouth to speak, but he had no voice. He tried once again, but it was just too hard. His eyelids fluttered closed as he lost the battle to remain conscious.

When he opened his eyes the next time, it was as if somebody had pulled the veil from his eyes. Things were brighter, clearer. His skull still felt like somebody had cracked his head open, but it no longer felt like somebody had turned the volume up on the world.

"Wyatt!"

He jumped at the shrill sound of his name. Charlie now sat where Linc had been what felt like just moments ago. His heart sank. He was in the hospital. How long had he been there? How long had he been unconscious? What had happened to him?

"Where's Linc?" he rasped. Charlie gave a surprised laugh then burst into tears. Wyatt's heart rate skyrocketed, sending the machine to his right into a fit of rapid beeps. Tears filled his eyes. "Is he… Is he okay?"

A nurse burst through the door, studying him as she came to check the monitor. "Oh, you're awake. Your color looks better today. How are you feeling?"

Wyatt ignored her, his gaze pinning Charlie in place. "Where is he?"

She wiped at her cheeks. "Wyatt, relax. Linc is fine. You're the one who almost died."

Wyatt settled back against the sheets, his whole body on fire. Died? What was she talking about? Why did everything hurt? The nurse adjusted his pillows then checked all the leads and wires before pushing something through his IV that made him feel cold and then warm. Why was his throat so raw?

He looked to the nurse. "Can I have some water?"

She nodded, leaving and returning with a huge white styrofoam cup with a straw. "You'll have to help him," she warned Charlie.

"Where'd he go?" he managed after the nurse left.

Charlie held the straw to his lips, and he sucked down half the cup. "He just needed to take care of

*intoxicating*

some paperwork with Jackson. He's been here with you every single day and night, boo. Honestly, he's going to be pissed that he missed the first coherent words you've spoken in a week."

Butterflies took flight in Wyatt's stomach. Linc had stayed. "A week?" he asked. Charlie nodded solemnly. "What happened?"

She frowned. "You don't remember any of it?"

Wyatt racked his pounding head. "I remember the stupid party. I remember my dad trying to make me work for Victor. I remember telling Linc I loved him and him saying we could leave…together. Then… nothing."

Charlie wept once more, her cheeks an angry red, like she was more frustrated than sad. "You fucking cut yourself. You went too deep, and you hit an artery. You almost fucking bled to death in my new car, you fucking dick. How could you do that to me? To Linc? What were you thinking?"

Wyatt's memory flooded back, like somebody flipped a switch. The razor blade. The car horn. Linc holding him while he died. "It was an accident."

"You accidentally took a razor blade to your arm?" she asked, incredulous.

He shook his head, like it would somehow take back what he'd done. "I just wanted to make a little cut, just to ease the pressure, but I was drunk, my elbow hit the car horn and it scared me. It was just an accident."

Charlie blew her nose hard, and when she looked at him once more, she seemed…resigned. "You can't keep doing this to us. To yourself. You need help."

Wyatt just closed his eyes. He was so tired. In his bones, he was tired. He felt like he'd lived a hundred lifetimes in his twenty-two years, and he just didn't want to do it anymore. He gave a slight nod. If that's what it took to get Charlie to stop crying, to stop looking at him like he was breaking her heart, then he'd talk to somebody.

"There's something else we need to talk about," Charlie said, her tone hesitant.

Wyatt studied her warily. "Okay."

She pulled something up on her phone screen. "I need you to understand that she was going to print the story with or without my input."

"What? Who was?" he asked, not following. Then it hit him. "That reporter. Did she print the story about my DUIs?" He couldn't blame her. It was a great story. But still. "Way to kick somebody when they're down," he muttered.

"No. Well, not exactly. She went after the much bigger story."

She turned her phone screen toward him. On the

*intoxicating*

front page was the headline: RED FAVORS BLACK AND BLUE. The headline made no sense until he saw the line below. *Explosive Abuse Allegations against GOP Senator.* Below that was a picture of Wyatt's back, covered in red welts. Wyatt was going to puke. Somebody had clearly taken the picture without his knowledge. It was from five years ago, after a house party incident where Monty had caught Wyatt making out with a boy named Jaden. He'd beaten Wyatt with his cell phone charger.

Wyatt's gaze jerked to Charlie, setting off an electrical storm in his head, his stomach sloshing. "How did she get that picture, Charlie?"

She dropped her phone into her lap and took his hand. "You refused to tell anybody what your father was doing. Whenever I could, I'd take pictures of your bruises. Just in case. Nobody believes the victim without pictures."

"You gave her that photo?" Wyatt's face flushed, his heart sinking.

"She was going to print the story about your DUIs... but then she was eavesdropping on you and your father in that conference room. She recorded you two. She heard enough to confirm you were gay, that Linc and you were a couple... By the time she came to me and asked for a statement, the news of your accident was everywhere." As Wyatt listened, a strange sense of peace washed over him. Maybe it was the meds the nurse had given him kicking in, or maybe he was happy he didn't have to lie anymore. But Charlie wasn't done with her confession. "When she said she was going to print what she knew, along with your DUIs, I offered her proof of his abuse—photographs, incidents I'd seen—in exchange for her keeping your record under wraps."

"So, the world knows I'm gay?"

"She didn't explicitly state it, but once the article hit, some guys you've hooked up with in the past were hot to out you online."

Wyatt laughed then winced. "God, why does my throat hurt so bad?"

"Because you haven't had anything to drink since before your surgery."

"Surgery?"

"Yes, you idiot. You almost died. They had to take a vein from your leg just to fix your arm."

Wyatt groaned. There was nothing he could say to defend himself. "I suppose my father has disowned me?"

Charlie snorted. "Your father is too busy trying to stay out of prison."

"Prison?"

*intoxicating*

She shook her head. "You don't get it. He assaulted you, Wyatt. You have photographic evidence…dates, times. Well, I do."

What was she getting at? "I'm not sending my dad to prison."

She rolled her eyes. "Well, do us a favor and don't tell him that because it's the only thing keeping Linc out of prison."

Wyatt's pulse skipped. "What?"

"Yeah, Linc may have kinda, sorta beat the shit out of your father in the waiting room while you were in surgery."

Wyatt couldn't help the grin that spread across his face. "He did?"

"That man loves you more than he loves his freedom. He would have happily gone to prison. Hell, he would probably die for you. He's a smitten kitten. Thank God, my parents have excellent attorneys. A little quid pro quo keeps Linc out of jail and your father from being charged with multiple counts of assault."

"He loves me…" Wyatt said, the words foreign on his tongue.

"There's somebody else here who loves you too…"

He frowned. "You?"

"Well, yes, but that's not what I meant."

Charlie stood and left without another word. A

metallic taste flooded Wyatt's mouth, his anxiety pumping adrenaline through his veins until he was light-headed. When the door opened again, Charlie was pushing an old wicker wheelchair. "Nana?"

Charlie parked his grandmother as close as she could. "I'll let you two talk alone."

Once she left, Wyatt stared at his grandmother warily. She was practically a stranger. She looked much older when she wasn't wearing a fancy gown with her hair and makeup done. Today, she just wore black slacks and a high-necked lavender blouse with a big black cashmere cardigan thrown over it, like it wasn't almost summer in Florida. He had no idea what she was about to tell him, but he wasn't in any shape to hear any more bad news.

Her mouth drooped at the corners, like he'd already somehow disappointed her, and she clutched her gnarled fingers together. "I owe you an apology," she said.

Wyatt blinked at her. "What? Why?"

Her eyes filled with tears, and she turned her head away, as if to collect herself. When she looked back, she said, "I let my daughter and that man force me out of your life. I know I was never the world's most affectionate…grandmother…but I loved you boys. You and Landon were the only joys in my life. When

*intoxicating*

he became sick, and they wanted to use your stem cells to treat him, I protested. I was afraid you'd get hurt, that the procedure wouldn't work and your father would blame you. You know your father doesn't like his decisions questioned." She shook her head. "But I was right. The procedure failed, and he blamed you. He took it out on you. When I said my piece, told him they needed to stop treating you like spare parts, they cut me out of your life, and I let them. I just gave up and let them have you."

Wyatt blinked, trying to process this new information. "I—" He didn't know what to say. "It's okay. I'm okay."

She shook her head vehemently. "No. Charlemagne showed me those pictures. All of them. He's been hurting you for years. I suspected you liked boys, even way back then. You were such a sweet and sensitive child and you had a flair for the dramatic. I should have protected you, but I just didn't know. But I should have. That place he sent you to. The things that happen in those camps. I should have fought harder for you. I knew my daughter certainly never would."

Tears sprang to his eyes, and all he could do was let them fall. "Why did you let him have power of attorney over your affairs if you hate him so much? Why let him paint you out to be crazy? Why didn't you fight him in court? You're obviously not senile."

She shrugged bony shoulders. "I just didn't care. I'm a lonely old woman, Wyatt. I didn't care about the money."

"Still, he didn't earn any of it." His father just took and took, doing nothing to earn the money himself. He was a parasite, feeding off others, using them to his own advantage every time.

She chuckled. "You sound just like Charlemagne. Her father will help me take back what's mine. That's sort of what I wanted to talk to you about. I wanted to let you know that you aren't without means."

"Means?" he asked.

"Money. You still have your trust fund. That was always yours. Your grandfather set it up when you and Landon were little, just before he died. He made it so your father could never touch it. He didn't trust him, either. We're not the Rockefellers, and my financial manager, Jerome, will need to approve all withdrawals from the account until your twenty-fifth birthday per your grandfather's wishes, but it's enough to keep you off the streets."

Wyatt gave a stilted nod, at a loss. "Thank you."

"Don't thank me. I should have stepped in years ago. I should have made an effort to be in your life."

He shrugged. "It's okay. You're here now."

*intoxicating*

She gave a watery smile. "I know I don't deserve it, but perhaps you might consider giving me another chance at being your grandmother."

Wyatt swallowed the lump in his throat. "Yeah, sure."

# thirty-three

## LINCOLN

THE MOMENT CHARLIE TEXTED THAT WYATT WAS awake and talking, Linc had cut his meeting with Jackson short. They'd worked out all the big-picture stuff; the details could wait. Linc needed to see Wyatt, needed to touch him and hear his voice. He wouldn't believe he was truly okay until he was back in Linc's arms.

When he pushed open the door to Wyatt's room, somebody had inclined his bed, so he was almost sitting up, but his eyes were closed. Linc tried to enter quietly, but Wyatt's eyes popped open anyway. One look at Linc and Wyatt burst into tears. Linc's heart plummeted into his stomach. He rushed to his side.

*intoxicating*

"What's wrong? Are you okay? Are you in pain?"

Wyatt just shook his head. "I'm so sorry. I'm so, so sorry. I lied to you. I knew I was going to end up cutting again. But I didn't mean to cut so deep. I wasn't trying to…kill myself. Not really. I swear. Not—I just wanted to cut a little. I didn't mean to scare you. I told Charlie I'd go to counseling. I promised and I will."

Linc tried to follow Wyatt's train of thought, gripping his face in his hands and wiping at his cheeks as he talked. "Hey, shh, stop. Stop. I-I know. I had no right to demand you stop cutting. I saw you spiraling, but I didn't know what to do. I know you didn't do it on purpose." He kissed him gently. "But Jesus, kid. You scared the fuck out of me." Linc choked on his next words. "I thought I'd lost you. I thought I'd lost you, and I just kept thinking I never told you I loved you. And I do. I love you so much. I thought I was going to sit there on the ground and watch you bleed out in my arms and you'd never know."

Wyatt looked at him funny. "But I knew. Deep down. When it mattered. When I think of everything you do for me…it makes sense. You take care of me. You make me food every day. You make sure I drink enough water. You don't let me drink energy drinks because they make me too jittery to put on makeup, and you make sure I go to sleep at a decent hour. You tell me every day that you love me, even if you don't say it out loud."

Linc wanted to wrap Wyatt in his arms and hold him forever. Instead, he gently gathered Wyatt against him, careful not to jostle his bandaged arm. Wyatt tucked his face against Linc's neck. He just breathed in Wyatt's scent, took in the feel of his warm body against him. He was alive. He was going to be fine. He had told himself this a thousand times over the last five days, but this was the first time he believed it. Wyatt was talking, crying even, his words making sense.

"God, I must smell like a swamp," Wyatt mumbled against Linc's shoulder. "My breath is probably lethal."

"I don't care. I just want you, stinky body, lethal breath and all."

Wyatt pulled back. "I love you."

"I sure fucking hope so because I'm not letting you go. Ever."

"Promise?"

Linc pulled back enough to sit on the edge of Wyatt's bed, taking his uninjured hand. "Yes, I promise."

Wyatt grinned. "Did you really beat the shit out of my dad?"

Linc scoffed. "It was always going to happen; it was just a matter of when. But, damn, it sure felt good."

Wyatt's face fell, his brows knitting together. "What

*intoxicating*

about the money for your dad? Now that old Monty's been outed as a child abuser, I don't think we have any way to blackmail him. My grandmother gave me access to my trust fund, but I have some stuffy dude in a suit who has to agree to my purchases, so even though it's my money, it isn't, like, totally mine."

"Baby, don't worry about that. I've got it covered."

And he did. Jackson fucking Avery was saving Linc's ass once again but not without a huge catch. One he really hoped Wyatt would be on-board for. Luckily, he had a secret weapon.

Wyatt narrowed his eyes. "Covered how? Are you going to become a male stripper? A prostitute?"

Linc grinned. "I don't know if I should feel flattered or insulted by the insinuation that the only way I could make money is by taking off my clothes."

Wyatt leaned forward, his puffy red eyes suddenly molten. "I'd pay good money to see you naked, Daddy."

Linc's cock twitched at Wyatt's husky rasp, but he just pressed a hard kiss to his forehead before gently shoving him back against the mattress. "Oh, no you don't. You will not get me all worked up in this hospital when your ass is out of commission for the next several weeks. Don't you want to go home?"

Wyatt's shoulders drooped. "Not to put too fine a point on it, but we don't exactly have a home."

"I wanted to talk to you about that." Wyatt nodded in a 'go ahead' gesture, still watching Linc, like he was waiting for the ax to fall. He couldn't help but laugh. "Jackson has offered me a job."

"I don't know how I feel about you guarding somebody else's body twenty-four seven," Wyatt muttered, lower lip pouting.

"You don't have to feel any way about it, brat, because he offered me a management position. I'd have my own crew. My team of security specialists. He even offered me a sign-on bonus that would cover my father's expenses."

Wyatt scanned Linc appraisingly, one brow hooking upward. "So, you'd wear a suit to work every day?"

Linc grinned. "Uh-huh."

Wyatt ran his free hand over Linc's chest. "I could be on-board with that. What would I do, though?"

"Baby, you're free. You can do and be whatever and whoever you want to be. You have a trust fund, and Jack is being very generous with my salary. You've got time to figure it out."

"This all sounds way too good to be true," Wyatt said. "What's the catch?"

"So, that's the thing… This amazing new job requires us to relocate."

"Relocate?" Wyatt parroted, like he was testing the

*intoxicating*

weight of the word on his tongue. "Like, to where? I'm sort of an acquired taste, Linc. You can't, like, move me to bum-fuck nowhere Indiana. I'll shrivel up and die."

"You are the biggest drama queen in the world," Linc told him affectionately, kissing him once more. "Has anybody ever told you that?"

"No," Wyatt said. "But, in all fairness, I'm usually standing next to Charlie."

"What if I told you Charlie has agreed to come with us?"

Wyatt tsked. "I'd ask 'Come with us where?'"

"Los Angeles," Linc said casually.

"You want me to move to fucking Los Angeles?"

Linc frowned. "Well, I thought—"

Wyatt waved his uninjured hand around. "Yes, totally. A hundred percent. Oh, my God. Your sister's in LA. You, me, Charlie, and Ellie in Los Angeles? This is amazing. This is the best thing ever. You're going to marry me, right?" Wyatt asked without pausing for a breath.

Linc's brain slid to a grinding halt. "What?"

Wyatt pulled a face like Linc was stupid. "Marry me? Make an honest man out of me? Take care of me forever?"

Fuck yes. A million times yes. Linc would go door to door until he found somebody ordained and marry

Wyatt today if that's what he wanted. He kissed Wyatt once more, the boy's chapped lips reminding him he needed to be careful.

He smiled at him, pushing the curls from his eyes. "Is that what you want? To get married?" Linc asked.

Wyatt nodded, eyes bright. "Please."

Linc leaned forward, pressing his mouth against Wyatt's ear. "Is that how you ask for things, sweet boy?"

Wyatt shivered. "No, Daddy."

"Then use your words and ask me again."

"Marry me, Daddy?"

"Since you asked so nicely…"

## *epilogue*

# WYATT

WYATT PICKED UP THE VIDEO CAMERA AND FLIPPED the screen so he could see himself. He messed with his hair until it didn't look quite so much like he'd rolled out of bed an hour ago, even though he had. It had been months since the accident, but he still tired easily, even though his stamina got better every day. The wicked scars on his left arm and right leg served as a constant reminder of what he'd almost lost and made him determined not to waste his second chance…or third. Jeez, maybe even more than that.

He hit play and grinned into the camera. "Hey, everybody, it's me, Wyatt Hudson, here today with an extra-special video. I promised you guys if I hit one million followers that I would finally give in and take part in the boyfriend challenge—well, husband in my case—and let Linc do my makeup on camera. Well, three days ago, I hit that magic number, so today is the day. I hope you enjoy."

Wyatt propped the camera up on the shelf. "Before we get into that part, I just wanted to thank you guys. It's insane how quickly life can change. I spent twenty-two years feeling like I would never measure up, never be loved, never have anything real in my life." He took a deep breath, overwhelmed by thoughts of his past, blinking back the tears pricking at the back of his eyes. "Sorry. I'm super sappy today. But it's been five months since the scandal broke with my dad and I don't even recognize my life. Four months ago, I started this YouTube channel for my makeup tutorials, and I've already hit a million subscribers. A giant scandal will do that, I guess, but I'll take it."

He laughed, then sobered. "Three months ago, I officially started intensive therapy sessions with my new shrink." He rolled his eyes. "I know, I'm so LA. Two months ago, they offered me my first chance to speak out against conversion therapy and help draw attention to the horrors that happen inside. It sounds crazy, but the more I talk about the abuse I suffered

*intoxicating*

by Victor Osborne, the less power it has over me. He may not be in prison, but he's also no longer running camps that hurt kids, and there's some comfort in that. While I haven't pressed charges, others have. Hopefully, they'll get justice and he'll go to jail." He paused, swallowing hard, his gaze darting toward the bedroom before turning back to the camera with a grin and holding up his left hand. "And one month ago today, I got to marry the love of my life."

He leaned into the camera.

"I'm not telling you all this to brag. I know not everybody has a trust fund to fall back on or a soft place to land, and getting out of an abusive situation is never easy. Sometimes, leaving means going into an even worse situation. Sometimes, the people who are supposed to love you, no matter what, kick you out. But I'm working with my grandmother and some very good friends to help people who feel trapped get out of their bad situations, no matter what their financial circumstances, and to help people who feel they have no place to go, feel safe." He blushed, suddenly awkward. "But that's for another day. On to the fun stuff."

He picked up the camera, panning it around the room. "This is our loft in the fashion district, and by *our* loft, I mean it belongs to my fabulous sister-in-law, Ellie. Now, you all know my best friend,

Charlie, is in New York, staring in that off-off-off Broadway production that's supposed to be, like, the next *Hamilton* or whatever, but you might not know that Ellie is their costume designer, so the girls are subletting their loft to us until they come back, which I'm hoping isn't for a very long time. Because I love it here. Isn't it cute?"

It was hardly more than two rooms. A small upscale kitchen with its natural wood and stainless-steel appliances bled into a cozy living room, which Ellie had decorated in her funky bohemian style. A brick half-wall separated the living room from the king-size bed and the door, which led to the bathroom. It was small and expensive, like everything else in LA, but Wyatt loved it. He loved it because it was his home with Linc. At least, for now.

Wyatt flipped the screen outward so he could turn the camera toward the hall, letting his audience see what he saw. As he came to the bedroom door, he stopped short, mouth suddenly dry. He'd heard Linc come in a bit ago, but he'd been in the kitchen trying to get enough coffee on-board to do his video.

Linc lay on the messy bed, still in his work clothes. Well, most of his work clothes. He wore black pants and his white button-down shirt, top button undone, and his sleeves rolled to the elbow, his legs crossed at the ankles. How could black socks look so fucking hot?

Papers surrounded Linc, his black-framed reading glasses perched on his nose as he squinted at something on his phone screen. Wyatt's dick couldn't help but take notice. He hit pause, setting the camera on the dresser before crossing the room. Linc looked up just as Wyatt snatched his phone and tossed it to the end of the bed, displacing Linc's papers as he straddled his lap.

"Hi," Linc said, amused.

"Hey, Daddy," Wyatt murmured, capturing Linc's mouth in a dirty kiss. "You're home early."

"Therapy today."

Wyatt paused briefly to look at Linc. "Did it go okay?"

He gave a half-nod. "Same as always, I suppose. Emotionally draining. Figured I'd work from home for the rest of the day."

Wyatt hummed his approval, returning to his previous exploration. "Good idea."

"I'm a little busy here, brat," he rumbled.

Wyatt rocked his hips against Linc's, moaning when he felt Linc already hardening behind his zipper. "You're supposed to be doing my makeup for my video today. My audience loves to see your face on camera," he said. He bit at Linc's jaw, then his lower lip, rapidly losing interest in his own project. "Besides, you can't lie here in your Daddy clothes and not expect me to jump your bones. You know what these glasses do to me."

Linc threaded his fingers through Wyatt's curls, tugging his head back to bite at his throat. "I forgot about the video," he admitted, grinding their erections together through the thin layers of material. "Wanna go do that now?" he asked, knowing full well Wyatt wasn't leaving that bed until Linc fucked him.

Wyatt yanked his shirt over his head, flinging it across the room, his fingers going for the buttons on Linc's shirt. "They can wait. I need you inside me. Now." Linc started to take his shirt off, but Wyatt shook his head. "Leave your clothes on, especially the glasses. I just want to do this." He lowered his head and licked over Linc's flat nipple.

"Fuck," Linc hissed. "You're being a very bossy bottom right now."

Wyatt slanted his lips across Linc's. "Yeah, what are you gonna do about it?"

"Pants off. Now," Linc growled.

Wyatt really had the best life ever. "Yes, Daddy."

THE END

# DEAR READER,

THANK YOU SO MUCH for reading *Intoxicating*, Book 1 in my Elite Protection Services Series. I hope you loved reading this book as much as I loved writing it. The second book in the series, *Captivating*, is available now on Amazon.

For teasers, mini-fics, updates, and extras, visit my website and sign up for my newsletter. I love to interact with you guys, so you can always hit me up on any of my social media accounts, like my Facebook Group: ONLEY'S OUBLIETTE, where you can meet other readers and have access to exclusive giveaways.

If you did love this book, it would be amazing if you could take a minute to review it. Reviews are like gold for authors.

Thank you again for reading.

# ABOUT THE AUTHOR

ONLEY JAMES is the pen name of YA author, Martina McAtee, who lives in Central Florida with her children, her pitbull, her weiner dog, and an ever-growing collection of shady looking cats. She splits her time between writing YA LGBT paranormal romances and writing adult m/m romances.

When not at her desk, you can find her mainlining Starbucks refreshers, whining about how much she has to do, and avoiding the things she has to do by binge-watching unhealthy amounts of television in one sitting. She loves ghost stories, true crime documentaries, obsessively scrolling social media, and writing kinky, snarky books about men who fall in love with other men.

*Find her online at:*
WWW.ONLEYJAMES.COM

Printed in Great Britain
by Amazon